Until his last mission, British military medic Luke McLaren kept his oath, 'Do No Harm'. When he fails to save his best friend, Mike, Luke's life implodes.

Mike's sister, midwife Kate Gibson, doesn't believe in happy endings. Not since her father deserted her when she was a child, and her brother got killed on a mission.

One night of make-me-forget sex and Luke knows Kate is the only woman he will ever want but can never have. Life goes on. He joins Sentinel Security, and Kate focuses on her clinical work in Africa.

When Kate asks for Luke's help to expose a bomb threat, he agrees. He has no choice thanks to his deathbed promise to protect her. With their hotter than hell connection reignited, Luke and Kate must face their demons and the enemy if they are to survive and claim a future together.

FAITHFUL

SENTINEL SECURITY BOOK 1

ELIZA RENTON

Cataloguing in-publication data is available from the National Library of Australia.

Edited by Leisl Leighton, Leisl Leighton Author Services

Cover design by Lana Pecherczyk – Bookcoverology

Printed and bound in Australia by IngramSpark

I am grateful to Serena Sandrin for valuable input on an early draft. To my brother, Duncan, for keeping me straight on military jargon, to Louise Wilson who patiently and honestly offered feedback on early drafts and members of my writing group, The Saturday Ladies Bridge Club, for their support.

For Ben, faithful by my side.

CHAPTER ONE
BURKINA FASO – WEST AFRICA

Luke McLaren leaned against the well-worn door of his wooden hut, the West African sun hot enough to make his eyeballs sweat and swore the next time he laid eyes on his best mate he'd kill him.

Mike Gibson had been a brother to him, ever since they'd survived SAS combat survival training. This morning, crucifixion was too good for him. Sodding green recruits got it. Gambling with Spanner ended in tears. Every fucking time.

It was a sodding mystery why Mike went all-in last night—upping the ante with his sister's care package. A cross between a Jaffa and a Ginger Nut – they were worth more than a month's pay. Right now, he craved the sweet piece of home.

The entire battalion hung out for Kate's addictive morsels. Thanks to Mike, Spanner got to stuff his face with the whole bloody lot. The arse took pleasure in shaking the tin in front of his nose as he headed to the Boss' tent, grinning from ear to ear.

For the last hour, he'd searched every inch of the place looking to ball Mike out, but there'd been no sign of him or his dog, George. Must have kept drinking after Luke called it a night and left them to their misery. If luck was on Luke's side, he might not have to kill Mike - the hangover from death enough to shame him make him regret his dumb behaviour.

Luke grinned. Mike with a thumping headache. Justice. He rolled a cigarette between his fingertips, not that he smoked, just loved to watch them burn. Placing the lit end under his nose he inhaled the smoke swirling in the morning haze, kidding himself this did less harm than a long draw.

Two days and his commitment to the Special Air Services unit ended, a job at London's major trauma hospital would seem normal after three tours serving Her Maj. He'd take a long hard look at the dream, the villa in Portugal, by the sea, the beach at his door. His bank account could cope.

Normal. The word had a reassuring ring to it. Nothing was ever routine in Africa. Terrified locals ran from Burkina into Mali fleeing from militant terrorists. Months ago, refugee camps surpassed capacity. With nowhere else to go torn apart families made a life in tents, makeshift housing, cobbled together from the deserted homes of those who had fled.

Every sodding day the same, from the crack of dawn until the sun collapsed exhausted into the horizon - running Burkina's People's Militia through hand to hand combat skills, weapons training, and trauma self-care.

Yeah. The end of his final tour couldn't come fast enough. Luke scratched his head, a bloody mystery why he'd joined the military.

He hadn't spoken to his mum in, make that couldn't remember when exactly. Hearing her struggle not to cry on the other end of the phone another cut to his heart.

Stuck here in the middle of nowhere, he craved sleep and sex - not fussed in what order. Neither was in the offing.

One last swill of bitter coffee—time for a quick burger before Knight's briefing. Anal and angsty, the Boss, a tick-sheet on legs, didn't tolerate tardy officers. Especially as *JNIM,* the local branch of Al-Qaeda recently upped their remote village raids.

A short briefing—Shut *JNIM*, and their poxy git leader, Seckou, down before they did more damage.

Ignoring the flies swirling over his head, the smell of charred meat, drew Luke's feet across the compound to the camp's corrugated canteen. Special orders never fazed Mahmoud, "Cheeseburger, rare, hold the onion, hold the fries." Him and *Burger King* ever-obliging.

Murphy's Law. Just as he parked himself on one of the upturned crates and wrapped his fingers around a stale bun, the emergency alert siren blasted across the camp. Stray dogs barked, birds shrieked and soared into the sky. *CASEVAC. Casualties.*

"IED blast, Doc, 'B' patrol pinned ten miles out. One *Alpha*, confirmed," Spanner spat the words across the compound, didn't miss a stride as he raced past, stabbing his index fingers at parked vehicles.

The burger toppled into the dirt, lunch for the chickens. Luke cursed, his feet gathering momentum as he tore from the canteen and raced to his hut.

Alpha, life-threatening injury.

Counting to ten, he grabbed his helmet from the hook behind the door, stuffed the front pocket of his flak jacket with extra tourniquets and grabbed his Bergan medical kit from beside the bunk. As always, he hesitated before shoving his Sig P229 into his hip holster – he'd vowed to save lives, not destroy them. Until now, he'd been lucky and never had to fire his weapon.

Luke grabbed the swinging door of the ambulance pulling out of the makeshift hospital.

"Get in," the Boss barked.

"Roger." Luke hauled arse in beside Spanner.

"Move the fuck over, Doc." Knight bowled in behind him, yelling, "go, go, go," at the additional service personnel swarming to their assigned vehicles.

Spanner floored the accelerator, sending a jolt through Luke's spine. Bracing one hand on the dashboard, he glanced over his shoulder.

No sign of Mike. Always up for messing with the dickers, he'd be pissed at missing the action.

Served him right – a shit load coming his way from Knight later. Luke grinned. He was looking forward to those biscuits for breakfast this morning. *Mind out of the biscuit tin.* "Who's out there?" his voice rose over the noise of the engine.

"'B' patrol. They left the compound early." Knight adjusted the head mic attached to his helmet.

Dread began its slow climb up Luke's spine, routine didn't exist in this hell. He pushed his foot to the floor, adding support to Spanner's efforts to get them there pronto. There'd been no rain for months. Their vehicle moved slow and rough over the dusty terrain. His lips were dry. Luke took a quick swig from his canteen and checked his watch. *Shit.* Seven minutes since they left Base. Time was fast running out for casualties.

"Stop," Knight ordered. "This will do us."

Spanner slammed on the brake, swerved, as stones spat on the windscreen. The vehicle screeched to a halt behind a pile of smouldering rubble. Guns blasted, to their left, smoke rose from a burned-out building. Last week it served as the church.

First out of the vehicle and on the ground, Knight raised his fist at right angles to his elbow. *Wait.* Luke yanked his eighty-pound pack from between his legs and onto his lap. Should be fifty, except Spanner insisted he carry the spare ammo. Shoot 'em up, patch 'em up in one glory bag. God bless the SAS and their sodding efficiency.

Knight tapped his helmet, *stay low.*

Luke jumped from the vehicle, the Bergan thumping against his lower back. He jogged behind him, staying close as they jogged along the narrow alley between a row of huts. The nozzle of his rifle jerked to the sky, an out-breath from firing.

Spanner swerved to avoid a man who came from nowhere with a child tucked under his arm. Luke slammed hard against his back.

Three, maybe four feet in front of them, two soldiers huddled around someone laying out in the open. A scan of the immediate area showed no others. Luke tapped Spanner on the shoulder and broke file.

"You got this, Doc?" Knight tossed the words over his shoulder.

The Boss signalled for his men to split into two ranks and head to where they could hear 'B' patrol taking heavy fire.

"On it. Leave me the corporal, take him." Luke pointed to the corpsman sitting in the dirt, nursing his head in his hands.

"Roger." Knight nodded. "You, you're with me." He dragged the man away by his elbow.

"Sitrep." Luke ripped open the front pocket of his Bergan and gestured for the corporal to forget the salute and deliver his report.

"Sir. Yes, sir, tourniquets applied, one on each leg." The soldier cleared his throat. "Field dressings secured. 10mg I/M morphine administered."

Face the colour of spearmint ice cream; he was twenty at the most. Best give him a job before he chucked over their patient. "Excellent work, private. Set up the stretcher." Luke nodded to the back flap of his pack.

It didn't take a genius to figure the injured man was fucked. Both legs —gone below the knee. The end of his femurs, jagged and bloody splayed at impossible angles. The remnants of his camo pants, soaked in blood, resembled torn Christmas paper. A boot lay next to the man's mangled left hand.

After their previous two tours in Afghanistan, hell's favourite sandbox, Luke still struggled with meeting the gaze of the severely wounded. One eye on the rapid rise and fall of the injured man's heaving chest, Luke snared his wrist and checked his pulse.

Swallowing the bile flooding his mouth he grit his teeth and lifted his eyes. His gaze met eyes the colour of an arctic sky. Luke froze. *Fuck, no.*

"Hey, Doc, fancy…meeting…you…here." Mike raised his head and stared at where his legs should be. "Shit."

117 bpm. Heartrate, too high. Keep it together. "You should be in bed after last night's balls up." Struggling to keep his voice steady, Luke swallowed hard.

"Wish I was, Doc."

Luke forced a smile. "Trust you to interrupt breakfast. Hold on, mate, we'll get you out of here."

Mike held his breath, plainly doing his best to swallow the scream welling inside him.

"Stay with me big feller." Luke cuffed the moisture from his eyes, steadied his hands and packed the stumps with field dressings. No training, or hours spent in trauma care, prepared him for his best mate's blood running through his fingers.

"This is bad… fuck." Mike shook his head. "Not like … this Doc. It's… okay. Let… me go. Please."

"Don't talk fucking shite and let me do my job." It was the pain. Mike didn't realise what he was saying. "Corporal, ready with that stretcher?" Bone-deep fear gripped Luke's heart as Mike clawed at his Bergan. "Okay, I got you." *Ketamine. Give him the Ketamine.* "This stuff is magic."

Mike tried to push the syringe away.

"Corporal, hold him steady."

Rat-a-tat-tat-tat. In the distance, Bullets cracked, screaming men, women and children raced for cover.

"No use, Doc," Mike whispered. His eyelids flickered.

Luke plunged the syringe into the idiot. "Look at me. Hang on. The Boss is on it. You. Are. Not. Dying. Here." Hands trembling – wrong time to get a case of the shakes - Luke packed more gauze into the ragged remains of his mate's legs.

Mike's face was ashen, his hollow cheeks lifeless. Shit scared he'd lose him Luke kept talking. "Stay with me, eyes open. Come on, Mike, stay with me."

"My sister, Luke… promise me, Kate, take care of her…"

"What am I, a fucking babysitter? You will have scored a shit load of R and R after this balls-up. Take care of her yourself." As fast as he packed Mike's wounds, they oozed crimson through his fingers.

"Luke…argh…Kate…promise."

Luke ran the numbers in his head, the golden hour for Mike fast disappearing. Knight and Spanner burst through the clearing as he reached in his bag for more Ketamine. *Thank Christ.*

One look at Mike and Spanner retched, his vomit landing beside the corporal who kneeled at Mike's head. Knight didn't blink.

"Zero, Charlie One Zero. Contact. Explosion. GI8082-O. T1. Copy." Standing next to Spanner, one hand resting on his shoulder, Snake, their Section Signaller, radioed Mike's TAG number, blood group and condition to the Base hospital.

T1 – it didn't get any worse. Back at Base, theatre staff stood by for immediate patient triage before surgery. Luke tried to work out their ETA, frantically repeating, calculating numbers, but the valuable total refused to stick in his brain.

"Doc...please... I'm finished...for the love of God...Boss?" Mike screamed.

"Easy soldier, let Doc do his job." Knight's hand settled on Mike's shoulder.

Mike's fingers dug deep into the flesh on Luke's arm. Each inhale more ragged than the last. "Please...Kate."

His mate's begging tore Luke apart. "I promise, okay, I'll take care of your skinny sister. Pay me with a tin of her biscuits." Mike's grip weakened on his arm.

Luke half-turned, another hit of Ketamine couldn't hurt. The nudge to his hip came as he finished grabbing the syringe, a split second before a single shot echoed in his right ear.

Mike stopped screaming.

Luke spun around in time to see his gun fall from his best mate's hand, Mike's eyes no longer seeing, his lungs no longer breathing, a single bullet hole blackened his temple.

"No. No!" His fist pounded the dirt beside Mike's head, refusing to believe the horror in front of him. Rage hotter than hellfire blazed through his veins. *What the fuck have you done?*

"Doc, Doc, get it together. Corporal, on my three, lift." Knight yelled for Spanner and the corporal to slide Mike's broken body onto the stretcher.

They were taking fire, needed to move, fast, but his body resisted, legs poured with concrete refusing to let him stand.

"'B' isn't his patrol. What the fuck is he doing here?" George, where was his dog, the mutt never left his side?

"Jesus, Doc. Unless you want to join Mike, grab your end and let's get the hell out of this hole."

Luke took the load, every cell in his body rattled with the certainty. *I killed him. I killed Mike.*

CHAPTER TWO
LONDON - ENGLAND

She must remember to call Mike. He was hanging out to hear the news.

Mission accomplished, she leaned back and kissed the three-year contract for the supply of Misoprostol.

Kate's stomach growled. Not unreasonable seeing as in the last twenty-four hours she'd eaten one packet of cheese and onion crisps. She kicked off her shoes, flopped on the sofa, blew air kisses at her mangled toes, and thanked them for their service. After being squished in three-inch heels for eternity, their loyalty deserved a medal.

After months of writing and re-writing proposals, to one of the UK's leading pharmaceutical companies, the bruised, turning blue toenails were worth it. Deal done. An essential donation of the life-saving drug for *Afrique Santé's* midwifery program based in Burkina's capital, Ouagadougou, *Wagga* to the locals. Secured.

Kate raised her imaginary glass and toasted the rain bouncing off the stairs leading to her basement flat. England ignored the calendar. It was the beginning of July, technically Summer. *Not going to miss you.*

Her eyes flicked over the photographs fighting for space between the wilted plants on the windowsill. Given the attention she paid them, they should be dead. Centre stage, Mike's photo beamed at her. *Good intentions don't make you a green-thumb, sis.* He loved to tease.

The laptop beeped, incoming. Kate groaned. The seventh email from Mother in the past two days. Uppercase words covering every grisly detail of the recent attacks in Burkina Faso shouted from the screen.

Highlighted in red:

Smaller NGOs pull out of the land-locked country. Every effort made to secure safe transportation for active personnel.

It was sad and irritating, but months ago, she'd given up trying to explain to Mother why she and Crystal refused to give up their work in Burkina.

She snagged the corner of the laptop with her big toe and closed the lid, not that it would make emails or truth disappear. Her best friend was waiting at Scarfes, their favourite bar in the Rosewood Hotel, probably well into her second cocktail. Time to join her, celebrate, and finalise their plans for returning to Africa.

Tic, toc, Micky Mouse chimed on the mantlepiece. Time for a sixty-second shower and a spritz of super deodorant before changing into something more comfortable, including flat shoes. Not as comfy as the pyjamas spread across the end of her bed, but they'd do until she snuggled under the duvet later.

Kate wriggled off the sofa. For the second time that week, she snagged her little toe on the leg of the coffee table. Tiny black dots hopped across her vision. On her way to the bathroom, she collided with the vacuum cleaner leaning against the wall, *for crying out loud.*

Kate swore out loud to the person banging on her door. At this rate, she'd never leave her flat.

Mother? No, she had a key.

Whoever it was, whatever they were selling, if they didn't stop pounding, Mr I-should-live-in-a-bubble upstairs would bang on her ceiling with his bloody broom.

"Okay, I'm coming." Face plastered with her best *I could give a flying fairy smile* she shoved aside the deadbolt.

"You're wasting your time. I'm a paid-up, card-carrying witch and I …"

Light, from the streetlamp, shone on the drizzle spilling over shiny black shoes. A sinking sensation began in her stomach as her gaze travelled to the faces of two, medal-pinned-to-pec, military officers filling her doorway. Their peaked caps pulled low over their foreheads.

'Run', every fibre, each nerve in her body screamed, but the massive boulder lodged in the pit of her stomach made it impossible.

'Good evening, Miss Gibson.'

Kate shuddered at the flat tone of the man's voice and braced her palm on the wall.

"No. Go away. You can't be here. You have the wrong address." Her insides in turmoil, the mobile she was clutching fell from her hand. Dread warred with the tears pooling behind her eyeballs.

"May we come in, Miss Gibson?"

"No. My friend is waiting for me. I'm late. The words didn't make it further than the tip of her tongue. Salty tears streamed over her cheeks, and her knees turned to rubber.

"Please, Miss Gibson." The larger of the two soldiers stepped forward, his solid grip on her upper arm the sole reason she didn't crumble to the floor.

"No, no." Her fists hammered his chest. The other officer caught her right wrist. No escape, no fight left in her, they led her to the sofa.

"Miss Gibson, please sit. Can we get you a glass of water? I am Lieutenant Colonel Richard Pearce of Her Majesty's Twenty-Second Special Air Services Regiment. I'm afraid we have bad news."

Unable to bear the weight of his touch, she wrenched her arm from his grip. "No. No." *Start again.*

Eyes darting from floor to ceiling, counting the squares on the rug in front of the gas heater, looking anywhere, everywhere. Not at them.

Her insides shook, and her teeth rattled.

"I'm very sorry, Miss Gibson, I regret to inform you …"

Kate sprung to her feet. "No. Don't you say it. Don't." Raising her chin, she refused, would not listen to the lie blazing from his eyes.

"Please. Sit." The officer cleared his throat and half rose from his seat.

Kate pulled her hand to her chest and gulped for air, willing the inevitable to find another home, someone else's sister.

"Miss Gibson..."

"Kate, I'm Kate. Oh, God no, please don't."

"We're deeply sorry, Miss G … Kate. Sergeant Michael Gibson was killed in action yesterday afternoon while on patrol …"

She would not scream. Kate bit the inside of her cheek and welcomed the blood pooling in between her teeth.

"Taliban insurgents attacked Sergeant Gibson's patrol while they were on clean-up detail in a village on Burkina's border with Mali. As per standard procedure, there will be a post-mortem, but we believe he died as a result of an IED—an explosion. You have our sincere condolences."

She may hear his words, but it wasn't true. "I told you, it is a mistake. George, where was George?" Mike and his dog were inseparable. He would never lead her brother into danger. He'd die first.

"George?" The officer tilted his head

What? She'd stopped speaking English. "His dog. Where was his dog?"

"I'm sorry . . . Kate." He shifted from one foot to the other as he spoke her name. "There was no mention of his dog.

Mike was training African locals, toilets, re-builds—no Rambo stuff. He swore when dad left them, he'd always be there for her and Mike didn't break promises.

"Is there somebody we can call? A relative? Someone who can stay with you?"

"What?" She blinked. "Yes… Crystal. I'll call her."

"Very well, a Family Liaison Officer will contact you tomorrow to let you know the arrangements for your brother's return to England. Miss Gibson, Kate, is there anything else we can do?"

"No." They'd done enough. "Thank you."

"Again, please accept our sincere condolences. We can see ourselves out."

Kate stumbled after them and slammed the door behind them. Her heart hammering in her head, she grabbed the phone off the coffee and punched in Crystal's number.

"Hi, hun. You stuck on the Northern Line? Damn Tube, we may miss running hot water in Africa, but never the damn trains. Right? I'm sitting here, lethal cocktail in my hand, getting truly smashed. How much longer?"

"Crys, I need you…"

"Kate? You sound weird, hun. Don't tell me you started celebrating without me."

"Crys…it's Mike."

"Mike? Is he there? I didn't know the boys were back from Africa. Spanner hasn't called. It drives me nuts how long it takes for their letters to get to London, and their internet is bloody non-existent. Slower than the bloody train." Crystal laughed.

Please, stop talking. "Crys. Oh, God…" Afraid she'd choke on the words locked in her throat, she grasped her neck

"What's going on, Kate? Are you coming, or not? Don't tell me the suits changed their mind and refused the Misoprostol?"

"Crys, it's Mike. He's gone. Mike's dead."

CHAPTER THREE
RAF – BRIZE NORTON, UK

Kate stood on the balcony of the visitor centre, wondering how long she could hold her breath against the wind roaring across the tarmac, amongst the usual mix of pigeons, sparrows and crows swooping and squawking at the intruders.

Dressed in clothes that owned a home at the back of her wardrobe, she stood sentry at Mike's Re-Patriation Ceremony. Did she have to agree to be her brother's emergency contact? If she'd said no, would this moment be more bearable?

Mike swore he'd never leave her. He'd promised. Promised.

Tears for the person who meant everything to her rolled over her cheeks. A strand of hair clung to the side of her mouth. She should have cut it or tied the mop off her face.

No doubt wishing Kate, not her beloved son, figured on the 'number up' list, Mother refused to attend Mike's ceremony.

"Sure, you don't want to sit, Kate?" Crystal squeezed her arm, wrenching her into the present.

Crys had been a gem since last Thursday night sleeping on the lumpy sofa bed, refusing to leave her alone, measuring days with endless cups of tea, handing her a wet cloth every time she heaved.

Perfect Crystal Starr didn't have a miserable bone in her. Her friend since primary school with straight blond hair and a mother who made doll's clothes.

"You okay, hun?" Crystal edged her towards the lone chair at the side of the balcony.

Arms plastered to her sides, eyes glued front and centre, she forced a grunt past the boulder blocking words held at the back of her throat. Afraid she might lose it if she looked at Crys, Kate gave her friend's forearm a grateful squeeze and focussed on the clouds gathering overhead.

Mike was the warrior. She was the sister who missed her brother's smile.

The flowers in front of the visitor's centre were plastic. *Bit naff,* she swore she heard Mike say. Kate stifled a giggle. Weird what made you laugh when every cell screamed 'cry'.

Finally, the military transporter poked its nose through the clouds, glided onto the tarmac, its powerful engine deafening as it taxied and rolled to a stop.

The door of the C17 lifted, and from its belly emerged Mike's Patrol Leader in full dress uniform, one white-gloved hand steadying the foot of the flag-covered coffin. They'd met before, but stuffed if she remembered when. Heads bowed, her brother resting on their shoulders, the rest of his patrol followed.

Kate shuddered.

Last summer, on leave before their final tour, Mike and his team came to London. How could she forget the lazy Sunday picnic in Hyde Park where Crystal met Spanner, and Mike introduced her to his best friend, Luke, a surgeon in civvy life. The team called him Doc.

Taller than the others he walked on the side of the coffin closest to her, his face a mask.

At the picnic, he hadn't said much, but his killer smile stayed with her weeks after they deployed. No smile now. Not this. Never this. Tears pooled at the corners of her mouth.

The wind gusting over the tarmac made the sombre march across the to the hearse slow. Aeons passed as the funeral director, hand on his top hat, his long coat flapping in the breeze, accompanied the cortège to the chapel.

The brief ceremony over, Mike's team formed a line and saluted as she and Crystal passed. Glad it was over, afraid she was on the verge of an embarrassing meltdown she didn't dare look them in the eye. A sorry sniff was the best on offer. Thank you was an insult to the pain in their eyes, to the sorrow that matched her own.

Head down, she huddled closer to Crystal and battled through the wind to the hired limousine. Neither of them said anything until they reached John Radcliffe Hospital, and the hearse made the turn to the morgue. She'd taken Mike as far as she could. Kate kissed two fingers and laid them on the window—*bye Mike.*

Post-mortems were mandatory for men killed in the line of duty. The Visiting Officer said it might take up to three weeks before they received the official death certificate. Thinking of Mike lying on a slab brought on vicious sobs that robbed her of air.

"Here, hun, right here." Crystal guided her head onto her shoulder. "We need air." She opened the window a crack.

The cold draught on her cheeks kept her awake as they drove to Mike's flat. He preferred to stay off-base. She wasn't looking forward to packing up his stuff, but Mother wasn't up to it. Her fragile mental health was a worry.

"You sure you don't want me to stay. My next shift at the hospital isn't until Sunday. I could call in sick," Crystal offered.

"I'm sure." Crys deserved rest and Kate craved time by herself.

Crystal tilted her head and raised her eyebrows.

Kate grabbed the end of Cry's scarf and pulled her into a hug. "Stop worrying. I'll be okay. Give me time to organise Mike's flat and complete paperwork for his regiment. I'll call you tomorrow."

"Love you."

"Love you too." Kate pressed her lips together. Too afraid she might change her mind and ask Crys to stay.

Mike's favourite aftershave hit her with the force of a double-decker bus as soon as she unlocked his door. *Spice and everything nice.* Her back braced against the closed door, she clutched her chest and took a second to pull herself together.

Her gaze wandered over Mike's collection of framed Disney characters lining the walls. Dad had given him his first print when he became captain of his high school football team.

His favourite photo hung proudly in the middle of the row – Mike and his squaddie mates at a charity fancy dress ball. He'd convinced them to go as Snow White and her dwarves. The memory made her smile, Mike struggling into a dress and his teammates all over six feet tall.

Kate swiped at the tear pricking the corner of her eye and marched her feet into the living room. A trick of the light had her catching her breath. She could swear Mike sat on the sofa laughing at the telly, inhaling a slice of pizza with extra cheese.

Straight after the terrorist bombings at the hotel in *Wagga.* He'd almost kicked down her door, hugged her so tight she almost suffocated. She was alive, and they had to celebrate.

Six o'clock in the morning, they shared a bottle of red, make that two, and cloaked themselves in shared memories and sentimental affirmations.

If Mike were here now, he'd tell her to put her bum next to his while they watched the football. Dad and Mike, Arsenal's loyal fans.

Reaching behind her, she snagged his football top from the arm of the sofa. A trace of his aftershave clung to the inside of the shirt as she slipped it over her head and welcomed the hint of life tickling her nose.

After packing Mike's clothes and emptying two tissue boxes, she was done. Balancing a strong cup of tea in one hand, she collapsed at the kitchen table and opened the large manilla envelope the Visiting Office had given her at the ceremony.

Late afternoon shifted into evening, and Kate's heart sank with the watery sun. She ought to check on Mother.

Calling their relationship strained was an understatement, but mum wasn't doing well. A good daughter would find a job in London, stay home, look after her.

For the past week, she'd been trying to figure out the best way to tell Crystal she wasn't going back to Africa. Not for a few months. Possibly never. Crys was more than capable of running *Afrique Santé's* training program.

Kate sipped her cold tea. The walls of Mike's flat drifted further and further apart until darkness and the sound of waves crashing underneath the pier surrounded her. Her father's voice echoed a long way off from where she was standing.

"I'll be back, Katy. Wait here. Good girl."

Why did anyone she ever cared for abandon her? Did she care too much, was she too clingy, needy?

Selfish. Kate despised feeling sorry for herself, detested how angry she was at Mike.

The persistent buzz of her mobile vibrated on the coffee table. Mother's ID glowed Martian green on her phone.

"Hello."

"Why didn't you call? Where are you?" Mother's grizzle crackled in Kate's ear.

"Sorry, I must have dozed off. I'm at Mike's. Remember? I told you."

"Weren't you supposed to call when you got to your brother's flat?"

Most of Mother's questions were rhetorical. As a nurse, Kate understood her anxiety, her manic preoccupation with her world.

"Can I call you back, mum? I left something on the stove." The lie flowed smoothly over her tongue.

She ran her fingers through her hair, regretting she wasn't more for her mother and able to forgive her.

"Soon, Kate." A loud click—dismissed.

"Bye, Mum." With any luck, Mike had a bottle of Merlot stashed on the rack under the TV.

Bottle and glass in hand, Kate was two steps from the kitchen when the sudden knock on the door made her jump. *Shit. I only have one brother to kill.*

Red wine sloshed over her bare feet and onto the carpet.

Not sure who it could be, she placed the bottle and glass on the coffee table and kept walking. At the door, she ran her fingers through the knots in her hair and vowed to make this quick. "Crys, that you?"

"Captain Luke McLaren, Royal Army Medical Corps. We met at the picnic."

CHAPTER FOUR

Doc. His deep baritone voice rumbled through the door. *Hell*. She ran her hands over the front of her skirt, knowing she couldn't face him. "I remember who you are. Sorry, but now's not a great time."

"I've brought Mike's gear, his duffel, from his locker."

"Oh … thank you. Look, I'm not dressed. The bag, duffel, it's safe, you can leave it, and I'll get it in a few minutes. Er, thanks for coming."

The pointy end of a long day chose that moment to stab her in the ribs. Suddenly, it was too much. Her throat was raw from shedding too many tears. It hurt to speak.

"Kate? Are you okay?"

"Yes … oh … no."

"I'm a doctor. Open the door. Let me help." Luke's voice rang with authority, smooth, professional concern.

Kate placed her palm against the door and laid her cheek on her hand.

"Open up, Kate. Please."

Fresh out of fight, she did as he asked, opened the door to eyes, the colour of a smooth malt whisky.

Not her best move, he may take it as an invitation.

She lunged for the duffle dangling by his side. The weight of it dragged her off balance. Fingertips pressed on the wall steadied her enough to avoid Luke's outstretched hand, his offer to help.

"Thanks. You didn't need to come. I planned to collect it tomorrow." She ran her top teeth over her bottom lip. There was no need to be ungrateful.

"You should eat," he said.

She hitched the bag over her shoulder, went to take a step back and stumbled again. This time, Luke steadied her. The gentle pressure of his palm on the small of her back warmed the constant chill settled there since last week.

Her gaze lifted to his face. High cheekbones, full lips, he was a handsome man, despite the scar in the middle of his chin. Under different circumstances, she may have welcomed his attention, invited him in for a drink. Had he been with Mike when he died? Not tonight. She didn't need to know tonight.

Luke watched her, and his kind eyes brought a flush of heat from her throat to her cheeks. Overwhelmed by his gaze, too full of concern, Kate stopped him before he could speak. "Sorry, I didn't mean to be rude." Grasping his forearm, she willed him not to say *everything will be okay*. Words sure to finish her.

Nothing surprised Luke. As a trauma specialist, he'd seen more than his fair share of unbelievable, until today.

Mike's sister opened the door, swamped shoulders to knees, in his mate's football shirt. Red curly hair, a shade lighter than Mike's spilt over her pale face. Striking blue eyes, brimming with sadness, hit him for six.

One thing for sure, Kate Gibson was about to drop. He hooked his arm around her waist, caught her weight and absorbed her tremble.

"Easy." Her head tucked comfortably under his armpit while the firm curve of her breast pressed snugly against his chest.

"What are you doing? Get off me. I don't need carrying!"

The solid punch from a fist, half the size of his, belted the air from his torso. Since when did boxing make the list of essential midwife skills? *Fair enough.* Never a man to venture where he wasn't wanted, he released her. "You need a drink, water."

"Yes. What? No."

Take the hint. Sod his deathbed promise to Mike. If he knew what was good for him, he'd head back to the barracks where his mate's wake had already started.

As he drove to the flat, he told himself over and over he shouldn't fucking be there.

Seeing Kate at Mike's ceremony, shoulders hunched, her eyes swollen from crying, he'd wanted to check on her make sure she was coping. Technically, it was the Boss' job, but he'd offered to be the one to tell her what happened to Mike before she read it on a cold, white sheet of paper.

You gave your word. Mike, the birdie in his ear. What could it hurt? Spend ten minutes making Kate a sandwich, put the kettle on before he fled. Palms up and out, he'd almost slipped past her when her eyes rolled to the ceiling, and she tumbled faster than an autumn leaf floating from a tired tree.

"Hup, I got you." Luke gathered her in his arms and settled her on Mike's beat-up sofa. Within seconds she sprang upright and teetered on bare feet.

"What is it with you? Kit bag—person." Kate slapped at his hands and pointed at Mike's duffle.

Her sudden sigh-smile lifted his mood. "My apologies, ma'am." *Leave.* He almost made it, took a step towards the door, turned on one heel and headed for the kitchen.

"Mike got any food stashed in the cupboards?" Half hoping he'd find a tin of Kate's legendary biscuits he opened the door closest to the fridge and rummaged behind the baked beans. *Bingo.*

"What's with the ma'am, soldier? Have you forgotten? We have met. I'm Kate. At the picnic, we didn't talk much, but…" Forget her? As if. A woman as stunning as Kate hibernated in a man's memory.

He'd barely spoken to her that afternoon because of the immediate and intense attraction he'd sensed between them. Keeping your hands off a mate's sister was part of the buddy code. Now, her head cocked to one side, twirling a length of hair between her fingers, did she deliberately tease him? Another time, another woman, he might explore the possibility.

"I remember you. And I'll call you whatever you want if you eat a biscuit and drink a glass of water. Deal?"

"Deal." She held out her hand. "Sorry, I was rude, before, it's been a tough couple of days. Let's start again. Kate, call me Kate."

Luke squeezed her hand, hoping to lift her gaze from the carpet—suddenly shy didn't suit her. "Okay, grub coming up, Kate."

"Thanks. How did you know Mike had biscuits?"

"Your brother shared your care packages." He winked, cadging another smile.

"In the Donald Duck tin—the one I gave him for Christmas." No smile.

Shit. He couldn't handle tears. Exit now and let the fuckers flow was the sane move. Call her in the morning.

"Sorry. You have to get back to base." She must have sensed his feet eager to hit the pavement.

The brush of Kate's fingers over his forearm sent a zap of electricity straight to his groin. Her gaze returned to counting the cracks in Mike's floorboards. "I've got some time. How about a cuppa. Sound good?"

Her chin lifted, and her eyes opened wider, blue pools perfect for diving deep. "Great, or do you prefer something stronger? No beer, but knowing my brother, I'll bet there's a bottle of whisky somewhere."

Still recovering from the unexpected shot of desire, he did his best to recover and continued opening cupboards. Mike's haphazard food filing designed to mess with a code breaker's head.

"There." Kate stood on her toes and plucked a bottle from behind the Weetabix and unscrewed the cap. "Say when." Under heavy eyelids, she stared straight at him, ignoring the glass as she poured.

He nodded for her to keep pouring. *Laphroaig.* He'd been hooked on the bevvy since med school when a mate said the smell reminded him of a burning hospital, the smell of fire and iodine assaulted his nostrils.

"When."

Given the circumstances, he shouldn't be attracted to Kate, but a sudden need to grasp her free hand powered over him. He stepped sideways, but the shift of his leg did nothing to ease the tension behind the zipper of his pants. *Not cool.*

Neither was the way his nipples hardened when her pinky finger traced a line on his tee-shirt right between his pecs. *Get a grip.* The faster he kept his promise, made sure Kate was okay and got the hell out of there, the better.

"Did I hurt you?" Her words hung on a long breath.

"Huh?" He gulped his scotch, trying to get his head around the sultry sadness attached to the thick eyelashes brushing her cheek.

"Before." Kate curled her fingers into a soft fist, and her second punch to his chest turned his brain to mush. "I don't make a habit of thumping men, especially the SAS." Her hand shook as she raised her glass. "Cheers."

Luke grasped her trembling hand, held it steady, and guided the glass to her lips. His libido fixed on her mouth, her half-smile.

"Sorry." Kate blushed.

Desire streamed through his veins, warring with his determination not to follow his instinct and kiss her.

"Don't apologise. Sit. Take a breath." Luke led her back to the sofa and sat beside her. Shock did things to a person, twisted their world.

Luke stared at the slim fingers interlaced with his, waves of electricity pulsing along his forearm, he opened his mouth to reassure her, tell her he understood.

"Believe it or not, I'm not usually pushy. This past week I haven't been thinking straight."

He could relate, though he didn't share. In the week since Mike's death, he'd drunk too much, fucked one too many willing women. *Yeah, but you didn't hold hands.*

"Thanks for bringing Mike's things. For bringing Mike home. He always said you guys were the best."

Mesmerised by the smile that blazed over him, Luke followed the graceful tilt of Kate's head, scanned the delicate collar bones cloaked in a cape of freckles, ploughed the depth of her gaze. A thousand questions behind her eyes. Vulnerable.

Sure, as hell, he shouldn't be attached to her hand. He was on a plane back to Burkina tomorrow. They were officially off the government payroll, Mike's repat their official march back into civvy life.

Thanks to a hefty donation courtesy of Knight's late grandmother Sentinel Security was set up, ready to go. They were supposed to be in it together. Him, Knight, Spanner and Mike. Luke swallowed the lump in his throat.

No way would he let the team go after Seckou without medical backup. Until they annihilated the bastard, he was part of the team. Another, one of a million, reasons nothing could happen between him and Mike's sister.

"Mike told me you were a surgeon at London Metro before joining the military." Kate sniffed.

"That's true. You're a nurse, a midwife?" Luke ordered his thumb not to brush the tear from her cheek and handed her a tissue from the near-empty box on the coffee table.

"Yes. I work in Africa mostly, before that at The Metropolitan Women's Hospital." Another sniff. "I love babies."

Thanks to Mike, he knew more about Kate than she'd feel comfortable with, but he didn't let on, it was better to keep her talking, besides he liked the sound of her voice, it held a power stronger than her slim body suggested. "Is that why you became a midwife?"

"Yes." She tipped her head to the side. "Why did you join the military?"

"The bombs in 2005, my sister was on the bus in Tavistock Square."

"Oh, Luke I'm sorry, was she …"

"No, lucky, relatively minor injuries, but she's never been the same since. I joined the medical corps, thinking I should do more than I was."

"And have you?"

He cleared his throat and quickly looked at his watch. "Depends on your point of view." Why he was telling Kate this stuff was a mystery, he never discussed his family with anyone.

"George, I was wondering about Mike's dog. I can't understand why he wasn't with Mike. Do you know why?"

It was one of the first questions he got answers to when they returned to base. "Yes, seems the dog had food poisoning. Vomit everywhere. Technically, they were on a sanitation patrol, helping to clear up a broken sewer pipe, so he let George sleep."

"Not my biscuits, I hope." Kate's fingers flew to her throat, skittering awkwardly over the thin gold chain caressing her slender neck.

"No. Never." Luke let out a long breath, matching Kate's relieved sigh.

"Mike loved that dog. Where is he now? Is he okay?"

"Yes, don't worry about him. He was up for retirement. Snake took him home. Sorry. Look, I better get going, I'm due at the base." Abrupt, but if he stayed longer, he wasn't sure he could ignore the strong urge to draw Kate into his arms, to hold her, take away the sadness that bled through the brave mask she wore.

"Yes. Sorry, I'm keeping you."

"Thanks for the drink."

"No. Thank you. I didn't realise how much I needed this." She touched his arm.

Luke shot to his feet, holding up his hand when she went to follow him. "No, don't get up, rest. Doc's orders." Lord, forgive him, he wanted this woman more than his next breath, and for the first time in his life, he wasn't sure if he was reading too much into a woman's touch. Kate's touch.

She stood to kiss him on the cheek. No more than a friendly goodbye peck. Except he could swear her fucking vulnerable eyes were asking him … *Oh hell*. Luke wound the curl falling over her face tightly around his index finger and tugged.

Bright as kingfisher wings, eyes glistening with tears locked with his, and he inhaled her freshness. *Fuck*. The scent of limes, sharp and present. *More*.

His lips drifted to the delicate edge of her mouth, eager for a taste, desperate to savour, but he wouldn't kiss her not unless she asked him. "If you want me to stop, tell me now." He closed his eyes, shifted left, right, and enjoyed the way her lips danced with his.

"Don't stop." Kate nuzzled her nose against his ear.

His mouth hovered at the base of her throat. "Now? Should I stop now?" Part of him hoped she'd slap him—scared shitless she might. Not a hint of resistance as he fought to keep his kisses gentle and stole from all things good.

"Mmm." Kate moaned.

The bite from her fingernails digging into the top of his arms sent shock waves below his belt. *Damn*. "Apologies," Luke murmured and took a step back.

"I don't understand. What's wrong?" Kate's hands dropped from his arms and gripped the edge of the sofa.

Nothing she'd done for sure.

"Luke, why did you kiss me?"

"I wanted to." The words of a randy teenager. He banged the side of his head with the heel of his hand, trying to knock some sense into his fucked-up skull.

"Then do it again." She grabbed his hand and pressed his palm to her cheek. "It's only a kiss. Please."

"No."

"Why not?"

Decades away in experience, five, possibly seven years younger than him, Kate didn't need his darkness, best to tell her what she ought to hear. "We fly to Africa tomorrow."

"Perfect."

CHAPTER FIVE

Upfront and on the table, Luke was leaving tomorrow. No wish wants or maybes. No fairy tales. Forever wasn't on her mind.

Dad had walked away with her universe when she was a kid. He left an ache she couldn't forget. News of Mike's death, been alone again, brought back the nightmares.

Numbness in her bones that weighed so heavily she barely moved from the couch except to pee. Hearing no goodbye, having no explanation did things to a favourite girl—left permanent scars.

She enjoyed sex, and the steamy release of it was what she needed right now and judging from the smouldering vibes coming from Luke he wasn't opposed to the idea.

Love 'em and leave 'em. Why not? Sexual healing with the stunning man nibbling the side of her neck as though she were the last sweet in the box, turned her bones to liquid. The desire reflected in the dark irises of his honey-brown eyes an adrenaline-charged strike to her bruised heart.

Greed for the power oozing from every pore of his skin, jealous of his strength, Luke's open-mouthed kisses, each rougher than the last, found her pleading for more. Burying her hands in the coarse hair licking the nape of his neck, Kate told her brain to take a hike.

Her turn to rule the kiss, Luke groaned, and she smiled, sucked tongue until her insides clenched. Gasping for breath, she raised her leg and hooked it over his thigh. Possessed, she rubbed her clit against the rough denim of Luke's jeans.

"Jesus, yes. Moan for me, Kate." Luke held her head and thrust his tongue deeper into her mouth, tasting her, claiming her. Brutal kisses, tasting of whisky and sugar, ripped moans of sweet pleasure from her grief-stricken soul.

"Now?" Luke's whisper loud and clear above the blood rushing in her ears.

Was he kidding? Her hands tore his t-shirt over his head. She'd never wanted a man this much in her whole life. "Yes. I want this." One night, away from hell.

Luke wrapped his arms around her, and her head found a home on his chest. A river of courage coursed through her blood.

"Bedroom through there?" Luke pointed to the hallway before scooping her into his arms.

Kate nodded, seized his pointing finger, and sucked it into her mouth. Luke's eyes rolled to the heavens. Impressive the way his cheeks hollowed into two lopsided dimples.

"Christ, what are you doing to me?" Luke lowered her to her feet, his breath sending chills along her neck.

She kicked off her shoes and dropped two inches. Luke's kiss hit her forehead instead of her lips, and they giggled like horny teenagers. "Sorry." She lifted her eyes to meet his.

"Come here." His voice was a low growl, mellow, like fresh honey sticking to her bones.

Luke's day-old whiskers scraped her chin. The burn outstanding. Even better the pinch of his fingers digging into her hips. The icy nothing of the last week replaced by a heat that sent her libido ballistic.

"Skirt, take it off."

Easier said than done. One deep breath, and with as much grace as she could fake, Kate wiggled out of her pencil skirt. Why hadn't she changed when she got home, slipped into that something-more comfortable.

She took her time, making the most of it, wanting more, craving every drop of the passion smouldering behind the dark irises of Luke's eyes. *Mine. Something for me.*

She peeled the stockings from her legs and slowly the power, her power of seduction took hold. Luke's breath hitched. Turning a man, this man, on, brought gasps of pleasure to her aching chest.

She was alive. She could prove it. Her hips swayed in time with a longing that snaked its way over each ridge of her spine.

How could this be wrong when it screamed perfect?

"More," Luke groaned.

"Now?" She couldn't resist the tease.

"Fuck yeah." His hand stroked the side of her hip.

Her trembling fingers grabbed the edge of her silk chemise.

"Too slow." In one smooth movement, he finished the job. The Doc had skills.

On fire, she arched against him and unhooked her bra. *I want your hands on my skin.* Her erect, aching, nipples stabbed at the frigid air between them.

Light from the hallway danced over the lines of his face and glittered in his eyes. Unbelievably sexy. She stepped out of her underwear and pulled on the buckle of his pants. "Your turn. Now."

Their lips quivered in a mutual smile.

Her hands trembled, but the zipper wasn't too much of a problem. A sharp tug before she eased the denim jeans over his hips, couldn't resist a feather touch of the dark hairs cloaking his taut, muscular thighs.

No underwear. Her breath hitched.

Beads of sweat pricked her forehead.

Fingers of one hand stroked the long hard ridge of his cock, while she rolled his balls in the other. Soft, delicate, such a sharp contrast to the rest of him. Kate's stomach clenched.

"Fuck!" Luke's erection pulsed in her palm.

"Promises, promises."

"Oh yeah. Hold on." He grabbed her thighs and wound them around his waist. His tongue lathed her nipple while his fingers pinched the other.

With any last chance of stopping this madness gone, Kate crossed her ankles and squeezed, sucked in a cry, and soared into the madness. She bit the side of Luke's neck. Hard. Ventured where she didn't belong.

***

Stop. Spiked on adrenaline, desiring Ms Gibson more than his next breath, they were through that gate. Luke grabbed her hand. If he didn't slow her magic fingers, he'd come before he got a chance to bury himself inside her. Kate first. He longed to see the flush of orgasm blaze across her face.

She shoved him hard, caught off balance he staggered backwards.

"What? You want me to stop?" *Fuck. Now?*

He rested his chin on top of her head and reigned in what little control he had left.

"Protection?"

He shuddered, licked her eyelids with the tip of his tongue and chuckled. "Don't worry, Special Air Service. Remember?" With a flourish, he pulled a wrapped condom from the pocket of his jeans.

"Ex. Special, fucking arsehole scout." Kate ground her pelvis against him, holding nothing back.

"Mmm. Say it again." He chuckled.

"What? Special? No."

He slid one finger inside her loving the way she clenched and sucked him deeper, added a second, then a third filling her tight sheath. More responsive than a hair-trigger, her hips rocked, following the rhythm he set. Her quiet whimper when he bent and sucked her pale, pink nipple spun him into orbit

"Open for me." His fingers deep in the wet heat of her body, Luke pinched her clit, and she came hard.

On fire, it crossed his mind that he would never have enough of Kate's hips grinding against him, lost in an erotic dance.

He kissed the bridge of her nose, licked the rim of her ear, and nibbled the pulse at her neck. "Look at me."

She did and tiny electric shocks built at the base of his spine. "I want to be inside you. Okay?"

"Yes, yes. Make me forget, Luke."

Jaw clenched, he fumbled with the condom packet.

"Let me." Kate's teeth ripped open the envelope.

Sexy as fucking hell, he couldn't drag his gaze away for the slim fingers taking their sweet time sheathing his cock.

"Jesus. Legs around my waist." He cupped her perfect arse cheeks, lifted her hips and thrust as deep as he could sink inside Kate Gibson.

Stretched tight around him, she peppered his face with kisses. Pinning her back to the wall, he fell into a rough rhythm designed to claim her sorrow. Listening to her whimper and moan as she climbed, reached for her release, he'd never fought so hard to keep it together.

He couldn't remember when he'd been so lost in a woman, always preferring to have them take their pleasure before he sought his own.

"Come with me, Kate."

"Yes," Kate cried his name.

Riding their climax together, Luke buried his mouth at the pulse point at the side of Kate's neck and poured all he was into her.

Knees trembling, jeans bunched around his ankles, he couldn't stand for much longer. He tightened his grip on Kate and shuffled to the bed, praying they made it without falling arse over tit.

With the smell of their lovemaking filling his nostrils, his breathing returned to normal. Kate slept by his side, the eerie glow of the streetlight streaming through the window landed on the soft skin of her perfect body.

Propped on one elbow, grinning from ear to ear, Luke stared at the beauty sprawled beside him and admired the ginger curls at the juncture of her thighs, her narrow waist, perfect pink nipples, the rise and fall of her breasts, moving in rhythm with her light snore. Long, golden eyelashes stroking her freckled cheeks.

Fucking gorgeous.

More content than he'd ever been, he rolled on his back, listened to the rhythm of her breathing finally joining her in sleep.

"Wait. Don't Go."

Dragged by a woman's scream, he was instantly awake. *Shit.* Luke turned on the bedside lamp and scrubbed his hands through his hair.

"Please, come back, no, don't go."

An arm landed across his waist. Kate lay next to him, her eyes shut tight, her head thrashing side to side.

"Kate, wake up." He brushed the hair from her cheek and stroked her forehead. Deep in his gut, he recognised her anguish, wished he could turn back the clock, bring her brother home. Alive.

"Don't go."

Having sex with Kate wasn't the 'taking care' Mike had in mind.

He'd come to tell her the truth, that Mike had shot himself with his gun. A gun he should never have been wearing.

The stuff of nightmares—Kate's brother died because of him.

Wrapping his arms around her, he rolled her closer to him, rocked her, whispered soothing words until she stopped shivering and settled. He'd never forgive himself for the pain he'd caused her.

Kate didn't stir as he rolled out of bed and dressed. Where were his fucking boots? He considered leaving them behind until he remembered where he'd kicked them, along with his shirt.

Praying she wouldn't wake, that he wouldn't have to face her, he snuck out of Mike's bedroom. After he shut the door to the flat, head in his hands, he sunk to the floor. *What have I done?*

CHAPTER SIX
ONE WEEK LATER

"Wait. What are you, bloody deaf?" The bus driver shot her a half-smile and pulled away from the kerb.

"There'll be another in ten." The woman rocking the Sainsbury trolly overflowing with red and blue striped plastic bags offered a toothless grin.

She didn't have time for the trip in the first place but needed a Boots for the bits that were hard to find once they got to the rural clinic.

Across the road, the entrance to the tube station yawned a welcome. She'd be warm, but the trip wasn't straightforward.

If her legs weren't acting like cricket stumps, she might have walked. It wasn't far. Instead, she stamped her feet and thumped her arms to her sides, trying to stay warm while she waited twenty minutes for the thirty-one to appear.

Packed, with the four-o'clock rush-hour crowd, she had no option but to take the stairs to the upstairs deck. Settled into a seat at the back of the bus, peering out of the window, Kate replayed Luke's story of why he joined the military.

Her eyes shot to the roof, wondering what his sister was doing, thinking on that day, a second before the bomb tore through the upper deck? She shuddered and hugged her shopping.

Luke did his best to hide it, the sadness underneath his anger. Empathy had drawn them together for a perfect one-night stand, exactly what she wanted, what they both needed.

When he left without saying goodbye, she should have been grateful, not irritated. Morning after conversations were awkward. Luke had saved her the effort of explaining that no matter how amazing the sex, it could not happen again.

The bus pulled up across the road from the station, and she shoved past the man sitting next to her and sent Luke to the back of her mind as she walked the short distance home.

The bloody stair lamp was out again, twice in one month. Kate fumbled with the key in the lock. Either the new bulb was faulty, or the landlord needed to fix the electrics—fat chance. The key finally budged.

Too late, she remembered Mother threatened to pop-in for a chat.

"Is that you, Kate?"

Who else?

The stench of boiling vegetables wafted passed her, up the iron stairs on to the street. She closed the door, familiar lethargy sinking over her. No amount of wishing would carry her a thousand miles from Camden Town.

"I've been waiting to hear from you all day. Please, Kate, tell me you got a proper job?" Mother hollered from the kitchen.

The, *or else* lingering in the air made the hairs on the back of Kate's neck prickle. The last year and a half she'd spent with Crystal training midwives in Burkina Faso didn't rate in Mother's world. Was it any wonder she'd never told her about their rescue work at the refugee camp, their partnership with Aunty?

"You should be thankful they considered you for the position, Kate. The Metropolitan Women's Hospital must have thousands of applications." The clash of metal pans punctuated the bloody obvious.

Mother had a point. Many nurses would sell both parents for the dream job—supervising midwifery training at the prestigious maternity hospital—top-end patients, including royalty.

Kate shuddered, unbuttoned her coat, placed it on the hook, milked every second while she reminded herself Mother was grieving. As if the fact made mum cooking dinner more bearable.

Her head throbbed, and her legs put rubber to shame. Content to curl up with a grisly thriller, she wasn't planning on eating.

The job was hers. Kate had worked at The Metropolitan Women's Hospital before; they were familiar with her skill set. Her experience supervising the midwife training in Africa proved a bonus and the Selfridges' power suit clinched it. Two hundred and fifty quid, too much for a garment destined for Oxfam.

"Yes, mum, I got the job." Light from the dingy fluorescent shone from the kitchen into the hallway.

Metal spoon in hand, her mother stood in the middle of the kitchen, surrounded by pots, pans, and cutlery. One look from the glassy eyes of the raw fish sprawled on the chopping board and Kate wanted to vomit.

Complicated. The best word to describe mum even before dad did a bunk. Elated one minute, suicidal the next, her moods rivalled the African *Harmattan* trade winds.

All through the interview, she'd told herself Mother didn't have anyone else. She may hate the idea, but perhaps she should in London. Kate was as shocked as the interview panel when she refused their job offer.

The rural hospitals in Burkina may not have The Metropolitan Women's Hospital state-of-the-art facilities, but what it lacked in shiny stuff, it delivered in human capital.

Guilt crushed an already buried heart. Any way she looked at it her had let her mother down, and no moment was the right moment to tell her she was returning to Africa. She should never have mentioned the job interview. Getting the job made matters worse.

"Kate, make yourself useful and pour us a drink. Where are you hiding the Gordon's? I swear I left a bottle the last time I was here."

She had. It went into the rubbish bin as soon as she left. "No. Don't think so." Kate rounded the kitchen bench and opened the fridge. "Fancy a lemonade?"

Her mother's pout accentuated the lines creasing the side of her mouth, making her appear older, sadder. "No, thank you. Set the table before dinner is inedible."

Argh. Kate wanted to throw plates at the wall. Without a sound, she pried two sets of knives and forks from the drawer. A trick Mike taught her, now a habit. When they were kids, the last thing they wanted to do was disturb Mother's afternoon nap.

"Kate, whatever's the matter? If your face drops any further, I'll be scraping your chin off the floor. You should be delighted you got the job."

She bit back a curse. "Please, mum. I'm fine. Tired, it's been a long day."

Last night, she'd gone to the local pick-up bar, something she never did, looking to replicate the blissful release she'd found with Luke. She didn't do long-term relationships, but one-nighters were never her thing

Luke had been different. Their attraction off the scale and his care and concern brought back fond memories of her brother. He was never short of a cuddle when she needed it.

After spending half an hour fixing her make up to hide the shadows under her eyes, she'd got half-way to the bar and decided on a movie instead. She had spent the entire time trying to figure out what language the actors were speaking, settling on Portuguese she finished her popcorn and left before it ended.

"You said you might pop in, mum, but I didn't expect …" She waved her hand over the kitchen bench. "Dinner, I didn't expect dinner." Kate opened a bottle of *Chablis* and poured two glasses.

Mother's withering look made her feel five years old caught licking the icing spoon. She shivered. "Did you go to the Harrods sale? Buy much? Their knickers are too dear for me even if the tag says half price."

"You should be earning a decent salary, able to buy whatever you want. If you hadn't spent the last year swanning around Africa." A fly, caught in the thermal from Mother's waving hand, ducked past Kate's nose. "It's beyond me how you expect to help others if you can't take care of yourself? I want you to buy a house."

Without taking a breath, Mother flew from Kate taking care of herself to embracing a mortgage to, "you need a man."

Pins and needles shot along her arm from the tight grip she had on the knives. "No, Mum. I don't need a man." *No permanent fixtures.* Of course, she might make an exception for a particular six-foot-four army medic.

"Please don't shout, Kate. I'm right here, standing next to you. When do you start at The Metropolitan Women's Hospital?"

Kate closed her eyes, guilt slapping the back of her head. She hated people who yelled. Loud words hit harder than chucked stones. "I don't." *Hell.* Way to go, Kate, hold up a placard saying, drop dead. She'd blame it on the wine, but her glass was untouched.

"What do you mean? You don't?"

"I'm not taking the job. *Afrique Santé* has renewed my contract." Without a man, she was tempted to add. "I wish you'd try to understand. I matter there, and I love my work at the clinic in Dori. Honestly, you don't need to worry and having your support would mean a lot."

Kate speared an overlooked piece of onion sitting on the kitchen bench with the tip of her index finger. "At this point in my life, I'm happy to rent. I don't need a house."

Mother rolled her eyes and kept stirring. Her chest heaved, and her mouth opened.

"Sorry I have to make a quick call." Kate moved fast, ignoring the barrage of comments trailing her into the bedroom. Sitting on the edge of the bed, she punched Crystal's speed dial number and willed her to answer.

"Hi, hun, is it done? Have you told your mum?"

"Yes. She's here."

"Crikey. In the flat? That doesn't sound good. How did she take it?"

"Honest Crys, what do you think? She is one stiff drink away from her you-are-a-failure, self-destructive-selfish speech. I will never own a house."

"A house? You lost me, hun."

"Forget it. It's not important."

"Make a run for it, drinks at Scarfes, my treat."

Crystal didn't have to ask twice. "I'm out the door."

"Dinner's ready Kate," Mother sang from the kitchen. "I want to talk to you about your grandfather' birthday. You forgot his birthday last year. This year it would be appreciated if you could make an effort."

Kate looked sheepishly at her shoes. Guilty as charged. "Yes, okay, but not now. I'm sorry. I didn't know you were coming with dinner. I've arranged to meet Crystal. That was her on the phone. You stay, make yourself at home. If you're here later, we can talk." Not likely considering her mother's bedtime was a sacred ritual.

"Call her back, tell her you're having dinner with me."

"Sorry I can't do that. We're meeting the CEO of *Afrique Santé*. They arranged it weeks ago." Kate winced, anything but the truth worked out better with Mother these days.

Scarfes was a fifteen-minute drive. Stuff the parking fee, she needed a drink. Heart pounding, she grabbed her coat and left Mother ranting at the dishes. She'd call her later and apologise again.

Crystal spotted her the moment she walked into the bar. "What's your poison?"

"I'll have what you're having," Kate half-spoke, half-mimed above the noise of the Friday, welcome-to-the-weekend office crowd.

"Are you sure, hun? You want what I'm having?" Crystal skulled the last of her drink.

"I'm sure, *honey*." Kate grinned.

Crystal sniffed the empty cocktail glass and winked. "One Nutcracker coming up."

"Cute." Kate flopped into one of the inviting, overstuffed armchairs in front of the fire. Thawing, inside and out, she enjoyed the image of Luke's full lips, his smile, dancing in flames.

"Here, get this down you." Crystal waved the Nutcracker under her nose.

The mix of coffee, almond and orange laced with vodka pried the final icicle from her soul.

"How are you, Kate?" Crys rattled the ice in her glass.

It had been a week since they brought Mike home. "Fine. Don't keep asking." A swell of regret hit the instant she snapped at Crystal.

"Okay, okay, not another word. Me, changing the subject." Crystal laughed, loud enough to turn heads. "I'm glad you're coming with me to Burkina," she whispered and poked her tongue at a couple sitting at the bar.

"Oh, that's mature."

"What?"

Kate shook her head at Crystal's feigned innocence and skulled the last of her drink. "Let's meet with Aunty as soon as we get to Burkina."

"OMG! How did you know? I didn't want you to worry, not with Mike's..."

"Worry? What do you mean?" Kate shifted forward in her seat and grasped Crystal's hand. "Tell me."

"Aunty phoned."

"When?"

"Right after...well, you know. Aunty said one of the girls at Dori clinic contacted her."

"What about, did she say? Which girl?" Aunty offered sanctuary to victims of teenage marriages at the refugee camp where she lived. The marriages were illegal in Burkina, but it was difficult for the gendarmes to police the smaller, more remote, villages.

They'd agreed to help Aunty by putting anyone who needed help in touch with her. It wasn't much, a minor part in a significantly more dangerous program.

"She's nervous. Another?" Before she refused, Crys eyeballed the waiter and signalled for two more Nutcrackers. "Aunty isn't sure how many more girls they can hide," Crystal continued. "She sounded scared, and I'm sure there was more she wanted to say, but she may not have been alone. I wasn't looking forward to telling her you'd decided to stay in London. She's always happy, relieved to see you. You'll sort her concerns, you always do."

"We'll do our best." Where was the waiter? A refill suddenly a marvellous idea. Kate refused to think about the day a husband, his mates in tow, came searching for his runaway wife.

CHAPTER SEVEN
JUST OUTSIDE BAMAKO, MALI, WEST AFRICA

The tilt of Kate's head, crazy red hair cascading over her shoulders, the passion reflected in her eyes as he eased into her heat. One fucking night with Mike's sister and invisible limb syndrome applied to his heart? *Grow a pair. Take another bucket shower.*

One leg bent, the other stretched in front of him, Luke slumped against the Land Rover. His head resting on the thick tyre, he refused to close his eyes because every time he did, Kate plagued him.

For him, what they shared would never be a mistake, but getting to know Kate was asking for fucking catastrophe. Leaving a note would have been pointless. What could he say? *Thanks for the blow-my-head-off sex, it's been terrific meeting you. I killed your brother. Have a great day, kiss, kiss.*

Thanks to the manic pace the Boss had set since they landed back in Mali, no one had enjoyed much sleep. He was doing fine, staying focussed on what needed to be done until Spanner let it drop that Kate and Crystal were heading for Dori.

A fucking three-hour drive across Burkina and he could ... What? Nothing. He swore to Mike he'd take care of his sister. Any time Kate needed him, he'd come running, but kissing her, steamy sex. Never again.

"Anyone got a light?" Snake reached for the pack of Marlboros sticking out of his jacket pocket.

"Here." Luke fished a book of soggy matches from his pants and tossed them over, knowing unless Snake wanted to alert the enemy, he daren't strike them. *Shit.* If Seckou was a half-decent terrorist, he'd had beady eyes on them since they arrived.

"Cheers, Doc." Snake tucked the matches inside his cigarette pack and cursed the rain that hadn't stopped since they bogged down in this shit-hole twenty-four hours ago.

"Man, I can't wait to get to Dori when we wrap up here. Deadset, no matter what it takes, Crystal will not leave my bed for a week," Spanner grizzled and reached for the bag of groundnuts lying next to Luke's pack.

What was he, fucking Tesco? "Hey. Find your own sodding nuts." Luke swung the bag behind him.

Spanner chuckled. "Hey, Doc, why don't you come with me? To the clinic in Dori. Catch up with Crys and Kate and …"

This time when Spanner snatched at the ground nuts, Luke let him have them. "Nope."

"Why not? Kate's a talented woman. Ah, ah, don't snarl, it does nothing for your chubby cheeks. Crys reckons everyone loves her and she's smarter than most people they've worked with here, or in London. Mike's sister …" Spanner's voice hitched. "Come with, Doc, let Kate work her magic on your lousy bedside manner."

Snake's turn to snort. Okay, okay so he should have been an anaesthetist, not a trauma specialist. Less blood and your patients didn't argue. "Shut the fuck up Spanner and keep your eyes on the Dickers."

"Standing by. Over." Spanner pressed on the side of his earpiece and shook his head. Still no sign of the shit head. "Let's make it a double, Doc." Spanner wiggled his eyebrows.

"One's plenty for me." Kinky sex was more Knight's style. "Now if you're talking a double scotch, I'm in. I'm fucking parched." Luke adjusted the strap on his helmet.

"Now you're being obtuse, Doc. I'm not talking about drinks. Me and Crys. You and Kate."

"Obtuse? Where've you been learning such big words?"

"Crys has been taking me in hand, bro'"

Spare me.

"Better let Doc check your eyebrows, Spanner, they're in spasm," Snake offered.

Spanner edged the toe of his boot into the side of Snake's upper leg a wide smirk sweeping across his face.

"No man, I'm telling you, won't happen." Knight was disappointed with him, which was worse than been blasted for being too chicken to tell Kate the truth. That had been the plan. He'd volunteered.

Luke gnawed the inside of his cheek and snuck a look around the rim of the tyre. Chairs and tables littered the space outside what must be the shittiest local in town. No one stayed longer than five minutes except for one wanker who'd been rocking on two legs of his chair for the last hour watching another man dig a hole. He bellowed orders. "*Dépêchez-vous,* hurry, deeper, or the rain will wash it away."

Luke scratched the side of his neck. Fuck knew what they were burying.

"*Merde,*" the man on the deck swore and placed his beer beside his feet.

Two black SUVs with tinted windows, missing plates, rolled onto the horizon. Seckou, the bastard. Had to be.

Raising onto his haunches, Luke waited for the Boss to give the order.

"Heads up." Knight's voice crackled over Luke's headset.

"Roger that. Look lively, gentlemen." Spanner raised his rifle.

About bloody time. A big bloke, Seckou had to be, circled to the passenger side of the truck. *Gotcha.* Luke was tempted to ditch their hideout and call the fucker into the open. Wild-wanking-west. A bullet in the brain courtesy of the Boss and they could all go home, escape the heat, turning his sweat to brine.

The man on the porch shuffled forward. *"Salaam-Alaikum."* Luke smelled his fear.

"Wa-Alaikum-Salaam," Seckou replied.

"You're early, brother. You said tomorrow."

Thank God for early. Luke rolled spit between his teeth and savoured a moment imagining boiling the bones of the Al-Qaeda hotshot who'd blown his mate to smithereens.

"Yacouba, are you not glad to see me?"

"Oui, bien sur."

"Enough of this shit, how much longer?" Luke gripped the handle of his Bergan and raised his chin at Spanner?

"Fuck knows. The Boss says, stand down, and I am riveted to the spot." He tapped his earpiece. "Roger that." Luke caught Spanner's answering nod. "You're in luck, Doc. Three, two... Go. Go. Go."

Let's do this. London calling. Bring it on!

"Back, back, get back." They were two feet from Seckou's vehicle when Spanner yelled and signalled for them to retreat.

A split second before the sky lit up in bright orange flame Seckou, the bastard, sprang from behind Seckou's vehicle aiming a mother-fucker RPG-7.

CHAPTER EIGHT

Kate had been clutching her hands in her lap for the entire drive to Heathrow. Her patience was at an end.

"Stay in the car, mum."

"What about Michael's flat, his furniture?" Drowning in crocodile tears, Mother, insisted on driving her and Crystal to the airport.

"Don't worry. Everything is taken care of; someone from the Base is happy to rent short-term. When I get back, we can decide if we want to sell."

"Do you know this person?"

"Yes, no, I met with him, checked refs, seems like a nice guy. Don't worry."

"Let me park. I'll come with you. We can have dinner and discuss what to do with your brother's clothes."

"No, we've eaten, and most of Mike's stuff is safe in storage." Mother didn't need to know the first thing she had done was stuff Mike's wardrobe into rubbish bags. The British Red Cross well pleased, sent a van to pick them up the next day.

"I wish you'd consulted me. There were personal items I wanted to keep. It's the least you could have done, let me choose." The waterworks began again.

Kate closed her eyes, resisting the temptation to stick her fingers in her ears and scream. "I'm sorry, promise, we can sort it later. It's getting dark I don't want you hanging around Heathrow. Besides the parking here costs a fortune. I'll call you when we arrive."

She didn't need to apologise. They were late. Any more delays and they'd miss the bloody plane, and hand-holding through check-in was not an option.

"Bye, mum." Half out of the car, guilt flooded her cheeks. Kate leant between the seats and gave her a quick peck on the cheek.

Crystal was no bloody help. Her face loomed on the outside of the car window cross-eyed and grinning. "Bye, Mrs Gibson, thanks for the lift."

Kate wrestled from Mother's grip on her coat sleeve.

Afrique Santé's representative waited inside Terminal Four guarding the boxes of Misoprostol. Everything checked in; boarding passes issued. Finally, they were boarding.

Oblivious to the drone of the engine, Crystal slept, her gentle snores raising the single curl draped over the bridge of her nose.

Head propped against the closed shutter, eyes dry and itchy, Kate stared at the tv screen. She'd lost count of how many re-runs of *Sex and City* she'd endured watching Carrie and her friends chase one blissful lay after the other. Half their luck. Kate sighed and drank the last of her luke-warm fizz.

She hadn't had sex since Luke snuck out of Mike's flat. Silent Ninja SAS feet were a myth. No one wearing size fourteen combat boots made it over Mike's floorboards without a squeak. No kiss. No care. *Exactly what you wanted.*

Tray table stored, Kate shifted her hips and stretched her legs under the seat in front of her. After circling in a holding pattern for an hour, all she wanted to do was lose the safety belt and stand.

Finally, the door to the aircraft opened. Tired didn't come close to the aching lethargy weighing on Kate's body as they joined the line through Immigration. Baggage loaded, they headed for Customs.

"At this rate, we'll be sleeping at Sankara airport." Crys put her weight on her elbows, forcing her trolly to stop abruptly. "Oops. Did I tell you the Sentinel boys are in Mali?"

"No." The carry-on bag slid from Kate's shoulder. The thought scared her half to death, mostly because she hadn't been able to get passed their night together.

"Spanner didn't say. Secret Squirrel stuff." Crys released the brake on the trolley and swung hard right. "Hey, that one, that lines shorter."

Kate drew in a deep breath and followed. Africa was a vast continent. It was highly unlikely she'd bump into Luke.

By the time they cleared customs, she was struggling to put one foot in front of the other. Next time Crystal offered her melatonin stash she'd accept.

The temperature hovered around thirty-five degrees in Burkina. A sharp contrast to the six degrees they'd left in London. Crystal lingered under one of the giant airport fans wrestling with the hair clinging to the back of her neck. Forty degrees was forecasted for tomorrow, no flushing toilets in Dori and running water twice a week if they were lucky.

The automatic exit doors flew open. Kate stood on tiptoe and strained to find Issouf, their driver, amongst the men holding name cards crowded along the barrier. Panicked, her blood pounded in her ears. What if he forgot they were coming?

"There he is. Issouf, here, over here." Crystal took off into the crowd, leaving her to wrangle the trolly with a mind of its own.

Aunty stood beside Issouf. Her hair secured neatly under the orange and violet *dhuku* wrapped around her head. Kate envied her ability to look elegant in the heat.

"Long trip, *chère*?" Aunty grinned.

"Too long." Kate sank into the arms of the queen of hugs. A squeeze with enough pressure to make you feel safe, not claustrophobic.

"Did customs give you any trouble with the *Misoprostol*?" Aunty peered over Kate's shoulder at the mountain of boxes.

Since they'd been using the drug, the maternal death rate had decreased significantly. Unlike oxytocin, it didn't need refrigeration—a bonus in Burkina where electricity was temperamental, unreliable, in remote areas.

"Not this trip. Paperwork in order. There are ten boxes. Three more than last time." Each one plastered with official stamps.

"I was sorry to hear of your brother's passing *chère*." Aunty pulled her in for a second hug.

Her friend's tears were more than Kate could handle, and she wasn't sure the cough she dredged from her throat hid the loneliness in her voice. "Thank you."

"Don't get sick on me, Kate." Crystal turned and smiled. "Lead on, Issouf. It's after midnight, and you don't want this girl turning into a pumpkin. I need my bed. By the way, how's that talented wife of yours?"

"She good, miss. Looking forward to seeing you. This way."

Crystal loved to nag his wife, Justine, for her family recipes. This trip she was after the secrets of Babenda. Kate clutched her stomach. Sardines were the hero of the traditional dish.

Issouf drove them straight to the Laico Hotel, seriously too upmarket for their budget, but Kate didn't argue when Crys insisted they enjoy one night of comfort before heading across the dusty Sahel.

In the lobby, two security guards eyed their bags while two more stood either side of the reception desk. Since the recent attack on the Splendid Hotel, no one took any chances.

"*Merci*, Issouf. *A demain?* Tomorrow." Kate shook his hand.

"*Oui*, what time?"

Crystal shrugged.

"Seven. Best get an early start."

Crystal groaned.

"What's with the pantomime? You had your chance." Kate chuckled.

"Okay, *à bientôt*." Issouf waved and stepped inside the revolving doors.

Although it was late, Kate was eager to listen to Aunty's concerns and relieved when she agreed to stay and share tea. Not wanting to rush her, they drank the first cup catching up on the last group of refugees settling into the camp.

"More?" Kate lifted the teapot.

"*Non. Merci.*" Aunty folded her hands in her lap, squeezed until her knuckles turned white.

A strong woman, it was unlike Aunty to worry. "Crystal says you're concerned there are too many girls at the camp."

"*Oui.* Yes."

"I'm sorry, we didn't intend to be gone this long, but we're here now, we can help."

"No apology necessary Kate. We manage. That is not what I wish to discuss. There is something else. *Un autre problème.*"

"Is it the Gendarmes?"

"No. We take care of the Gendarmes." Aunty rubbed two fingers and her thumb together. Anywhere in the world, money, the universal language. "Do you remember Amina?"

Kate nodded. How could she forget the pregnant teenager she'd met on her last visit?

A local nurse, Sedi, asked for her opinion on the girl's health? At six months, she was underweight and shouldn't be suffering morning sickness. Together they worked out a diet and discussed the benefits of ginger and vitamin supplements.

"I visit her at the clinic in Dori. Sedi wanted me to explain how it would be at the camp. Amina was *agitée*, frightened. I tell her everything is okay that you and Crystal will bring her to me. That's when she say we are in danger."

Kate steadied the cup perched on her lap. "What kind of danger? Has her husband found out we're bringing her to *Wagga*? Did he hurt her?"

Anger whipped through her body. If he'd hurt the girl... Unable to sit without fidgeting, she sprang to her feet and circled Crystal's chair.

"No. I saw no bruises, no marks, but her husband is angry that his wife visits the clinic."

Kate shook her head. Par for the course in Dori. Locals shunned alien, non-Muslim midwives. Home deliveries were the norm, but Amina was on the watch list for specialised care.

"She say it is something else and that she must talk to Kate."

"Me? Why?"

"*Je ne sais pas.* I don't know. I tried, but she go quiet, refuse to say more." Aunty placed her empty cup on the table.

"You have no idea what the problem might be?"

"*Non.* I told Amina, you be coming back, to come to the clinic on Thursday to speak with you. At eleven. *C'est bon?*"

"Yes, that's more than okay. Thank you."

"I am sorry Kate, Crystal, but this will be the last girl we hide at the camp." Aunty's black eyes glistened with tears.

Tempted to say she understood, which she did on one level, Kate grabbed her hand instead. Far from their reality, neither she nor Crys could pretend to have any idea what it was like to be forced into marriage or live in a refugee camp.

"*Merci Aunty.* You are an angel. I mean it. You have done everything possible to help these women. I will call you as soon as I've spoken with Amina."

"*Merci chère.* Now, I must get back to the camp. I will see you both when you return to *Wagga. Que Dieu soit avec toi cherie.*"

Kate didn't believe in God, but Aunty was a devout Christian. "Thank you, Aunty. Issouf will drive you home. Take care."

Kate closed the door and flopped on to her bed.

Crystal lifted the lid of the pot of tea. "One more cup, do you want it?"

"No, go ahead. I won't sleep if I drink any more caffeine, and I need to sleep." Using the heel of her hand, she scrubbed at the thick shawl of tension, clinging to her shoulders, and kicked off her shoes.

Crystal grabbed her overnight bag and dragged herself to the bathroom.

"'night Crys." Kate doubted she'd be awake by the time her friend finished showering.

"*Dormi bien.*" Crystal blew her a kiss.

Kate nodded. French wasn't Crystal's strong point. It tickled her when she found the courage to use a few words. "You too. Sweet dreams."

"What's going on Crys? If Yacouba hasn't found out Amina's planning to leave him, why is she afraid?"

"Got me, hun, but my brain nodded off hours ago. It's two in the morning, rest, we'll see Amina soon."

CHAPTER NINE

Next morning, Kate waved a finger at the air conditioner and accused it of making too much bloody noise. Defiant, the monstrous whir persisted. Thanks to the mosquito net, she had no itchy bites. There was always a plus.

Odd, the one eye she'd managed to open found no trace of Crystal. She was not an early riser.

After a quick shower, dressed and dragging her case behind her, she headed for the lift. A good morning nod at the other person heading for the lobby, she pushed her sunglasses onto her nose waited for the doors to open.

It didn't take long to find Issouf in the car park loading extra supplies into the Land Rover.

"Good morning, Issouf. *Avez-vous, bien dormi*?"

"*Oui*, I sleep good, and you?"

She'd need several coffees before she came close to rivalling Issouf's ear to ear grin. "Great," Kate lied. She handed him her bag to wedge beside their other supplies. "I rang reception and asked them to bring the heavier boxes to the lobby. Do you mind getting them?"

"*Bien sur.*"

"Thanks, Issouf. Have you seen Crystal?"

"Yes, she is helping the boy. He hurt his knee." Issouf made tumbling motions with his hands and nodded at the steps leading into the hotel.

They both laughed. "Lollipops involved?" Crystal kept a never-ending supply in her pockets ready to dish out any time disaster struck, or a tear leaked from a child's eye

"We have plenty of time, Miss Kate. The hotel has prepared food. We won't have to stop until Kaya."

"Coffee, please tell me, they gave you coffee?" Kate crossed her fingers against her chest.

"*Oui*, we have coffee." Issouf pointed to the flasks on the back seat lying next to bags of groundnuts and bottled water.

"You're an angel, but are you sure Betsy will make it?" Kate half-joked and kicked one of the worn tyres. "This pile of junk is way beyond its due date."

Driving at night could be dangerous. The last thing they needed was a breakdown on one of the deserted stretches between towns.

"*Oui*. We will get to Dori." Issouf waved at the sky—communicating with invisible guardians. "There is a message for you at reception, Miss Kate."

"Me?" She wasn't expecting any messages. Luke? Her stomach did a backflip. "*Merci*, Issouf. I'll pay our bill and grab it. Don't forget our boxes." It was getting late, time to tear Crys away from lollipop duty.

"Good morning, Madame. How can I help you?" The receptionist peered over the top of her computer screen.

"Good morning., I'm checking out, Room 721. I believe you have a message for me." Kate placed her credit card on the marble counter.

"*Oui*. The gentleman call late last night. I ask if I should disturb you, but he said no." She reached into the pigeon-hole for the neatly folded piece of paper.

Hey Crys, how are you, sweetheart? Got your message. Impressive work getting the grant. We're still up the fuck in Mali, but I'll find you in Dori. Soon. X Spanner.

Kate smiled, mildly irritated by the flicker of disappointment that the message wasn't from Luke. No plans or promises—fine with her. Exactly what she wanted, relationships meant commitment, a promise to stay. She swore to herself she wouldn't be hurt by another person deserting her. That didn't stop her wishing the best for Crys and Spanner. Her friend was nuts for her man.

Bill paid, she thanked the receptionist and returned to the Land Rover, thankfully, Crys wasn't far behind, bursting onto the concourse, a tell-tale rim of pink around her mouth. Children weren't the only ones partial to strawberry lollipops.

"Sorry, medical emergency." Crystal giggled. "I'd have been here sooner, but it took a few minutes to find my patient's big sister."

"I bet. I'm surprised you're up so early."

"Breakfast called."

Kate smiled and pointed to the front seat. "My turn in the back."

"You sure?" Crystal hesitated.

"Sure. There's less chance of you throwing up in the front."

"Sorry. I've been this way since I was a kid. We never got far in any car without mum stuffing a brown paper bag in my hands." Crystal clambered in next to Issouf.

The Land Rover's engine spluttered. If they made it to Dori without breaking down, it would be a bloody miracle. Kate wedged one leg between the boxes of *Misoprostol* stacked on the back seat and ignored the jagged pieces of seat frame digging into her spine.

Traffic was murder leaving *Wagga*, on top of the usual bottleneck, an accident near the toll booth forced four lanes of bikes, cars, and lorries into two.

Nothing bothered the street vendors. Slabs of water and washing powder perched high on their heads they weaved in and out of the vehicles. Kate reached for her purse, rolled down the window and called over a small girl dressed in a bright pink shirt and pale blue skirt. Another bag of groundnuts couldn't hurt.

Damn. "Sorry, Crys, I forgot, I picked up your note." Kate fished the crumpled paper out of her pocket and handed it over the back of the seat.

Crystal's face lit up brighter than fireworks on Guy Fawkes as she sunk into her seat and devoured Spanner's words. "Aw, he's such a hun. I miss him. What about Luke? He been in touch?"

"No." Why should I?" Telling her friend Luke visited Mike's flat the day of the funeral was a mistake. It brought out the matchmaker.

Crystal didn't push, simply nodded slowly, smiled, and went back to her note. Kate yawned, squashed her face against the window and faked sleep. Lost herself in the sharp, brutal lines of Luke's face, lines that softened when he came. The crevices that softened when they kissed.

Behind closed lids, Kate rolled her eyes. A mutually satisfying, adrenaline-fuelled, one-night stand, nothing more. Falling in love with any man you kissed was reserved for teenagers. The sooner they reached the clinic, and she could get lost in her work, the better.

Once they were away from crowds surrounding the capital, Issouf drove hard and did his best to avoid the potholes. It was late evening when they reached Kaya, their last stop for petrol. Kate gripped the strap hanging above the car door and shifted to the other side of her numb backside.

Patients were due at the clinic early tomorrow. Crystal didn't argue when she insisted they keep driving. Smart and eager to learn, local nurses were more than ready for the update of their practical skills, and Kate didn't want to miss Amina.

"Wake up, Kate, we're here. Damn, where did I put the bloody key? I'm sure I shoved it in my pocket before we left *Wagga*." Crystal hopped out of the Land Rover, stumbled, and shrieked when a black goat shot in front of her.

Smaller than the mangy creatures who graced England's countryside, the Burkina variety were not much bigger than small dogs.

"Sorry I scared you sweetheart. Go on, shoo." Crys knocked on the clinic door. "Hello, anyone here?"

Kate could have sworn Sedi said she'd wait until they arrived, but there were no lights on inside the clinic. No sign of life. "Try again. Maybe there's someone out back?" Kate shivered. Nothing beat pitch-black darkness for raising ominous shadows.

"*Voilà.*" Issouf dug his fingers deep into the crack between the front car seats and twirled the lost key around his index finger.

Crystal sighed. "*Merci*, Issouf. You're an angel. I was getting ready to break in."

Kate shivered. Ever since their chat with Aunty, deep unease had found a home in her stomach refusing to pack its bags and look for another nervous Nelly. A twig snapped. Kate whirled towards the sound, convinced someone was watching them.

Oblivious, Issouf quickly unloaded their luggage and stored general supplies in the shed. When he headed in the same direction with a box of Misoprostol, Kate stopped him.

"Sorry, Issouf. Let's put the drugs inside the clinic. I'll help." It must be the absence of light making her overly cautious. No matter what Mother might think, the village had a low crime rate, and they'd had no trouble at the clinic.

Unloading complete it was time for Issouf to head for home. A sudden itch between Kate's shoulder blades made her zero in on the spot between two trees.

"*Bon nuit.* I will return in the morning, Miss Kate."

"Goodnight and thank you, Issouf. Say hello to Justine for me." Kate rubbed the back of her neck, determined to pull herself together and stop imagining bogeymen lurking in every trick of the light. "We won't need the vehicle why don't you take it."

"*Merci.*" Issouf shook his head. "I will walk." Issouf disappeared into the night, leaving the clinic swiftly darker, lonelier.

Despite the balmy night, a shiver ran the length of her spine. "Come on, Crys, I'm exhausted, and I want to check the steriliser and meds trolley before we crash."

Any reassurance Kate absorbed from linking with Crys' arm vanished as they passed the reception desk and groped for the light switch.

A loud crash shattered the night, and the wind howled through the branches of the trees.

Her torch flickered and died.

Without any landmarks to anchor her, Kate seized Crystal's hand and dragged her to the exit. Relief swamped her when she recognised the man looming outside as Issouf, pistol in hand. "*Reste la*. Stay here."

No problem. The few self-defence classes she'd taken at Camden Rec hadn't made her any braver. Against an opponent, she doubted she could keep open long enough to do any damage.

Five minutes later, Issouf re-appeared, gun holstered, cradling a small animal.

"Oh, sweetie. You scared me to death." Crystal rescued the scrawny culprit from Issouf's arms.

"Sorry, Miss Kate, I found three of them in the vegetable garden." Issouf hung his head.

"It could have been worse, Kate. We can fix it tomorrow," Crystal cooed over the shivering animal clasped to her chest.

Wishing she possessed a molecule of Crys' patience, Kate smiled. *Bloody goat.* For the second time that night, they said goodnight to Issouf. In the distance, a motorcycle roared, the local lads heading home. There it was again, the centipede crawling up her spine. A tingle. A warning?

She took the goat from Crystal's arms and set it on the ground. "Go on, get out of here." Tomorrow, she'd ask one of the village men helping with the clinic renovations to build a fence around the vegetable garden. He could fix the slamming shutter at the same time.

A swift bang of her torch in her palm and it shone dim yellow over the shadows clinging to the narrow path to their rooms. Kate took a few calming breaths to settle the growing ball of fear lodged tightly in her chest.

There were two locks on her hut door, she used them both, rolled her lips and dismissed the chill nested in the hairs on the back of her neck.

Panadol. Sleep.

CHAPTER TEN
VILLAGE OUTSIDE DORI, BURKINA FASO

Someone was watching them, Kate was sure of it. Sitting on the low, wooden fence surrounding the women's clinic, she placed a hand on her trembling left knee and sipped her lukewarm tea.

Wait to hear why Amina insisted they were in danger was driving her nuts.

Rising with the sun was meant to energise her, shake off the cloak of exhaustion. Another night of little sleep was a worry. If she didn't get quality time in bed soon, her clinical judgement might suffer.

Thanks to the hydralytes Crystal gave her last night, the gremlin in her head had stopped knocking holes in her skull, but listening to the baby crying versus sucking concrete? Sucking concrete won every time.

No argument, the clinic vaccination room deserved an A for traumatic. The day's tight schedule confirmed it would take more than one cup of coffee to make it through the day.

She took a second, breathed slow and deep, before walking to where screaming babies were receiving their jabs.

Crystal stood next to a trembling Sedi, sticking a needle into a baby's plump forearm, terrified most newbies. Crys did her best to distract the unwilling victim with squeaky toys and a cuddly bear.

Kate smiled—all over before mother and Sedi realised.

"Hi hun, with this racket going on, I wouldn't blame you for staying in bed." Crys rolled her eyes in a circle around the room.

Another toddler cringed in her mother's arms. Her big brown eyes fixed on the syringe in Crystal's hand.

"Very funny. Just grabbing another cuppa." Kate toasted Sedi. "Superb job."

"Amina's waiting for you in the assessment room." Crystal tickled the child whose two tiny legs pummelled her stomach.

"Already?" For no real reason, Amina arriving early for her appointment spooked her. A mosquito swooping out of nowhere confirmed her sense of vulnerability. Karma be damned, feeling no guilt, Kate swatted the bloodsucker.

Killers in the shadows, questioning every move people made. What the hell was wrong with her?

There was a simple explanation. Amina's husband decided it was too far for his pregnant wife to walk in this heat and put her in a shared taxi. With a snort she reminded herself, in her work, many things were possible.

She smiled at the workmen lining the walkway between the clinic buildings. Thanks to their efforts, the clinic was looking great. They had finished the new eco san toilets ahead of schedule and already begun work on the enclosed bin area.

Inside the examination building, there was no sign of Amina. Wondering if she'd decided not to wait, she was about to retrace her footsteps and check with Crystal when a shuffling sound came from the treatment room on her left.

"Amina, is that you? It's me, Kate."

"*Oui*, here."

"Can I come in?" Kate rested her hand on the half-opened door.

"*Oui*. Yes."

Amina sat by the window, a blue scarf covering her head, her eyes fixed on the trees outside the window, elbows locked, her hands pressed flat into the bed. Ready to bolt.

The girl was no heavier than when Sedi recorded her weight the last time they saw her at the clinic.

Barely visible against her brown skin was a ring of dark spots spiralling down one side of her neck—a similar band around her wrist. Aunty said there were no signs of abuse, but there was no mistaking the bruises.

Kate's insides tensed, who had hurt the girl, how could she get her hands on them? She was a nano-second from demanding who had done this to Amina, but that could spook her, make her leave. Scraping her tongue along the edge of her teeth, she forced herself to stay calm.

Not wanting to spook Amina, she scraped her teeth along the edge of her tongue and let go of the tension balling in her fist. "It's good to see you. How are you?"

The girl refused to look her in the eye. Kate shifted her weight, took a small step and switched to French.

Er…*ça va*? Good." Amina understood English but preferred French or her native Mossi.

"*Oui, ça va*. Good." Amina's eyes darted her way.

Progress. The huge breath cradled in Kate's upper chest escaped.

Excellent. "I'm sorry I'm late. Aunty said you'd be here at eleven. *Onze heures*." Kate tapped her watch.

Amina blushed.

Great going, Kate. The last thing Amina needed was bloody Big Ben chiming the hour. Crystal was much better at this stuff. "I'm glad you're here. Aunty said you wanted to talk but let's check you and baby first? Okay? *Détende-toi*. Relax, lie back for me."

Despite her, *everything-will-be-okay*, smile, relax had to be one of the most overworked and useless words in a midwife's vocabulary.

Kate took a pair of surgical gloves from the box on the table and quickly tossed them into the bin. She couldn't perform an internal exam.

If Yacouba found out a non-Muslim nurse violated his wife they'd both be dead meat. It would be best to fetch Sedi, but what if Amina ran?

She shifted to the monitor on the metal trolly and settled for taking Amina's blood pressure. One fifty-five over one hundred and seven—too high. "Will you lift your top for me?"

Amina curled her fingers around the hem of her shirt, pulling it firmly over Kate's hands when she slid them underneath her blouse. "Has baby been moving?"

"*Oui.*"

"*Merveilleux.*" Kate closed her eyes, interlaced her fingers, and measured the height of Amina's uterus. A wave of sadness washed over her. The baby was small, too small.

Fighting her inner critic, she bit her bottom lip until she winced. She'd been working in Africa for a long time. Cultural differences were sometimes hard to understand.

Amina was too young to be a mum, to be shackled to a man three times her age, especially one who didn't seem to care his wife was sick.

"Thank you." She slid her hands from underneath Amina's shirt. "Aunty said you wanted to talk to me. *Oui?*"

"When we go?"

"To Aunty? The day after tomorrow. Can you be ready?" Leaving may be preferable to living with an abusive husband but moving to the refugee camp was a big step.

"Salif must come too. My brother. He need help. Seckou want him to do terrible things. If he says no, Seckou will kill him. *Il le tuera.*" Amina grabbed her hand and continued pleading in Mossi.

"Slow down, Amina. I don't understand. *Pardon, Je ne parle pas, Mossi.* Who is Seckou?"

"*Mon oncle.* He live in Mali. He plan the attack." Amina's eyes darted around the room as though she expected her uncle to appear any minute.

Attack? Kate's blood ran cold. Thoughts swirled in her head, none of them terrific, from feet planted firmly on the ground to swimming in deep water in a heartbeat. She was a midwife, not a rope-swinging heroine with breasts of steel.

"They going to blow it up."

"Blow it up?" Kate, Polly bloody Parrot, shook Amina's arm and switched to French. "Amina, *où est la bombe*? Where?"

"I not sure."

"What do you mean you're not sure? Think Amina. *Qui, Quoi?* Who? What? Please, Amina. *Très important.*" She had to calm down, screaming at the girl was getting her nowhere.

"You promise, Salif come or I not tell you."

Without thinking, Kate grabbed the girl's shoulders. "Amina, stop playing games."

"I not play games. Salif must come." Amina winced. Tears streamed over her face.

What did she know about bomb threats except what she remembered from standard emergency protocol? Find the nearest table and hide underneath it.

Kate dug her hands in her pockets and begged her mind to stop racing so she could work out what to do next. *Tell somebody.* First, she had to make sure Amina didn't panic and disappear.

"Okay. Bring Salif with you tomorrow. Issouf, our driver will take you both to *Wagga*."

Later, she'd explain to Aunty why there'd be two more mouths to feed. Oh, and one was a boy.

Amina sat up. Afraid she was going to run, Kate shifted in front of her.

"*Merci*, thank you, Nurse Kate."

A tear pricked at the corner of her eye when Amina grabbed her hand and brought it to her lips.

"No problem. Now, tell me, Amina, what bomb?"

"Tomorrow, I tell you when we come."

Paler than when she arrived, it was useless trying to question Amina further. Kate couldn't risk her not showing tomorrow.

"Come on. It's pouring. I'll take you home." Rain lashed at the bamboo blinds covering the window.

"*Non*, I walk."

No way. Amina lived on a farm six or seven miles from the clinic. Kate grabbed her hand and shouted to Sedi at the end of the corridor. She was putting instruments into the steriliser, more than likely relieved vaccinations were over for the day.

"Sedi, please tell Crystal I'm taking Amina home."

The ride shouldn't take long, on the way Amina may relax and tell her more about this bloody bomb. She and Crystal weren't capable of disarming terrorists, but unlike London, the nearest police station wasn't just around the corner.

Market Day was in full swing. Nothing stopped for the rain. Amina's small village buzzed with traders and locals scurrying for supplies.

"Here, let me out here." Amina rattled the door handle.

"Easy, you'll hurt yourself. Let me pull over. Is this where you live?" Kate parked in front of a tin shelter where a group of women sat peeling vegetables.

"I walk from here. *Moi, Salif.* We see you tomorrow," Amina tumbled out of the Land Rover and headed along the muddy path.

A man, waving something in his hand was chasing a boy across open land heading for Amina. *Bloody hell.* The man had a Panda, a machete.

"Salif," Amina shouted.

Seatbelt undone, she was out of the car running towards them before she realised. Hoping to distract the man, she waved her hands in the air and shouted.

"*Bonjour. As-Salam-u-Alaikum.*" Her cry vanished into the howling rain. "I'm Kate, Kate Gibson, a nurse from the clinic. *La maternité.*"

He turned and lowered his machete. One of the women at the table lifted her head. "She be okay. Yacouba shout, but he no hurt her."

Kate stared at her in disbelief. "Then why does he have a machete?"

"*Allez la.* Go." The woman tipped over a bucket. "You make things worse if you stay."

Kate tapped her pants with the flat of her hand, searching for her phone. *Damn.* She'd left the bloody thing at the clinic. "I'll bring help."

Confused and shaken, a thousand possibilities raced through her mind, none of them good. Mind a blur, skidding and sliding she climbed into the Land Rover and tore towards the clinic.

Chin resting on top of the steering next to her tightly gripped hands Kate squinted, strained to see clearly through the rain lashing the windscreen. *Oh hell*. Horn blaring, she shouted for the goat to get out of the way.

Despite the danger racing towards him, the damn thing froze. Kate slammed her foot hard on the brake causing the Land Rover to swerve and crash into the fence. The sudden impact thrust her forward. Her head smacked into the windscreen.

She must have blacked out for a moment because the next thing Crystal was there, running her hands over her shoulders.

"Bloody hell Kate, are you trying to kill yourself? Don't move, hun."

Kate flinched as Crys hands continued their examination of her neck and torso. "Nothing broken. But, what were you thinking Kate, driving like a lunatic in this rain?"

"Crys, stop digging your fingers in my ribs. Give me a minute, and I'll be fine."

"Okay, but let's get you out of the rain. Any dizziness, can you walk?"

She'd vomit if Crystal didn't stop waving her hand in front of her face. "Crys, there's a bomb."

"Put your arm around my neck."

Kate grabbed her friend's shoulders. "Listen to me Crys, Amina says there's a bomb."

Crystal blinked, laughed nervously. "No way, you're kidding, right?"

When Kate didn't reply, her friend turned pale.

"Where when?"

"I wish I bloody knew. Amina won't say until she and her brother Salif are safe at the camp."

"Bullshit. S'cuse my French. We should call the police, let the gendarmes handle it."

"No." Her voice was sharp, stressed. "Sorry, but Amina's not talking, and I'm guessing, neither will the people in her village. Either they're fully aware of what's happening, or they're as scared as Amina."

"Okay, take a breath, let's get these cuts cleaned up. What do you want to do?" Crystal ran her thumb over the bump on her head.

"If I haven't buggered Betsy, send Issouf to check on the farm to make sure they are okay. I told Amina to bring her brother here tomorrow. God, Crys, I'm not sure who we can trust."

"I'm with you. My vote. We call Spanner and the boys."

"Spanner?" Her friend had a one-track mind. "He's miles away."

"Not that far. Got any better ideas? He will know what to do." Crystal smiled nervously.

"I guess so." It was a sensible idea if Luke wasn't with him. She took Crystal's arm. It had to be the bump on her head, not seeing him again, that turned her insides to jelly.

"Let's get you inside before you collapse."

Kate's fingers rested on her forehead. "Hardly, it's just a bump."

"The size of a golf ball. What if it's a concussion? You did your best, hun."

"I should never have left them. I'll go with Issouf." Before she could climb back into the Land Rover, Crystal re-threaded her arm through hers.

"Over my dead body."

CHAPTER ELEVEN

Kate sat under the Acacia, an ice pack pressed against the bump on her head, her mind working overtime. One hand on the sweat trickling between her breasts, she closed her eyes and pictured snow.

The sun beat through the clouds—the sultry air heavy with the next downpour. There hadn't been a cloud in the sky the day of that lazy picnic in Hyde Park.

Luke had insisted she had the last shortbread. The smile that came with it impossible to get out of her head. He sat beside her all afternoon, holding off the rain, making the sun shine.

Kate sniffed. Far too close, even before they had sex.

"There you are, I brought you these." Crystal rounded the corner of the hut, two Panadol in her outstretched hand.

"Thanks, you're a lifesaver."

"Did you get any sleep?"

Kate laughed, more a snort at the ridiculous idea. "Some." She hadn't seen her shrink for years, but now her recurring nightmare had returned. Night air, a crow on her back, whispering words of loneliness and dread making it doubly hard to sleep through the night.

"Up you get." Crystal made her walk a straight line, waved a finger in front of her nose, fussed until Kate bit her bottom hard enough to draw blood. She was a nurse, for Christ's sake, capable of knowing if she had a concussion.

Last night, Issouf returned from the farm, but there was no trace of Amina or her brother. Over a pot of strong tea, she agreed with Crystal that they should tell someone about the threat. It was a dumb idea to think they could handle the situation by themselves.

Crys had wanted to call Spanner right away, but she convinced her to wait to see if Amina showed in the morning. For all they knew, she could be lying, a threat, blackmail, to make them bring her brother to the camp.

"I need to grab a box of dressings from the supply." One arm interlaced with Crystal's Kate tugged her close to her hip. "First, lets' check on the Land Rover."

Fingers crossed, as Issouf had driven it last night, there wasn't too much damage. The vehicle sat at an odd angle in the dirt. Kate's heart sank.

"Wow. Wrecker Gibson. Oops, sorry hun, not funny." Hands on hips, Crystal circled the vehicle. "Damn goat. What the hell? Some twat has slashed our tyres."

"Slashed? Are you sure?"

"Well, I'm no car mechanic, but take a look. What cretin would do this?"

Yacouba. His name came through Kate's head loud and clear. The son of a bitch must have returned last night when she was convincing herself every bump and thump in the night was in her imagination.

"Sorry, Kate, we can't wait any longer. I'm calling Spanner." Crystal's phone was out of her pocket before Kate could argue.

"Ringing now." Crys shoved her phone into her hand. "Tell him, Kate."

Me? Unwilling, but resigned she took the phone. It kept ringing, grateful for the reprieve, she was about to hang up and suggest they tried after Amina came to the clinic when Luke's baritone, sexy as a samba, rumbled in her ear.

"Spanner's phone."

"Er. Luke, hi. Why do you have Spanner's phone?" Schoolteacher Kate reared her head.

"Kate?"

"Yes."

"I'll get Spanner." Great, Luke was as keen to speak to her as she was to him.

She held the phone out to Crys, who shook her head and waved her hands. Kate sighed. *Great.* "You'll do, sorry, I mean, it's fine, Luke. I can tell you."

"Tell me what?"

"I think we are overreacting. I don't want to bother you, but Crystal..."

"No, bother," Luke interrupted.

Maybe she imagined it, the irritation, his tone as distant as frigid Alaska. *Adults, we're adults.* "Second thoughts, let me speak with Spanner." Trying to keep her frustration in check, she rolled the tip of her tongue behind her teeth.

"Busy now What's the problem?"

"Okay. It may be nothing." Say it often enough, and she might convince herself.

"I see."

What the heck did he see? Could the man be more bloody irritating? "It's our Land Rover. It won't start."

"Did you check the petrol gauge?"

Two women without a brain between them—they should join a circus. Crystal circled her hand over her head, urging her to get to the point this time.

"All good. Issouf, our driver didn't forget to fill up with petrol." She stifled a groan when Crystal's mouth dropped open. *Yep, he asked.* "It's the tyres."

"A flat? Get your driver to change it."

Argh. Even bimbo Kate could change a flat for Christ's sake. "Luke, every tyre is flat."

"Say again."

Fair enough, she swallowed and reigned in her patience. Phone reception was crap, she raised her voice and enunciated. "Crystal. Believes. Someone. Slashhhhed. Our. Tyres."

"What the fuck?" She clenched her jaw, not at his curse at his raised voice. Shouting always scrambled her brain.

"Luke, lower your voice." From the muffled voices at the end of the line, Kate guessed he was bringing Spanner up to speed.

It made no sense to string this out further. "Luke, there's more."

"More? Hang on I'm putting you on speaker."

"Yes." She took a breath, reigning in her patience. The quickest way to get this conversation over with was to lay everything out in the open.

"Our work at the refugee camp in Burkina. How much do you know?" Luke grunted, effectively no answer. "We're helping Amina, one of our patients, to get to the refugee camp in *Wagga*.

Yacouba, her husband is abusive, and she's pregnant. I'm sure she's overreacting, but she insists we're in danger." Kate clutched her vibrating knee. "Luke, are you there?"

"Listening."

Kate took a deep breath. "Amina says her uncle is planning an attack but refused to give details until I promised she could bring her brother, Salif, with us to the camp."

Kate pinched the bridge of her nose and ignored the gulp of air at the other end of the phone.

"Go on, Kate." A steely tone had crept into Luke's voice, a more distant side to the warm, compassionate man who'd held her at her brother's flat.

"I wanted her to tell me more, so I gave her a lift home." She paused, remembering the look of fear on the boy's face and the man charging after him. "Amina's husband, Yacouba, was there, he was chasing Amina's brother."

"Did he touch you?" Luke hissed.

"No, he was too far away. He had a Panda. A machete."

"I know what a fucking Panda is."

Shouting again, the sudden rise in Luke's voice, brought on the familiar urge to cry. She held the phone away from her cheek. "Luke, please, stop shouting, or I will hang up. Amina and her brother are due at the clinic this morning. Issouf was taking them to *Wagga*, but now the tires have been slashed, we're not sure what to do."

"We'll get to your vehicle. First, tell me exactly what Amina said."

"I'm not sure she's telling the truth, but she says her uncle, Seckou I think she called him, is planning to set off a bomb. She promised to tell me more today."

"Seckou. The bastard's everywhere."

"Fuck me," Spanner cursed in the background.

"What?" Kate ignored Luke's growl. She had no idea what the heck was going on, but Amina was due any minute.

"Sorry. It doesn't matter. Go on, Kate, I need more."

No kidding. "I don't have any more Luke. Forget I called. I'll drive to the Gendarmerie in Dori and let them take care of it."

Kate curled her toes in her boots, mentally kicking herself for listening to Crystal and not calling the locals earlier.

"Kate, listen to me, don't hang up. Take Crystal and go inside the clinic. Tell your driver, Issouf, right?"

"Yes."

"When you're safe inside, get him to call me. We're on our way. Do you have weapons?"

Shocked by his question, her chest tightened. "No." As a medic, he should know better. They were nurses, not soldiers. Then she remembered Spanner gave Crystal a pistol for her birthday and knowing her the weapon hadn't left its box. "Luke, we have clinic this morning. I'm not waving a gun around while children are here."

"Answer me. Do you have a weapon?"

Bloody hell. Did he know how much he was scaring her? "Yes, yes, Crystal has a pistol."

"Good. Send your patients home. Staff too."

"Luke, we can't do that, there's a baby due today. We can't send the mother home."

"Okay but keep Crystal's pistol with you."

"Kate, promise me you'll shoot any fucker that comes near you. Any of you." Spanner's words in the background raised the tiny hairs on her arms.

"Sorry, Spanner, I can't promise." Mike taught her how to use a pistol, but she found it hard to squash mosquitos. Her chances of shooting anyone was zero. *You do whatever's necessary to protect your patient.* Kate rolled her bottom lip and hoped Luke was overreacting.

"We're coming, Kate." The tight ball in her stomach relaxed slightly at Luke's reassurance, and she let go of the tension balled in her fist. "Pack. Keep Amina and her brother there. We'll question them when we arrive."

"Where are you?" she asked.

"Djibo. ETA three hours. It depends on the road."

"Okay. Thank you." Without waiting for his reply, Kate hung up and returned Crystal's phone. "They are in Burkina. You said they were in Mali."

Crystal shrugged. "Thank the goddess."

"Luke wants us to stay inside the clinic and send the others home."

"Sounds like a plan. You find Sedi. I'll organise everyone else."

As they made their way inside the clinic, Kate resisted the tug on her emotions, the way she did every bloody time the longing for Luke stirred inside her. Still raw from that night, the night, she wasn't sure she could handle seeing him again so soon.

Cheer up, Kate, think positive, no vaccs today. Sedi is with Chinara. Her waters broke last night, and her contractions are seven minutes apart. That was before we discovered the mutilated tyres."

"Thanks."

73

A couple of beds in from the door, Chinara lay on her side, clutching her abdomen, her face contorted with another contraction. With such a narrow pelvis, her delivery was unlikely to be smooth. Sixteen, and this was her second pregnancy. Her husband insisted it was a boy. *No pressure.*

"That's it. Breathe." Sedi held Chinara's hand until the contraction passed. *"Alors, rendons-nous plus à l'aise."* Sedi's voice trembled.

"Well done." Kate applauded Sedi. She was doing her best to make Chinara as comfortable as possible.

In between contractions, they helped her change out of her sweat-soaked gown into a fresh one. Kate drew the curtain, took the damp cloth out of the bowl, and handed it to Sedi to wipe over the girl's cheeks.

"Not long now, Chinara. Sedi needs to check how far you are dilated." Sedi froze. "Don't worry. You'll be fine. You've got this." The young nurse smiled—unconvinced. She was more than capable but needed to believe in herself. More practice meant more confidence.

Sedi didn't need her breathing down her neck. She promised to return as soon as she found Issouf and asked him to call Luke. Damn. Kate registered the sudden movement to her left a split second before the crash of steel and smashing glass split through the calm in the clinic.

Putting on a brave face as much for herself as Chinara and Sedi, she peered through the slit in the curtain, screening the bed. A man she didn't recognise held Crystal by the hair and pressed a gun to her temple.

"Arrêtez. Stop. Leave her alone!" Kate swerved, caught her foot in the chair leg, and stumbled into the path of another man. His hand grabbed her from behind and crushed her head into a shirt rank with stale sweat. Frantic, she lashed out with her foot, aiming for his shin but missed.

"Putain. Whore."

Out of the corner of her eye, there was a flash, a glint of sunlight reflected off the Panda Yacouba raised above her head. Arms clutched her arms around her waist she braced for the blow.

Amina came from nowhere and sprung on his back, her skinny arms clenched around his neck, her fingers clawing at his mouth.

Terrified he'd slash his wife, Kate grabbed Amina's shirt and tried to pull her off him. "Amina. *Ayo*." She screamed one of the few Mossi words she'd learned. No.

Yacouba jammed his elbow into his wife's side, hurled her to the floor, and raised his boot over her head.

"No." Searching for a weapon, Kate picked up a kidney dish from the trolley and threw it at him. Not the best. Where were the damn scissors when a girl needed them?

"*Chienne!*" Yacouba's fist smashed the side of her jaw. His eyes gleamed. No mistake, he enjoyed striking her.

He levelled the Panda over her heart, pressing the tip of his blade into her skin until blood trickled over her shirt.

"What do you want?" She swallowed the spit welling in her mouth.

"Please, Nurse Kate, do what he say." Amina cradled her tummy.

Kate reached for her hand and drew her to her feet. "Amina, it's okay. Yacouba, please. Amina, sit down, that's it, right here."

"*Tais-toi*. Shut your mouth. She sit when I say." Seizing Amina's wrist, Yacouba pulled his wife from Kate's grip." The tip of his Panda found a new home between Amina's shoulder blades.

Tears streaming down her face, Crystal wrestled from her captors hold and moved towards them. Kate held up her hand—it didn't need two of them getting killed.

"If you don't want my wife to die, move. *Allez*," Yacouba yelled.

"Okay, okay, I want to help you Yacouba, but Amina needs hospital care. Please, let her stay here."

A few feet from the exit, she stopped walking and turned to face him. Where was Issouf? She had to stall Yacouba long enough for Issouf to realise what was happening and help.

"This is not a game *putain*?" Yacouba punched Amina's upper back. "*Vite*."

"Take it easy." Her voice shrill, Kate's adrenaline levels were through the roof. If Yacouba let go of her elbow long enough, she'd pound his arse in the dirt and say cheers to his misery. "Okay, okay. Don't hurt Amina, your baby."

"You no hear me? Shut your mouth." Yacouba's spit hit the side of her neck, and she retched.

"Move."

"Okay, okay. Let me get supplies, drugs, for Amina. You do want your baby, *oui*, your boy. Please." Kate had no idea what sex the baby was, but the idea of a clone brought a glint to Yacouba's eye.

"Deux minutes. Allez, vite."

Two minutes, she'd take it. *Think.* At the drug cabinet, Kate shoved six bottles of *Doxylamine* and *Pyridoxine* into a paper bag and frantically looked for something to use as a weapon. She settled on a couple of boxes of *Temazepam.* That should put the bastard to sleep.

"Enough. *Allez.*" Yacouba signalled for his men to follow them to the exit.

Kate called over her shoulder to Crystal. "Take care of the others."

With the heel of her hand, she wiped away Amina's tears. "Don't be afraid. We'll go together. I won't leave you."

CHAPTER TWELVE

The tick of the dashboard clock pulsed in rhythm with Luke's rising blood pressure.

Kate was right to blast him for yelling, he seldom lost his temper, but in what fucking universe did anyone, with no combat skills, face off a prick carrying a machete?

The dusty Sahel rolled by his window. His knees smacked against the dashboard, Spanner was known for his mad driving skills, but it would take almost three hours to reach the clinic.

When his mate shoved a CD in the player, he couldn't keep a grip any longer. "I wouldn't do that." Spanner's penchant for vintage Garage Rock did sod all for frayed nerves.

"Fuck me, Doc. Get a grip. You're losing it and what's with yelling at Kate. That takes mega balls." Luke didn't need Spanner's sarcasm. "I'm in the shit box for days when I lose it with Crystal. We're talking severe withdrawal of privileges."

Spanner sharing his domestics sure as shit didn't lighten Luke's mood or quiet the pounding of his heart. "It beats me how you're so calm. Aren't you worried for Crystal?"

"Bridge too far, Doc. You know she means the world to me."

Great. Spanner's jaw tightened. He'd hurt the ugly warrior's feelings. He was head over heels for Crystal. Any other time, he'd apologise if—oh yeah, the bomb. "Did you miss the part where Kate mentioned explosives? Seckou?"

"No. Hey, I get you're on edge mate, but the chances are this Amina kid is wagging Kate's tail. It's not like you haven't come across forced marriages. Can't blame the girl for leveraging her brother, hell I'd throw in my mother too, if, okay, maybe not my mother."

"Spanner. Shut. The. Fuck. Up. Kate, Crystal too, must have a sodding death wish—end of story. You and I know, a red cross painted on their bloody foreheads won't stop Al-fucking-Qaeda messing with them."

"True. But there's no getting away from it, Kate, and Crystal are hard-wired to help, and nothing will change that fact. Before you go blazing off into the sodding sunset, I vote we swing by the Boss and him know we're heading for Dori."

The bloody voice of reason. Spanner, at his most irritating. They may not be in the military anymore, but old rules applied at Sentinel. "Where is he?"

"Pow-wow with the gendarmes. Something must be up because the local hotshots arrived from Gao this morning."

"Let's go." His patience shredded Luke adjusted the collar of his shirt. Last night's rain had given way to a steamy cloud that hung like a sodden shower curtain inside the Jeep.

"Yeah, yeah, hold tight." Spanner swung the vehicle hard right.

On a routine supply pick-up, they were ten miles out from Sentinel's compound, enough time for him to plan their route to Dori. If they were lucky and the Boss didn't object, hell, Luke could care less if he did, he could be at the clinic by mid-afternoon.

By the time they strode through the door of Knight's war room, his nerves were shot. As a trauma surgeon staying calm was his prime asset, but the knot around his heart tightened. Kate was in danger, and his pulse shot thumped in his fingers.

The Boss' eyes narrowed, not impressed with the interruption. The scowl on his face a sure sign he was near to losing it with someone. As they'd just arrived, Luke guessed the meeting with the gendarmes wasn't going to plan.

"I'm leaving." Luke stepped closer to Knight's desk.

Knight nodded for the gendarmes to give them the room. The ugly one playing ping-pong eyeballs with his mate jostled Luke's shoulder as he passed.

"What's got your underwear in a twist?" Knight raised an eyebrow and eyeballed Spanner. "Enlighten me, sergeant."

This is bollocks. "Talk to me, Knight. I don't need Spanner running interference."

Spanner stepped forward and laid a hand on the front of his chest. "Easy, Doc. Kate called. Her and Crystal are in trouble."

Knight finally looked at him, a frown creasing his forehead. He reached for the map on the table. "Where are they?"

They were wasting time, and if the churning in Luke's gut had any say, Kate didn't have any to lose. "Outside Dori, at the clinic." Luke placed his finger on the map, unable to figure out why it was an issue. The Boss was there when he promised Mike he'd take care of his sister.

Knight folded his arms across his chest and nodded at the chair opposite him. "Sit. Tell me why you insist on running off half-cocked."

Luke remained standing. "You're gonna love this. Guess who's landed smack in the middle of Dori?"

Knight's hooded eyelids lifted, and his pupils flared with anticipation. The Boss was a quick study.

"You, got it, Boss. Our mate, Seckou." They had been waiting for the bastard to surface, ever since his spectacular exit the last time they had him surrounded.

"Kate's unclear on the details, but one of her patients says there's a bomb. Their vehicle's out of action. Tyres slashed. Patients unable to leave the clinic."

Knight walked around his desk and slapped a piece of paper on Luke's chest. "Guess there is a God. Cop a look at this."

The words, *Seckou on the move, headed for Burkina,* jumped off the page.

"You've got your pass, Doc. I take it you are going with him?"

Spanner nodded. "Someone's got to watch his six."

Luke strode towards the door, shivers zapping the length of his spine. He could take care of his own fucking back.

"Spanner. SITREP as soon as you get to Dori," Knight demanded.

"Roger that, Boss. Come on, Doc, what are you waiting for, Christmas?" Spanner shoved past him swinging the keys to the Jeep above his head.

It was a long fucking drive until they reached Dori, and the sweat on his neck dried faster than he could wipe it away.

Kate. The woman who peeled layers off his soul. He hadn't called her since that night they'd spent together. Best not to start what would end in tears. When she found out his part in her brother's death, she wouldn't want anything to do with him. Meanwhile, the image of Kate pointing a gun at an attacker almost broke him.

"Damn it, Doc. Wake up for fuck's sake."

His eyes snapped open and fixed on a lorry tearing straight for them. Beside it, a small bike ate the dust spraying in a wide arc from its tyres. The passenger, red hair sailing behind her, clung to the driver. *Kate.* Deadset, if he didn't have a sodding heart attack, he'd claim a miracle.

Spanner drew his weapon. "Take the wheel."

Bullets whizzing over their heads, heart hammering in his chest, Luke shifted underneath Spanner and fought to keep the Jeep from careening off the road.

Mud and dirt shot across the windscreen, the wipers whipping back and forth did shit to raise visibility. Seconds later it shattered, sending shards of glass raining over them.

Tyres screeched, brakes squealed, the lorry swerved, just missed the front wheel of the bike, and slid to a halt in front of a large barn—one exit, no cover. The motorcycle skidded sideways. The sudden move tossed Kate into the air.

"Fuck, no." Kate hit the ground. Heart in his mouth, Luke braked and hurled himself into the open. "Cover me." *Get to Kate.*

Spanner cursed, followed him out of the Jeep, gun blazing.

Birds squawked overhead. The rear door of the lorry slammed on its hinges. A wiry Burkinabe, grasping a heavily pregnant girl in a headlock, landed two feet on the ground. *Son of a bitch.*

"Hey, over here." Trying to get the wanker's attention, Luke waved his hands. To his right, Kate, face contorted in pain, staggered upright and took off towards the girl.

"*Non.* Yacouba. Don't hurt her," Kate yelled.

"Get down," Luke bellowed over the gunshots. One minute she was running the next Kate clutched her upper arm. "Fuck. She's hit."

Luke's legs turned to treacle. He caught her a second before they both hit the ground. Ignoring Kate's groan, he rolled on top of her and shielded her from the spray of bullets whistling over their heads. "Kate, talk to me."

"Luke? Don't. Yell. At. Me." Her ice-blue eyes flickered. Her words slurred.

A patch of crimson spread across the sleeve of her shirt. Where the fuck was Spanner? Twenty feet to his right, chasing the girl and the man holding her by the neck. *Shit, shit, shit.* He needed him here. "Let them go."

Spanner hesitated then ran towards them and slid to his knees beside him. Too much fucking blood. He seized Spanner's hand and covered Kate's oozing wound. "Hard. Press hard." Her shallow breathing scared the shit out of him. "Don't you go into shock on me. Right here. Keep your eyes on me."

"You okay?" Kate's fingers cuffed his chin, then fell limp at her side.

"Hey, that's my line." He grasped her hand and pulled it to his chest. Damn, if tears didn't prick at his eyes.

"Amina?"

"Shh. Why did you do that, sweetheart?" No sane person ran in front of a bullet. She stared at him, her eyes brimming with questions, always with the questions.

"Don't call me, sweetheart."

"Okay, sorry. You can spank me once we get you to safety." Nonsense fucking words meant to keep her conscious. Carefully he slid one arm beneath her legs, the other under the small of her back, and lifted her into his arms.

"Luke, Amina?" Kate's head lolled against his chest. Blood everywhere. Had the bullet nicked an artery?

"She's okay." Later for the truth. Kate needed a hospital. He pressed her closer to his chest, catching his breath when the warmth of her blood seeped into his shirt.

"S'okay, Doc, they're gone." Spanner kept his eyes on their surroundings and opened the Jeep door.

Sitting on the back seat of the Jeep, Luke cradled Kate's head on his lap. He interlaced their fingers and prayed to a God he was sure didn't exist.

"Where to, Doc?"

"The clinic, it's closer than Dori. How long?"

"Fast as I can."

"Call ahead, tell Crystal we will need to transfuse."

What seemed like an eternity passed before they reached the clinic. Careful not to jostle Kate in his arms any more than necessary, Luke kicked open the clinic door. Lines of worry creasing her face, Crystal was waiting for them.

"You okay, baby?" Spanner asked.

Crystal nodded. "Fine, hun. You?"

"Crystal, with me." Blinking away the sweat dripping into his eyes, Luke swallowed his mounting fear and struggled to stay professional. He cleared his throat. "Gunshot wound to the upper arm. No suspected broken bones—heavy bleeding. Pupils dilated. Rapid pulse. Shallow breathing."

"Don't worry. I'm a bleeder. Ask my dentist." Eyes half-open Kate gasped.

"Do you have your wisdom teeth?" he jabbered, relieved to hear her voice.

"All four." Her words slurred Kate's pulse fluttered under his fingertips.

The rattling in Kate's ears drove a truck through her insides. Her stomach rolled, bile rose to the back of her throat, she swallowed hard trying her best not to vomit. Not in front of everyone. What would Mother say?

"Stay with me, Kate, stay with me," Luke ordered.

Where did *Doctor-I'm-in-Charge* think she was heading? The message to lift her finger and wave it at him failed to make the journey from her brain. Slithers of light bled underneath eyelids too heavy to lift.

Ouch. A sharp jab and the upside-down dream of scream spiralled into Kate's worst nightmare. A metallic smell assaulted her nostrils. Blood. Was it hers? Amina? *No, no, no.* No one heard her.

"Crystal with me," Luke shouted.

Darkness, like a savage animal, clawed at the edges of her vision. Luke's voice drifted away. No sight, no sound.

Wait.

CHAPTER THIRTEEN

Every muscle, every cell and vein shivered through Luke's body.

Seconds before he'd been on autopilot, treating Kate's wound, stabilising his patient. Thank God, the bullet hit no major arteries—broke no bones.

Luke loosened the ties of his surgical mask and drew aside the bedside curtain, taped the lock on the IV line and adjusted the flow, opiates for the pain, antibiotics to take care of any infection.

Kate was alive, and nothing would stop him from touching her.

Selfishly, while she slept, he brushed his lips over the silky skin covering her forehead and traced the black shadow beneath her eye with the edge of his thumb. She smelled of fresh limes and antiseptic, an odd mix.

Her little finger twitched. *Come on Sleeping Beauty, flash me those ball-busting blues.*

Semi-conscious, Kate's hands thrashed and clawed at her IV line while her eyes darted furtively around the cubicle.

"Steady, lie still, you're safe." He held her wrists lightly in one hand and stroked her forehead.

"Luke?" Thanks to the knockout cocktail, her voice wasn't much more than a whisper.

"At your service. Lift up." Her head bobbed on her shoulders. He centred her head on the pillow. "Better?"

"Thirsty." Kate licked her lips.

"How are you feeling?"

"As though someone shot me with a cannon." She waved a limp wrist at her left arm.

"Close. It was a nine millimetre."

"Sorry, Doc. I don't have a clue what that means."

"Consider yourself lucky there was no major damage, but you lost a lot of blood."

"Amina, where's Amina?"

Luke's grip tightened slightly enough to keep her from having another go at ripping the IV from her arm.

"Easy. Stitches. You need to rest. I'll give you something to help."

"No, thanks."

"Doc's orders." Luke reached for the glass and pills beside her bed. "Steady. Small sips."

Her hand clipped the side of the glass, spilling water onto the sheets.

"Prefer a shot?"

"No."

Admiring Kate's mix of vulnerability and grit, he placed the pills in her palm. "Didn't think so. Swallow."

Defiance gleamed in her eyes, the spitting image of Mike. His staunch adherence to the negative had got them through 'the long drag' during training, a gruelling hike in the Brecon Beacons. Once a Gibson dug their heels in, it took a Sherman Tank to move them.

Her slim body offered no more resistance than fairy floss as he settled her against the pillow. The tears glistening at the corner of her eye hit him harder than a kidney punch.

"Mmm."

"Sweet dreams, Kate."

"Luke?"

"Sleep, I'm not going anywhere." The legs of his chair scraped across the tiled floor. For the hundredth time, he checked her pulse, amazed how the steady beat of her heart soothed his own.

He fought the temptation to climb into bed next to her and fold her in his arms. Never let her go.

Kate's eyes closed. Exhausted, he settled for staying close. Turning his cheek, he lay his head on the sheet next to their joined hands and counted her breaths.

Around seven-am, he woke to Crystal rattling a tray of fresh fruit and cereal next to his ear. His neck ached—stiff from lying in the same position for six hours.

"Morning. You need to eat. Not even Superman can survive without food."

"Thanks, Crystal." Luke peered over her shoulder, expecting to see Spanner. Sure enough, he wasn't far behind her, balancing two more trays in his hands.

"I'll leave you to eat. Last night, during Kate's surgery, Chinara managed to pop a baby into the world. I'm on bath duty. Tell her when she wakes—she'll appreciate the news—and remember, eat, no hero ever starved to death. I'll be back soon to check on our patient."

"Will do. She should be awake soon." Luke laid his palm on Kate's forehead. She was paler than the sheet covering her slim body, but there was no sign of a fever.

"I'm not worried, Doc. I know our girl's in expert hands."

He pointed at the tray. "Thanks." No way could he stomach the eggs, but the baguette might fill a hole, and the coffee was welcome.

Minus her shadow, Crystal returned an hour later.

"My turn."

Luke drank the last dregs of his now cold coffee and waved the empty cup above his head. "Okay, I surrender. Where's Spanner?" While Kate was resting, he'd check for an update on Amina.

"Knight's here. I think they're catching up." She rolled her eyes. "Go on. I'll take care of our girl."

It was a hundred degrees outside, hot enough to cook pizza on the sizzling corrugated roof. The smell of burning rubbish, wood and acacia seeds filled Luke's nostrils. Above him, one of the village lads knocked coconuts out of the tree. Another day in Paradise. If it weren't for the redhead with a bullet wound in her arm.

Holding a can of Kabisa, Spanner sheltered under the roof of the shower block. Soft drink for breakfast. Luke smiled.

"How's our girl?" Spanner swigged his drink.

"In pain. Will be for a few days. That's manageable but can't say the same when she hears the news we lost Amina."

Spanner whistled. "I'll leave that in your capable hands, Doc."

"The Boss arrived while you were in surgery."

"Yeah, Crystal said."

"Snake's with him. They're setting up camp."

Luke let out a shaky breath, the cooler air blowing over his face some relief from the cloying humidity. Having Snake with them beat any secret weapon. As well as being an excellent Comms man, the cocky git was a menace sniper. "Any sign of Amina's brother?"

"Salif? No. Zip." Spanner tapped the empty can on his chest. "How's the ticker?"

"Cut the shit, Spanner and eat your corn flakes." Luke flipped a soggy flake from the front of Spanner's shirt. He was in no mood for counsellor fuck for brains.

"Hey, I'm saving that for later." Spanner grabbed his forearm. "You worry me, Doc, you're not usually so fucking touchy."

"We got more on Seckou or where Amina's old man may have taken her?" He could have her hidden anywhere. After years of massive drought and failed crops, Burkina's starving villagers were a perfect recruiting ground for Al-Qaeda fuckers.

"No specifics, but Issouf confirmed Yacouba, Amina's husband, owns the farm where they shot Kate."

"So, what's the prick's connection to Seckou?"

"Other than a brother-in-law. Not sure."

Spanner eyed the pack of matches Luke rolled in his hand. "Haven't kicked holding the cigs?"

"Nope." Luke glanced at his watch. "I should check on my patient." Twenty-three minutes since he left Kate, but who was counting?

"I'll come with. Crys wants help with some boxes." Spanner fell in beside him.

"Doc, you better prepare Kate. Tell her, unless we locate Amina and Salif soon, odds are we won't find them in one piece."

The girl was pregnant for Christ's sake. Spanner was right. Once Seckou found out what Amina told Kate, she was a rock around his neck. It made no sense keeping Amina, or her brother, alive. More bad news, he still hadn't told her about Mike.

"You and Kate—you're keen on her, right?"

Luke shrugged. *Back to this.* "I prefer women who dodge the crowds at Selfridges' sale, mate, not bullets." Brave words for a guy owned by dread and lust. From the hairs on his head to the tips of his toes, he needed to see Kate. Now.

Hey, Doc, stick with my sister.

"Yeah, yeah, got it covered." Spanner shot him a look. He was chatting with a sodding ghost. "Don't ask."

"Talking to yourself? A sure sign a person's in love."

"Get fucked." There was no denying his attraction to Kate. Hell, he'd watched her melt at his touch, but anything more was Spanner's wishful thinking.

Luke drew back the curtain surrounding Kate's bed. Unable to believe his eyes he stopped dead. The bed was empty sheets tossed aside.

No way she'd left the clinic through the door, they'd have seen her, and she sure as shit wasn't up to climbing through any windows.

CHAPTER FOURTEEN

Kate Gibson attracted mayhem like fire to a match. Cursed with the same act now, think later, spontaneity as her brother what gave him the daft idea she would stay in bed?

"Luke?" Crystal's voice chased him along the corridor.

"Where's Kate?"

"Sorry? She was in bed five minutes ago."

His stomach somersaulted. Maybe Kate needed to use the bathroom, if so, why the hell didn't she ask for help? "Wait there." The rapid beat of his heart told him before he pushed open the door to the toilet. It was empty.

Was Kate in pain, needing meds? The blood pulsed at his temples as he ran to check the pharmacy. "Kate. You here?"

The sound of crickets trapped behind the blinds greeted him. In case she'd passed out, he stepped inside, checked behind the shelves. *Shit.* She couldn't have got far.

Behind him, Spanner had joined Crystal. Luke noted his arm slung protectively across her body. He wasn't the only one on edge.

Calm down. Kate couldn't get very far, not with an IV in her arm.

Ignoring the militia of chills marching through the hair on his forearms, he stalked towards the bed curtain fluttering a few feet ahead.

"Relax." Kate's voice echoed his plea for composure.

Sweat pricked his upper lip.

"You'll soon get the hang of it. You're doing great." Oblivious, Kate sat chatting to a woman breastfeeding her baby.

Luke recognised the woman cradling the child as the woman who'd given birth last night. He took a breath, allowed his heart rate to slow, then signalled the all-clear to Spanner who pulled Crystal closer. Any excuse for a grateful kiss.

"You should be in bed." His voice was surprisingly steady, considering his panic over the last five minutes.

Kate smiled. "Good morning."

Grateful Kate was safe. His anger dissipated replaced by a burning desire to smother her with kisses and insist she never scare him again. She should be in bed, it had only been a few hours since her surgery, and the sun pouring through the window highlighted the slate grey of her skin.

"I can't find Amina. Where is she?" Kate's toss-away question while she stroked the baby's head.

Hell. He treated torn, bleeding bodies smack in the middle of war zones, but confessing to Kate they didn't have Amina, took a whole other set of balls. He pointed to the small head peeking above the light pink blanket. "What's her name?"

Kate tilted her head. "The mother or the baby?"

"Both." His heart jumped boulders watching Kate flash the double dimples tagged to the side of her mouth. A smile to turn ice to fire.

"Chinara, meet Dr Luke. And this darling is her daughter, Omolara. Can I have a hug?" Kate reached for the baby.

"Great name." Fuck, what else could he say? Mesmerised, he stared into the joy glowing in Kate's eyes. The joy, missing at Mike's flat, showered over him, lightening his heart, demanding his cock's attention. Embarrassed, he shifted behind her chair.

"Yes, Omolara. It means a child is family in Yoruba. Chinara is from Nigeria."

Luke didn't miss Kate's wince or the way her fingers lightly tapped her wounded arm. "Let's get you back to bed. I need to check your dressing, find you a sling." He held out his hand.

She refused, her mind-blowing smile no consolation as she braced her hands on the arms of her chair. Sharp creases marred her perfect forehead. "I don't want to leave her." Her deep blue eyes flared with defiance.

Coward, he didn't have the heart, or the balls, to insist she left even when she struggled to stand. He practically leapt in front of her. One arm supporting her elbow, he helped her sit before she keeled over and did more damage.

"Okay, five minutes, while I find a wheelchair. Or I can carry you. Your choice."

"No wheelchair, they give me the creeps. You can carry me if you promise not to drop me."

"Promise."

Kate could weigh a ton he'd carry her to London. London, safe, out of harm's way. Luke tapped his watch. How soon could he make it happen?

She nodded and smiled at the young mother. "I'll pop back later, Chinara—a *plus tard*. We can bath Omolara together."

Luke empathised with the young mum who cringed at Kate's mention of holding her tiny baby in the water. The small child in her arms was no bigger than the length of his hand and forearm.

"Don't worry, you two, it will be fun." Kate drew in a sharp breath.

"How are *you* feeling, Kate?"

She raised her fingers and wiggled them in front of him. "With my hands."

"Cute. Want to try that again?"

"Truth?"

He nodded. "Always."

"I'd sell my soul for a shower." A faint smile. "You?"

"Ditto." Luke scratched his head and watched Kate's smile flicker. In a flash, he bridged the small gap between them. Coming home, no other words for the sensation driving the frost from his bones.

"Okay, time for bed." He waved goodbye to the baby. "Hold on to your pole." He didn't want the IV drip pulled from her arm.

Careful not to put pressure on her injured arm, Luke helped her out of the chair. He waited while she grabbed the IV pole. "Got it? Okay, one, two, three." Luke scooped her into his arms and slowly walked her to her room, the pole rolling alongside them.

"Oh, I almost forgot. Luke, you didn't answer my question. Where's Amina? Tell me she's safe?"

Forgot? Not likely. He doubted much got past Ms Gibson. "Kate, Amina is—"

Saved by the fucking bell. Crystal twirled past them carrying a tray of meds and grinned. "Our runaway found. You gave our boy here a scare. Watch your pole."

Kate laughed. Luke sighed, knowing his reprieve would be short-lived.

Not the first time, since he found her, Kate shivered. They were in Africa, one hundred and two in the sodding shade. "Cold?

Before she could answer, the wiz and thud of a bullet zapped the air and smacked into the window beside Kate's head.

Crystal screamed.

"Take cover," Luke ordered ignoring Kate's groan as he took her to the ground.

Safe, for now, Crystal ducked behind a nearby cupboard.

"You there, Doc?" A door slammed. Spanner, crouched low, pistol drawn, scanned the corridor trying to get a bead on the threat.

"Here. All good," Luke confirmed. Afraid he'd crush Kate, he eased into a crouch. "Kate. Are you hurt?" He ran his hands over her body, checking for injuries. Her eyes were open, her breathing steady.

"No. It's my arm." Kate bit her bottom lip. The other arm."

Luke couldn't resist a smile. No longer attached to her IV, blood trickled down her arm, pain creased her forehead. He reached for the towel on the gurney alongside them. "Here."

"Crystal?" Kate called to her friend.

"She's fine." Frantic, over the pounding in his ears, Luke considered his options. One. Find the shooter before he fired another shot. Two. Throw Kate over his shoulder, bank on Spanner taking said shooter out, and run for it.

"Behind you, Doc," Spanner yelled.

Luke spun toward where Spanner pointed. A slim male stepped from the shadows waving his fist above his head. Luke lurched for him praying any stray bullets found him before Kate. The small, lethal object in the lad's hand was the last thing he expected.

Luke cursed. "Grenade."

CHAPTER FIFTEEN

A blinding flash, smoke billowing along the corridor. Impossible to see beyond the wavering edges of the clinic walls. Terrified, the roof would collapse at any second. Her guts groaned. Kate's breakfast curdled in her stomach.

"Kate, talk to me." Luke's plea competed with the ringing in her ears.

"Okay, I'm okay." Kate swiped the blood escaping from the missing IV over her elbow.

"Where is the fucker?" Spanner yelled.

"Can't see shit, mate," Luke answered.

The wobble in his usual calm, confident voice scared her. Eyeballs ricocheting left, right, Kate struggled to locate Luke through the smoke swirling everywhere. He'd been right beside her before the explosion.

"There, Doc, by the desk," Spanner's voice. He was okay.

"Got him," Luke answered.

A shadow materialised out of the disappearing haze, male? Hard to tell. What was he doing? Why wasn't he moving?

Huddled beside Omolara's bed, Sedi shielded Chinara's baby from the slim figure pointing a pistol at them, begging with him not to hurt the baby. "*S'il vous plaît, ne blesse pas le bébé.*

Kate pressed her fist against her mouth. Amina's brother, Salif, waved his gun. He was trembling, his hand shaking. Any moment the gun might go off, and Sedi and the baby harmed. "No, don't shoot."

Luke turned in her direction—every muscle rigid with tension.

"Kate. Stay where you are. Spanner, for fuck's sake."

"On it, Doc. I've got him. Take care of the women."

Luke hurried towards them. Kate didn't protest. They had to work together, deal with this without anyone getting hurt.

Drop your fucking weapon. On your knees." Spanner was on Salif in three strides the muzzle of his pistol burrowed into Salif's neck.

Bloody hell.

"Go," Spanner yelled at Sedi.

Too stunned to move, she hesitated.

"Run, Sedi," Kate echoed Spanner.

Luke's eyes narrowed, his message clear. *Don't move.* Sedi tugged the tiny bundle closer to her chest and staggered from the clinic. Terrified, Spanner would hurt Salif, she reached for the handrail above her head and scrambled to her feet.

"Stay where you are," Luke commanded.

Her legs wobbled. Luke must know she'd love to do what he asked, but she couldn't let Spanner hurt Salif.

"Doc, call for back up, now."

"Roger that. Boss. Get. Here. Over," Luke bellowed into the lapel mic on his shirt. The headsets they wore a permanent fixture to their bodies.

Desperate to reach Salif, Kate curled her fingers over the rail and dragged her body along the corridor.

"Stay where you are." Luke lunged for her.

Sick of his bloody orders, she twisted her torso and broke free of his grasp. Convinced Salif wouldn't shoot her she kept moving.

"Please. Salif. *Tu es* Amina's brother? Yes? I saw you at the farm. Put the gun down we won't hurt you. Right, Luke?" Kate glanced behind her and caught his gaze. *A little help here.*

She offered Salif her hand. Spanner turned purple. Fair enough. The situation didn't do much for her blood pressure either, but she couldn't be sure he wouldn't kill the boy.

Even if her passionate night in the sack with Luke had eased the numbness claiming her after Mike's death, it didn't mean they were close enough she could be sure which way any of the Sentinel team would hop.

"*Écoute-moi* Salif, Spanner will lower his weapon. You too, it's okay. I know you won't hurt us. *C'est vrai?* True?" Her heart skipped several beats. Spanner held his pistol firm. "Please, Salif. I promise, my friend, won't shoot you."

Luke was beside her, the frosty mix of fear and fury in his eyes turned her blood to ice. He was a doctor, why wasn't he doing more to help her.

"You have until the count of three… *un, deux…*" A sharp click, she assumed it was the release of the safety on Spanner's weapon.

"No."

Luke shook his head and blocked her hand when she lunged for Spanner's gun.

"Damn it, Kate."

The honey warmth in Luke's eyes turned pitch black.

No fight left in him, Salif released his rifle and crumbled to all-fours. Spanner swept his right foot in a wide arc and kicked the weapon to Luke.

While he was slightly off balance, Kate seized her chance, dragged Salif to his feet and rushed him to the nearest chair. Terrified, his body trembled under her fingers. "Luke, a glass of water."

He stared at her but made no move to fetch water. Mike called him his best friend, but had Luke failed him too? Sniffing in a couple of breaths she checked herself. She was scared, the only explanation for doubting Luke. Neither he nor Salif would hurt anyone.

"Seckou know Amina talk to you. He will kill my sister." As if they needed any proof, a tear trickled from the corner of Salif's eye, despite his efforts to stay tough.

Kate knelt beside Salif. "I'm sorry if I caused trouble, I shouldn't have brought Amina home from the clinic, but I wanted to help. *Dîtes-moi*, where is she? Where has Seckou taken her?"

"Get up, Kate. Come to me," Luke snarled. "Take my hand. You're bleeding."

The blood ran down her arm. Luke was holding his breath, doing his best not to shout. The man was learning.

"Why you no listen? No one can stop Seckou." Salif's hands scrubbed through his hair and over his ears.

"A minute, Luke." She waved Luke's hand away. "Salif, tell us where Amina is."

The clinic's tin roof shuddered, and the door rocked on its hinges. Kate jumped, sucked in a breath, and waited for a second grenade to explode. A flash of lightning highlighted Knight's massive frame blocking the doorway. She raised her eyes to the ceiling. *Better the devil, you know.*

"I hate fucking rain," Knight roared. Gun held steady in both hands he nodded at Luke. "Having fun, Doc?"

"Good of you to drop in Boss." Spanner grinned.

Their banter was irritating but oddly comforting.

"What the fuck, sergeant? I've got more important things to worry about than playing nursemaid to you numpties."

"My sister. You will save Amina. *Oui?*"

Knight stalked towards them. "Strewth, Spanner, shoot the whiny fucker."

"No. Luke, please, help me. Spanner put away your gun." Kate shifted, didn't think as she placed her body in front of Salif.

"Out of the way, Kate," Knight hollered from the doorway.

Luke froze, an image of Mike's broken body, Kate lying beside him, eyes fixed on nothing, took his heart rate through the roof. He cuffed the sweat pouring from his brow. Even if the Boss meant it, which he doubted, no way would Spanner shoot an unarmed boy.

Why was he here? He should be at school, not waving loaded weapons at people. He tapped his chest with his fist. "Salif. Look at me. Listen to me. No one wants this to end in tears."

Luke glanced at Kate. Her full lips sucked into a thin line, ready to keel over any second.

"We will help your sister, but you must tell us. Your sister told Kate, Seckou, your uncle, has a bomb. Is it true?" Luke breathed a sigh of relief when Kate took a step back, barely putting an arm's length between her and the boy.

"Get my sister. You help me. I help you."

Not appreciating the lad's defiance Spanner raised his gun. Luke glimpsed the panic in Kate's eyes a millisecond before she threw herself in front of the boy and blocked Spanner. She did, she expected Spanner to shoot the boy.

"Go, run," Kate yelled and flung her full weight against him, taking him by surprise. He stumbled.

She was hanging on by a thread. Luke flung his arms wide as she sidestepped around him.

"Go." Kate's scream chased Salif from the building.

"Fuck me. Spanner, don't let that kid leave." Knight glared at Kate, jaw clenched.

Point made. Luke braced, ready to protect her if the Boss made a single move towards her.

"Let him go." Kate grabbed his arm.

"I've got you." Luke led her to a gurney. The intensity of the last seconds was finally catching up with her.

"Let me go. Knight will hurt him. Please."

"No, he won't, but we must talk to him. Lie down, let me check your arm."

Kate sat and swung her legs on to the gurney. Hoping she'd lie down, he laid a palm against her chest, but she clawed at his shirt, desperate to see over his shoulder.

He turned his head, Knight and Spanner stood empty-handed in the doorway.

"Luke. Please." Oblivious of the blood trickling down her arm, she tried to haul herself off the gurney.

The woman had the strength of a rogue bull. His patience at max, Luke uncurled her fingers from his shirt.

"What part of lie still don't you understand or is bleeding to death your immediate plan?"

CHAPTER SIXTEEN

She'd failed Amina again.

Darkness spread from the corners of Kate's eyes, drawing her deeper into the black. How long she was out, she wasn't sure, but her guilt was front and centre when she eventually regained consciousness.

"You're awake?" Crystal's voice sang through the cobwebs inside Kate's head.

Crys' cheerfulness was uncrushable. She stood at the foot of the bed, a tray of food in one hand, a glass of freshly squeezed orange juice in the other. The drink she might manage, the solid stuff no way.

"How did I get here?" Surprised when her voice came out no better than a croak, Kate wiggled her elbows deeper into the mattress and tried to sit. *Whoa.* No mistake, her body preferred horizontal.

Crystal rolled her eyes at her pathetic attempt. A clean white bandage covered her arm. She vaguely remembered Luke giving her something for the pain. "Mmm, that looks delicious," she lied. Where did you get the pineapple?"

"Justine, who else?" Crys wiggled her nose and pinched a wedge from the bowl. "I love that woman. She threw in a jar of her delicious honey, too."

Judging by the orgasmic glaze covering Crystal's eyes, one or two spoonfuls had already found their way into her hibiscus tea. Issouf's wife swore by the stuff, a cure for all ills.

"Hands off. I'm the patient." Kate slapped her friend's hand. She'd smile if it weren't for the needles stabbing the back of her eyeballs. One day soon she'd go back to shouldering one not two heads. "How long did I sleep? Salif...?"

"Don't worry. Salif got away before anyone could shoot him. Knight is fit to be tied."

Kate grinned. Stuff tying the Boss in knots. She'd love to hang the arrogant man.

"Amina, have they found her? Where's Luke?"

"Er . . . Too many questions, hun. You're making my head spin. Come on, lean forward, let me fix those pillows." Crys smoothed the edge of her sheet and offered her arm. "You must be feeling better. There's colour in your cheeks."

"Getting there, thanks." If she didn't count the tadpoles swimming in front of her and the fact Crys hadn't answered any of her questions.

"Did Luke say when he'd be back?" She'd startled awake several times in the night, grateful he was there, watching over her, his soothing voice calming her nerves until she fell back to sleep. Drawing in a long sip of orange juice, she vowed not to miss him when babysitting duties ended.

"I'm not sure." Crystal made hard work of fluffing her sheets. "Sedi showed me where the chickens hide their eggs. Eat up, when you've finished with Humpty Dumpty here, I'll help you shower."

Crystal's persistent vagueness was aggravating. "Enough with the culinary chit-chat, tell me what's going on, Crys. Luke. When will he be here?"

"Luke's with the others discussing the plan." The words shot from her mouth. "Shit. Don't tell Spanner I blabbed."

"Plan, what plan?"

"The one for our move."

"Move?" Kate choked on a mouthful of egg. Pushing the tray aside, she threw back the sheet and swung her legs over the side of the bed—dumb move.

The bitter taste of orange juice flooded the roof of her mouth. "What move?" She pinned her gaze on Crystal, not taking her eyes off her until she coughed up an answer.

Crystal hmphed.

"Fine, I'll ask him myself. Give me my clothes." Crystal sidestepped as she reached past her for the pants lying on the arm of the chair.

"Keep it up, and you'll tear your stitches. Again." Luke, the man who never failed to stop Kate in her tracks, propped one hip on the edge of her bed and snagged her wrist. "Okay, Slugger, let go of the pants."

"Sorry." Kate rolled her lips together. She hated losing her temper and regretted the hurt written on her friend's face. It wasn't her fault the boys were pushy. Silently, she promised her a session at the day spa when they returned to London.

Luke's palm flattened on her forehead. She didn't have a temperature, which was impressive considering his touch played havoc with her insides. Kate held on to her anger, head thumping, arm throbbing, she fought the urge to peck him on the cheek.

Luke's palm landed between her shoulder blades as he stretched for the orange juice. "Drink."

"Grr."

"Really?" He frowned but kept the cup steady.

Wimp. Sit up straight. Confront his bossy arse. She'd stay in Dori until they found Amina. "Crystal said you are leaving, I understand if you and the others can't stay, but until Amina's found we are staying in Dori."

She cocked her chin in Crystal's direction, expecting support. "We should have gone to the gendarmes in the first place."

Kate wanted it to be the truth, but now she'd seen Luke, her insides turned to mush, her brain flicked to panic mode. Could she really manage if Luke left?

"Finished?" Luke rested the juice on the tray.

Her fingers trembled and he cradled her fingers to his chest. His heartbeat slow and steady under her palm.

"Take a deep breath. With me. That's it."

She didn't want or need the concern etched in Luke's face. "Thanks, I'm fine." She shook her hand free and forced herself to ignore the comforting rumble of his voice.

"I'm staying, Luke. Aunty sent me to help Amina. I messed up, I should have made her tell me everything, never left her when I took her home, but I did. I won't…"

"Doc, we need to move." Knight stood at the foot of her bed.

Kate shivered. None of the guys was under six feet, but Knight towered over all of them.

"Give us a minute," Luke said.

She preferred this Doc to the bear who yelled. The one who angled his body to shield her from Knight even if she was more than capable of handling bully boy.

Her frustration with Luke forgotten, Kate shoved the idea of softening the tight lines framing his mouth with a kiss to the back of her mind.

"Soon, Doc. Crystal, you're with me." Knight crooked his finger.

Keeping one eye on Knight, Crystal hovered at the end of her bed and offered half a smile. "It's for the best, hun, let them do their job. I'll get my stuff together and meet you out front."

Traitor. Kate pulled the edges of her nightdress closed as the blood rushed to her cheeks. "What about the clinic?"

"All good. Crystal took care of organising most of it this morning. She's given Sedi instructions on how to care for Chinara and her baby. They'll be fine. We're not going far, Kate, just moving you and Crystal to a secure location."

"Where?"

"A hotel in Dori. We…Sentinel, will stay until you're well enough to travel to *Wagga*."

"And Amina?"

"Knight's on it. We will find her." Luke squeezed her hand.

She refused to surrender. "Please, Luke, I'm not a child. The bullet injured my arm, not my brain, don't leave me out of your plans. If we are leaving, I need to get a message to Aunty at the refugee camp. She is expecting Amina tomorrow."

"No problem. As soon as we're at the hotel." Luke held on to her hand as she wiggled to the edge of the bed. "Deep breath. Lean on me."

Giddiness returned as soon as her feet touched the floor, she'd be lucky to stumble a few steps before she fell. The most delicious man she'd ever met said to lean on him. Kate sighed. History proved it was a mistake to depend on anyone.

Sure, it was tempting to accept Luke's support until she remembered he was a one-nighter, exactly what she'd needed at the time. The fact that she was hurt by his leaving without a word was annoying, disconcerting. There was no room in her life for a relationship. She had a job to do, find Amina.

"When guns go off, people die, Kate. When you were hit, I . . ."

Their faces were a breath apart. Kate was sure Luke meant to kiss her. His strength, so seductive, she could easily lean into it and later regret her spontaneity like she had that night at Mike's place.

"We'd better go." As she pulled away, his breath stroked her cheek, warm, seductive.

"You want Crystal to help you dress?" Luke released her fingertips, and the loss hit her with the chill of an arctic gale.

"No. Thanks. I can dress myself." She steadied her breath and dismissed the energy pulsing between them. Their undeniable chemistry soared off the charts—wrong on many levels.

"Ten minutes. I'll wait outside, sing out if you need me."

In twenty, Luke returned. Pleased she'd managed to get dressed without getting dizzy she shoved the rest of her clothes in her bag. "I can't find my brush."

One of his hands tucked a strand of matted curls over her ear while the other stretched behind her for her bag. *Now, he'll kiss me.*

"I got it, thanks." A move too fast to beat him to the handle made her knees tremble.

"Hold tight." Luke scooped her into his arms before she had a chance to bat his hands away and stand steady.

"Hey!"

"Sorry, not the most elegant. Don't worry. I didn't drop you the last time. It's easier to carry you than watch you faint."

"I won't faint." She wasn't sure it was true. She was certain being this close to Luke's solid chest was giving her hot flushes."

"Listen to your doc." The corners of Luke's mouth curled into a half-smile.

She sucked in a deep breath, ready to challenge. The warm strength of Luke's arms was disconcerting, uncomfortable, disappointing when he lowered her into the passenger seat of the Jeep and fastened her seatbelt.

He reached into the medical bag in the back and shoved a Percocet and a bottle of water into her hands. "Take this. Good to go?"

"Yes, thanks."

Luke released the clutch and put the Jeep in gear. "Did you swallow it?"

She unscrewed the top of the water bottle and took a long gulp. "Yes, Luke." To make her point, she batted her eyelids and wiggled her tongue.

"You sure you want to poke that at me?" His voice deepened.

Oh, yes, damn sure. "You're worse than my mother."

"Trust me. I am not your mother. Rest. Close your eyes."

Trust. *Never in a million years.*

CHAPTER SEVENTEEN

Cowboys, the bloody lot of them.

Abdicating responsibility to Luke and the Sentinel team irked beyond belief. She should demand Luke turn around and take her straight back to the clinic, but without her health or the contacts to find Amina, thinking she could rescue her, was plain stupid.

Good girl Kate concentrated on the scenery slipping by the window and counted the shrines by the side of the road. Anything to distract her from the terrible things that might be happening to Amina.

The cocktail of heat, blood loss and fear curdling in her stomach threatened to spill over as they pulled up at a roadside motel. Tiny lizards sunbathed on the rocks clustered around a paved courtyard surrounded by colourful plants and low-level shrubs.

Crystal should have beaten her there, but there was no sign of her or Knight.

"Wait here while I grab our key."

Our key? Not happening. Luke disappeared before she could open the window, left her sitting in the car seething. The next thing, he was tapping her shoulder. Damn Percocet made it impossible to keep her eyes open.

"Can you walk?"

"Yes. No more fireman Jim. Give me your arm."

The space between Luke's eyebrows narrowed—she was getting used to his growly face.

"Steady. Foot here." Luke tapped a small patch of even ground with his boot.

His feet were huge, which for some reason made her laugh. Emotions running haywire, she clung to Luke's arm and allowed him to lead. The last thing she wanted was to fall flat on her face. Kate kept hold of Luke's arm as he put the key in the lock.

"Where are you sleeping." She made a point of looking in both directions. "Next door?"

"One key, love." Luke swept his hand in a wide arc and ushered her through the open door. "Much safer, if one of us shares the room with you."

Kate raised an eyebrow. "Why you?"

"Whoa." Luke wrestled himself from the grip she had on his arm. "You know me. I thought it might be easier, but if you prefer one of the others, no problem. Let's get you settled, and I'll see what I can arrange."

Luke had a point. Sleeping in the same room as Luke may make her horny as hell, but he was too honourable to do anything uninvited. "You'll do."

"Glad we got that settled."

She couldn't resist a smile when he laughed.

Inside, an overhead fan buzzed loud enough to scare mosquitos but was bloody useless against the heat and humidity. A quick scan confirmed the room had space for a table, two chairs and a bed. One bed. Turning her head needed work. The room turned anti-clockwise before she found her balance.

"Steady. Hold off on the dancing for a day or two." Luke pointed to the bed. "Sit."

With one hand on the mattress, she swung the noodles below her waist on to the thin sheet.

"Hungry?"

The perfect domestic scene. It was tempting to lose herself in a fantasy of Luke and Kate. Except there was no them. Ever. "Let's wait for the others. We can eat together."

"Up to you." He shrugged.

The night they had sex; she'd run her hands through his military haircut. The memory of the surprising softness of the short bristles against her fingertips, drew her back over and over, the same way his high cheekbones and perfect ears did.

After two or three weeks in Africa, the tight black curls brushed the collar of his shirt. Free of army rules and regs, she hoped Luke would keep his hair long. It suited him.

Crystal had mentioned Knight's plans to form Sentinel Security after their final tour was over, telling her Luke and Spanner were involved.

"Toss me a pillow." Luke lifted his arms.

She hurled it at his chest. "Taking a nap . . . on the floor?"

"Cute. I assume you're familiar with patient care."

His eyes smouldered, luring her in. She pushed the heat rising in her body back where it belonged. Infatuation was Crys's thing, not hers. Sure, she dated, but there was one toothbrush in her bathroom. Hers. At the first hint of someone wanting to get close, she found an excuse to end it—no point hanging on for the inevitable break-up and a chance to hurt.

"Lean forward. I won't hurt you." His breath blazed through the hairs on her neck.

Luke's eyelashes brushed his cheek, begging for a lick every time he blinked.

"Okay, now back."

Forward, back, up, down, her ear played see-saw against Luke's chest. Pillow finally in place, Kate lay back against it, struggling not to grin.

"Okay, can't promise this next part will be as easy." His gaze dropped to her arm.

"I can take it. I'm a nurse, remember?" Blood, puss, and gore didn't bother her, but she kept her eyes on the view of the courtyard as he changed her dressing.

"Done. No sign of infection." Luke cut the tape and put away the first aid kit.

Silence followed as he stood staring down at her. Kate held his gaze. Luke swallowed, shifted. "I should call Knight."

Spell broken. "You go ahead. I need to use the loo." She refused Luke's offer of help, hobbled to the bathroom, slid the door shut and stared at herself in the mirror.

Death's mother. No other words for the reflection glaring at her. No one would notice under her baggy pants and shirt, but at a guess, she'd lost half a stone since Mike's death. Cradling her head in her hands, she repeated Crystal's calming mantra. *Fuck, fuck, fuck!*

Half an hour must have passed before she plucked up the courage to come out of the bathroom. Luke smiled and tucked his phone into his pants pocket. "Everything okay?"

"Yes." On shaky legs, she made her way to one of the chairs at the table. "Who was on the phone? Any news of Amina?" Her stomach clenched. It sucked, not knowing if she was safe, alive or dead.

"Sorry." Luke shook his head, rose from the bed and picked up his duffle.

"Do you play?" He held a pack of cards in one hand, a wooden box and several broken matches in the other. "Cribbage?"

"Crib?" She laughed. "I took you for Poker man. Texas Hold 'em?"

"No, I never gamble." He shook the box, and a warning sprinted across his face.

Hit a nerve? "My dad had one." She pointed to the box. "I found it in Mike's stuff when I cleared out his flat. I'm amazed you still have the pegs. My dads were long gone by the time I was old enough to play. He used burnt matches."

Overwhelmed, remembering the two most adored people in her life, the next sentence tripped over her tongue. "Mike? Does he ever talk to you?"

Luke covered her hand with his. "Yes. Worse, I answer."

It took several swallows to stuff her tears where they belonged.

"Here. Dealer's choice." He let go of her hand, offered the cards, and lowered himself into the seat opposite.

"Okay. Rummy. Three of a kind, four of another, right?"

"Or a run, same suit."

"You should have kept that to yourself, Doc, given yourself the upper hand." A dimple appeared on the left side of his mouth, and the massive cloud resting on her heart lifted.

She shuffled the cards, glanced up, caught the hint of a smirk. "Hey. Don't mock. It looks awkward, clumsy, but I get there. Mike always laughed at my cack-handed shuffle."

"You're left-handed?"

"Isn't every genius? Ready to have your arse kicked, Doc?" She dealt the cards, and the twinkle in Luke's eyes stole the edge of her fear.

"I'd love to see you try." Luke peered underneath the card on the top of the pack.

He must have practised the lazy roam of his eyes caressing her torso on many women because it was perfect. Tingles shimmied through her pelvis.

"Bloody 'ell, I've got a hand like a foot." Luke groaned.

"That's what Mike used to say."

"I remember."

Their fingertips grazed, and loss, overpowering as a tsunami, swamped her. Refusing to allow grief to claim any more of her, she bit her tongue until she tasted blood.

If Luke noticed her passing meltdown, he didn't react, simply took the next card. "Hey, you're cheating. It's my turn."

"Who, me, cheat? No way."

"Yes, way! Count your cards. How many do you have?" She tapped the eighth card in his hand.

"Tough." Luke caught her wrist.

"Tough? Oh, you are going down, mister." She tossed her cards in the air and made a move for his extra card. Pain strong enough to put her teeth on edge shot through her arm.

"Easy." Luke sprang from his seat, a single stride, and he was by her side, his hand resting on her shoulder.

His mouth hovered close to hers. Kate angled her body slightly and clasped her hands around Luke's neck. Her body moulded perfectly to the front of his. Dumb move. She didn't care. His erection pressed against her chest and flecks of gold sparkled in his eyes. *Magic.*

A moan escaped from inside her, from a place kept dark too long. *Closer.* Why deny how much she was attracted to Luke? Sex with him cured all ills. "You are so sexy. I'm thinking ..."

"Yes?" Luke lowered his head and brushed his mouth against hers.

"More." More of his warmth, his comfort. Her hands skimmed his shoulders. She was a nanosecond from ripping his clothes off when her bloody phone rang.

"Leave it." Luke nibbled her chin.

Her nipples were tight, aching for his touch. It took every ounce of will power to pick up her phone off the table and answer the call. "Hello."

"*Tais-toi,* shut-up, listen."

Salif. Heart pounding, she struggled to steady her voice. "What do you want?"

"The English, he is with you?"

"Yes. Can I call you back?"

"No problem, fine. Can I call you back?" She offered Luke a weak smile hoping to distract him from the tremor rattling her body.

"Say nothing. *Dix minutes,* I wait no longer."

"Will do. Bye." She drew a breath in through her nose.

"Who was it?" Luke asked, his gaze glued to her face.

"Crystal. She's forgotten her toothbrush, wanted to know if I had a spare." Guilt washed over her in accusing waves as the lie tumbled from her lips. "Maybe I can swap it for a hairbrush." A nervous giggle bubbled out of her as she gathered the carpet of discarded cards.

"Crystal? Where are they?" The playfulness in Luke's voice had disappeared.

Did he suspect? She'd never been great at lying, and Salif hadn't whispered. "She didn't say."

"Aha."

Until she heard what Salif had to say, she'd keep his call to herself. Earlier she was convinced Spanner would shoot him. Luke might be hurt if he got caught in the middle of Knight and his crew and the men they were after.

She couldn't bear it if she were responsible for anyone being injured, worse, killed. No, best to wait, keep her head.

Another infuriating bleat. This time Luke rolled off the bed and dragged his phone from his pocket, it was like living in a bloody telephone box.

"Boss? I'll be right there." A grin wider than the Sahara sprawled across his face. "I won't be long. When I get back, we can finish our game." Luke's words landed square on the button he'd intended to press.

She didn't like lying to him, felt more than a little two-faced, as she had made him promise not to keep things from her. Through the parted slats of the blind, she watched Luke disappear before returning Salif's call.

"The English, he has gone?" Salif was hard to hear, his voice muffled.

"Yes, but he will be back soon. Is Amina okay, what do you want?" A thousand questions piled in her head. She closed her eyes and waited for Salif to speak.

"Oui, *ma soeur va bien*, okay, but you must come with me."

A shiver ran down her spine. Kate went to the window, back to the wall, she peered out of the window. "Salif, where are you?"

"Come outside. Seckou will kill Amina if you don't come with me." Salif's voice was louder, closer.

She fumbled with the door handle even though the voice in her head said it was a stupid thing to open the door.

"You lie. He is here."

One step and she was at the window, peering into the dark courtyard searching for Salif, seeing Luke walking towards their room.

"Salif." She wanted to yell, but her voice was a whisper. Salif was gone. Anger at Luke for scaring him away stole the last of her energy. Tears welled in her eyes, had she lost the last chance of seeing Amina alive?

CHAPTER EIGHTEEN

Leaving Kate alone didn't sit right with Luke, yesterday he'd failed to protect her, and he wasn't planning on a repeat. Plus, he would bet his last matchstick, she was keeping shit from him.

One night of sex, spending every waking moment since dreaming of being inside her again, didn't mean he knew her. He hated fucking secrets.

One hand on the door to Knight's room, he closed his eyes, stealing himself from what might have happened if Spanner handled Salif.

Inside, the Boss nodded and waved his hand at the men clustered around the table. Luke eyeballed each of them, familiar with everyone except the smaller, heavier man opposite him.

"Gentlemen," Knight stood, his hands spread flat on the table. "Now everyone's here we can begin. Doc, you know Issouf, Kate's driver. Meet Oumar, ex-militia. He and Snake ran training in Mali. He's been heading up surveillance for us at the farm."

"Oumar, good to meet you."

Snake hunched over his laptop his fingers working double time on the keyboard. No one denied his talents when it came to all things technical. Word was he'd made a fortune in the dot.com world before joining the military.

He didn't look up, leaving it to the beady eyes of George to check him out. He blinked—a nod in dog.

The African tapped one-finger to his forehead.

Luke took a seat, his focus locked on Knight. "Where were you, Boss? Kate's been looking for Crystal." Luke crossed on ankle over his other knee and leaned forward.

"She's next door taking a long bath. One of Oumar's men is looking after her," Spanner answered, his eyes skirted the door to his right probably wishing he was the one on guard duty.

"Attention, kiddies, here's what I've got?" Snake tilted the screen. Eyes fixed on the screen George leaned heavier against his thigh.

Military dogs were highly trained, often a one-man dog. Luke suspected George would always be Mike's best friend. For now, he seemed to be settling in well with Snake.

"Hold on a sec, Snake," Luke interrupted. "Spanner, Kate got a call, said it was Crystal." Luke waited.

Spanner shook his head.

"Didn't think so." Confirmed, Kate lied. She didn't trust him and, yeah, it fucking hurt. Not that his feelings mattered. What counted was who had called and why she lied about it.

"Focus, gentlemen." Snake thrust his laptop into the centre of the table. Images of every angle of Yacouba's farm flickered on the screen.

"Get in there, Doc." Spanner nudged his elbow against Luke's shoulder.

"Sweet." Luke whistled. "Who secured the cameras?"

Spanner stood, the legs of his chair scraping across the tiled floor and tipped his head at Knight. "The Boss. Who else?"

"Why didn't he say so?" Luke mouthed the words at him.

Spanner shrugged and headed for the fridge. "Fuck knows, man."

Knight cleared his throat. "Snake, how many tangos?"

"Let's find out." Snake checked the thermal images. "Oumar, what's your take?"

"*Huit, peut-être, dix*." Oumar rocked precariously on one leg of his chair.

Knight drummed his fingers on the table. "Ten. Good enough."

Spanner returned with several malt beers on the table, the clink of the bottles sliced through the growing tension. The Burkinabes rarely touched alcohol. "Sorry, Doc, no *Laphroaig*," Spanner's apology at odds with the smirk on his face.

He'd give a week's pay for the smooth burn of his favourite whisky, but duty called. Plenty of time to relax when Seckou was dead, and Kate was safe.

"Thanks." Luke swigged the malt, the nutty taste a syrupy distraction from the unease worming its way along his spine.

"Oumar, we'll need you, Issouf, and three others, here." Knight drew a red circle around an area on the map. "*D'accord*?"

"*Oui*, okay. My men wait for my signal," Oumar answered.

Judging by the way his thumb caressed the hilt of the dagger tucked in his belt, their new mate, Oumar, was no stranger to wet work.

As for Issouf, he must be more than Kate's driver, ex-military too if Luke had to guess. Luke circled his head, but the devil holding him by the back of the neck refused to release his grip.

"Snake, Spanner. You take positions here and here." Knight drew his attention back to the map. "Doc, you'll hang back with the vehicles. Take point if and when needed."

Apart from a few trees, there was zero cover for working on casualties. "It's wide open. Contingency plans," Luke asked.

"Adapt as necessary." Knight eyeballed them each in turn. "Copy?"

George agreed, barked and licked his lips. It was hard to reconcile the sweet face of the springer spaniel with the ace sniffer dog. Get in, secure the girl, get out. The team did its best work when shit hit the fan.

Spanner scowled at his *Malta*. "No offence, Issouf, but how the hell do you drink this stuff?"

Issouf cackled, his black eyes sparkling. Spanner surrendered his bottle into his outstretched hand.

All very cosy, but he was eager to get back to Kate. "Knight, we done here?"

"If Snake has nothing more."

"Nope, all good Boss."

"Okay, we'll call it a night. Rendezvous at o-seven hundred. Doc, have you told Kate? She up to speed with Seckou and the circumstances of her brother's death?"

Trust the Boss to bring this up now. "No, not yet." Luke wiggled his jaw. His temples throbbed.

He'd been waiting for the right moment, ever since he'd taken on the task, afraid to start the conversation in case Kate insisted on knowing every shitty detail of how her brother died.

"Do it. Tonight. Or I will." Knight's threat followed the empty bottle he tossed at the bin.

Aced it in one. "Goodnight."

In a few hours, they'd lock in any last-minute changes, complete their mission and end this. The hotel courtyard was quiet, aside from the odd rat scurrying through the undergrowth. Too quiet. Nothing to distract him from the woman he couldn't get out of his mind, no matter how hard he tried.

The Boss was right, damn him, the sooner Kate heard about Sekou, the better. First, he'd get to the bottom of what she was hiding, but go in hard, and she'd clam up, worse still demand he get that other room.

As soon as he entered the room, plans to interrogate her flew out the window. Kate lay curled on the bed, head propped on her hand, eyes watering. Tears or fatigue it could be either.

Every neuron fired, pulsed through his body. *Touch her, comfort her.* Stroke the curtain of curls framing her face. He balled his hand into a fist. Sleepy suited her—alluring as hell.

The tears staining her cheekbones, turned his insides to mush

"Hiya," her voice was huskier than usual.

"Do you need something for pain?"

"No, thanks. I'll ask if I do." Eyes shining with moisture, Kate patted the space beside her.

It was an invitation he should but couldn't resist. Sitting as close as he dared, he put his arm around her. To reassure her, to soothe himself.

The soft weight of her head nestled against his shoulder ripped his insides to shreds. "I swear if anyone ever makes you cry again, I'll kill them."

Her grin threw him off. Did she doubt he meant it? He couldn't blame her, but she shouldn't question. He'd do anything to protect her.

She fixed her gaze on his.

"Thanks, that's an incredible promise. I hope you never have to keep it. It scares me that you might."

He'd never seen a sight as erotic as the gentle rise and fall of her breasts as she inhaled and placed the tips of two fingers to his lips.

"Kate."

"Shhh. Lets' not talk about it. I'm very grateful for all you've done for us these past few days, but this, whatever this is between us, it's a bad idea. What happened at Mike's was great, no denying, but we need to concentrate on what we're here for—finding Amina and keeping her safe."

What could he say? Kate's honesty cut straight to the heart of it, his heart, and it ripped him apart, knowing she was right. Kate Gibson couldn't mean anything to him other than the oath he swore to Mike.

A shuffle outside the door stopped him from telling Kate agreed, but it didn't mean he wouldn't protect her with his life. A split second later, the door opened.

Spanner looked sheepish and so the dick should for bursting into his room without knocking.

"Shit timing, arsehole."

"Hey, sorry, Kate. Knight wants a word with Doc." His eyes circled the room, doing a shit job of not looking at Kate.

Luke sprang from the bed, shielding her from Spanner's gaze. "Step outside I'll be there in a minute."

He wasn't the jealous type, and he held no claim on Kate, but the hairs on his forearms bristled. He gave himself a mental slap. A sharp reminder Spanner had eyes for Crystal, and unlike the Boss, he was a one-woman kind of guy.

"Wait here I'll be back." Despite what she'd said earlier he wanted to wrap her in his arms and insist she rest. "I'll be back."

"What's going on? Have they found Amina?" Kate wrestled with her injured arm until she was sitting on the edge of the bed, hearing her wince broke his tentative grip on keeping it together.

"What's going on? That's good coming from you."

Robbed of all patience, Luke rounded on Kate. The look of shock on her face was a kick to his gut.

"I've told you before not to yell at me." She shoved at his chest and covered her ears.

Christ, she blistered his brain. Not knowing what else to do, he chose the dumbest reached for her hands.

"Get off me." She ripped herself free.

Luke wanted to punch the wall, better idea, wipe the stupid smirk from Spanner's face.

"Kate. We're here to help, you called us. Remember? Impossible if you withhold information?" *Sodding hypocrite. Seckou, Mike, tell her.*

"I don't understand." Kate wrapped her arms around her waist, pulling away from him.

Luke let her go, but nothing stopped the harsh words coasting from his mouth. "Enough with the bullshit. The call, earlier, it wasn't from Crystal. She's next door. How do you expect us to keep everyone safe if you lie to us?"

"Oookay. I'll tell the Boss you're tied up. We'll see you in the morning." Damage done. Spanner skulked out the way he came.

"I don't want to fight Luke. I'm a nurse, not a soldier, but nothing will make me desert Amina. Not before she is safe."

Gibson genes got you killed.

"Tell me, Kate, before I go out of my ever-loving mind, who called?

And leave out Crystal's fucking dental hygiene."

Kate's gazed dropped from his face. "Salif. He was here."

"Are you kidding me? When?"

"Before you came back, I didn't see him, but he was here."

"For Christ's sake, why didn't you tell me?"

"I wasn't sure what he wanted. Oh, God, I don't know, he wanted me to go with him."

"No fucking way."

"Yes, well. Moot point. You came back before I could decide." Her hand began to beat on his chest, softly at first, but as her tears turned to sobs, the blows to his chest more frantic.

"Okay, take it easy. I haven't been entirely upfront with you either." The biggest understatement of his life. He held her wrists lightly. Loose enough so she could escape if she wanted to. "There are things you ought to know."

"What? No, Luke please, don't say it, don't tell me Amina is …"

"No Amina's at the farm. Knight's organised a raid for tomorrow morning. That's why Spanner was here." This time he didn't resist, call it a medical intervention, Luke covered her hand to stop her thumping her thigh.

"The Boss agreed to help you because—"

"Oh, tell me. It wasn't out of the goodness of Knight's heart." Kate pulled her hand from his grasp.

"No. Kate. Your brother died while on a routine clean-up patrol in a local village. There'd been minor raids, but no one suspected JNIM of using the village as a base. They surrounded the perimeter with IEDs."

"Luke, please, I'm not sure I can take the gory details of my brother's death. Why are you bringing this up now?" Her lips quivered as she fought those bloody tears.

"It's important, Kate. The leader of the JNIM cell was …"

A split second before he spoke the bastard's name, Kate's eyes lifted level with his. "Seckou?" she whispered. One fist beat against his chest.

Too damn smart for her own good. "Yes."

CHAPTER NINETEEN

Snuggled against Luke's chest, Kate lay full clothed where she'd fallen asleep. She'd thought about it but making him sleep on the floor would have been too mean. Instead, she'd welcomed the warmth of his arms as he rocked her to sleep.

They agreed. Purely platonic. Emotionally expensive.

The news Seckou was responsible for the IED that caused Mike's death, and Amina's kidnapping was too much of a bizarre coincidence.

Adding to her fragile trust issues was the nagging certainty Luke hadn't told her everything. Destined for inevitable burn out if she didn't shove the possibilities to the back of her mind, she enjoyed the best night's sleep she'd had in a long time.

As the world crept alight, she snuggled deeper into Luke's armpit. Forgiving herself, it wasn't as though they were naked. The outline of his nipple pressed against his shirt falling tantalisingly in line with her lips. She watched the gentle rise and fall of his chest and matched her breathing with his.

"Good morning." Luke's sleepy growl rumbled over the top of her head.

"Morning." She raised her chin and gazed into unsettlingly deep brown eyes heavy with sleep.

"How's the arm?" Luke's fingertips traced the edge of the dressing.

Not wanting to think about her injury, she concentrated on withdrawing from his warmth. "There's a briefing, right? Better get up before Spanner comes looking for you?"

"Funny, Ms Gibson."

"I need a shower. Hand me your med bag. While you're gone, I'll take care of this dressing." Reluctantly, she uncurled from the support of his arms. Anxious to know what Knight was planning, she nudged his thigh with her foot.

"Okay, no need to get violent." With a long sigh, Luke walked over to his bag and placed it on the bed next to her.

"Luke. You will let me know what Knight is planning, everything he says?"

"Yes, but it cuts both ways, Kate. No more secrets." He snatched their room key from the bedside table.

"Deal."

"Ten minutes, get dressed."

Ugh. She'd spent the night next to Luke in blood-stained pants. As fast as she could, she stripped and entered the shower. The shock of hot water hitting her lower back made her jump.

Not having full use of her arm meant the simple task of washing and dressing was a performance, a tug-of-war involving limbs and clothing. It was a miracle she found any clean underwear.

Teeth clenched she gingerly unravelled the wet bandage. The circle of red skin surrounding Luke's neat stitches was inflamed, sore. She'd keep her eye on it, check for infection.

Luke returned as she finished re-dressing the wound and lowered himself into the chair by the window. His eyes trailed the length of her torso before they fixed on the dressing. Nothing overtly sexual, no reason to go weak at the knees.

"Good job, Nurse Gibson." The frown that followed guaranteed she'd hate the next words out of his mouth. "Time to move."

Bingo. "Move where? Aren't we staying here? Safer, you said."

"Change of plans, Knight's arranged transport to *Wagga* for you and Crystal. You will be safer there.

"What? Where will we stay?"

"Knight has a villa, Sentinel's first safe house." Luke chuckled. "Two men from the 'B' team will be there, to guard and protect you and Crystal while we go after Amina and take care of Seckou."

Frustration mixed with disappointment that again they didn't consider it necessary to consult her or Crystal made her furious. The worse thing was, she hated to admit it was the best for Amina and that was the important thing.

Luke didn't need to play nursemaid. Forcing a smile, she swallowed the outburst lurking behind her teeth and gave up the argument. Knight may be an overbearing arse, but if anyone could find Amina, it was Sentinel.

"I can hear you thinking. You're pissed you can't stay here for Amina. Right? The Boss won't stop, Kate, none of us will, not until we find Amina and end Seckou. We owe it to Mike."

At the mention of her brother's name, loss gnawed at her bones. "Okay, you win. Give me a few minutes to get my stuff together. I presume Spanner's told Crystal?"

"Yes." Luke was out of his chair before she took her next breath. Two strides brought them nose to nose. "Do you think I'm happy letting you out of my sight? It's tearing me apart that I can't come with you. And, for the record, Kate, no one wins in this scenario."

Was he going to kiss her? No. She had her pride. He couldn't have it both ways, one minute telling her how much he wanted to be with me and the next practically marching her out the door.

She spun away from him and faced the wall. Salty tears burned her eyes, but she'd take another bullet before she let Luke see them fall.

"Please, Kate, let me do, let us do, whatever it takes to protect you. Look at me. If you won't think of yourself, think of Crystal, Amina."

Luke had played his ace. She didn't want to look at him, didn't want to feel comforted when his hands landed on her shoulders, and he gently turned her body to meet his.

"You're pale, sit for a sec." Luke stared at her, his brown eyes, bottomless pools. God, she wanted to trust him, but hope crumbled quicker than the wall of Jericho any time she leaned against it.

Luke stiffened, the warmth of his body no longer surrounded her.

"Sorry," he whispered

For what she wasn't sure.

"Let's go. You okay to walk?"

"Yes."

Luke grabbed her bag and helped her outside and into the Jeep where Spanner and Crystal were waiting. He fished something from his pocket, a bright piece of batik, colourful, a sharp contrast to the shadows in her heart. "What's this?"

"Here." He slipped it over her head.

"A sling? Why I don't need it."

"Wear it for me. Doc's orders."

He gave instructions to the driver and, without another word, turned his back and left. What never began, ended. Not wanting to examine why that bothered her, she used her hand as a pillow against the door frame and stared, unseeing, out of the window.

"Kate, are you comfortable? Take my spare cardie for your head."

"Thanks, Crys." Resting her head on the folded garment, she took a drink from the water Luke had pressed in her hand. Liquid splashed over her chest. Unlike Issouf, their new driver drove fast. Her bum took a beating every time he rolled over a pothole, and her head hit the roof of the car.

"*Pardon*, I don't know your name. Is it possible to go slower, avoid the trenches?" She held her body stiff, trying her best not to bounce in her seat.

Crystal rolled her eyes. "*Alors.* Excuse me," she raised her voice above the wind howling through the open window. "Slow down. *Ralentis.*"

Kate smiled, appreciating the support, not that it did any good. She was sure the driver was deaf. Odd Knight sent someone who didn't speak English. Kate shrugged. Guess there wasn't anyone else available given they'd need everyone for the rescue mission.

The dusty window reflected the worry lines creasing her forehead. How had Luke managed to destroy her defences so quickly?

Determined not to allow herself to go any further along a track of what-might-have-been she slipped the colourful sling over her head and grasped the water bottle with two hands.

Her head began to swim, picturing Luke bleeding somewhere. Plus, the damned heat wasn't helping. A low groan escaped her lips.

Crystal grabbed her hand and gave it a reassuring squeeze. "Driver, *pardon*, I don't know your name. Any chance we can grab breakfast before we get much further? My friend, Kate, needs to take her medication. We don't have to stop for long—we can get food to take away."

"*Oui*," he replied. More a grunt than actual words.

They both swallowed a giggled. Guess the driver did speak English. Kate swore Spanner ordered him not to stop, but she wasn't complaining.

Ten minutes later he spun the steering wheel hard to the left, screeching to a halt outside a lean-to café. "We eat here."

Not the Primrose Hill Deli, but a strong coffee might help see her through the rest of the trip. Kate rubbed her sweaty palms over her skirt and put Crys' cardie on the seat beside her. The parking area was empty, apart from a beat-up sedan, there were no other vehicles. Unusual, there was always a bike.

"No hungry munchers. Guess we'll be out of here in ten. That will keep grumpy balls happy." Crystal nudged her ribs.

Their driver left them and sprinted ahead, phone to his ear.

"Give me your elbow, Crys." Kate bit back the pain pulsing the length of her arm. As they got closer, a woman, with a grizzling baby strapped to her, crashed through a beaded curtain.

"Coca-Cola, beer?" The woman bounced on the spot, jiggling her baby in his make-shift harness. Drool dribbled over his chin. Teething. Next to vaccinations, the worst.

"Non. Bissap, please. Kate?"

"Coffee for me." Crystal was the one with a taste for hibiscus tea. She reached for the child's puggy hand. *"Bonjour mon petit, pourquoi pleures-tu?"* The boy's breath hitched while he considered her question. "There, there, no more tears." He sniffed, tired, but no sign of giving in to sleep.

"Have a seat, Kate. What do you fancy to eat? How about fried eggs on a baguette?" Crystal waved the one-page menu.

"Not fussed. I'll have what you have. First, I need the loo." A splash of water on her face may help.

"Want me to come with you?" Crystal lowered her menu.

"No, I can manage." Kate rolled her eyes. Elegant, the two of them wrestling with her knickers in a toilet no bigger than a shoebox.

Kate ran her fingers through her hair. She'd have to chop it off if it got any more matted. "Sorry to ask, but can I borrow your brush. I can't find mine."

"Sure, take this for now." She reached into her cloth bag and handed her a brush. "I'm sure I have a spare in my other bag, it's yours when we get to *Wagga.*"

"Thanks."

"Go on, don't get your knickers in a twist

A man stood by the outhouse smoking a cigarette. A queue. She didn't relish waiting in this heat. She shifted the piece of batik hanging around her head and slipped her arm back into the sling.

A sudden gust of wind made her tremble. Every instinct screamed, forget the loo. Unsteady on her feet, she spun around and slammed into their driver. She hadn't noticed him that close behind her. *"Oh, pardon, excusez-moi."*

The toe of his boot ploughed into the top of her foot, making it impossible to move.

Too close, too big, the man's yellow eyes bored into her. A jungle cat towering over its prey.

"Salif, *allons-y*."

A flicker of hope ignited inside would Amina's brother help her? Kate did her best to free her foot and opened her mouth to scream.

The sharp sting between her ribs was enough to stop her struggling.

"Move again, and I gut you, *putain*."

CHAPTER TWENTY

Thunder rumbled overhead, the universe's comment on Luke's latest cock-up. As soon as the Jeep pulled away from the hotel, Luke missed Kate more than water.

Too piss-weak to tell her the truth of how Mike died, he stalked off, telling himself he should be glad she was gone.

His promise meant watching out for Mike's little sister, a phone call, every couple of months, a Christmas card if he remembered. Simple, until Kate opened the door to her brother's flat and the chemistry between them ripped him open like a can of sardines.

They had no future. Secure fucking Seckou. Bring Amina to safety. Quit Sentinel and return to London. That was the plan.

"Gear packed? Don't worry, Doc you'll have plenty of time to make it up to Kate when you catch up in *Wagga*." Luke shrugged from Spanner's hand on his shoulder. Happy Jack did nothing to lift his black mood.

"I don't need to make anything up to her. We're not close, not together like you and Crystal." Thoughts of Judas and thirty pieces of silver clouded his mind.

Spanner smirked. "Sure, anything you say Doc."

Snake and Issouf climbed into their vehicles while Spanner finished loading weapons into the truck.

"Let's roll," Knight barked.

Oumar and his team were already in position at the farm. Game on.

A slim figure, the dogs of hell on their tail, dashed from the clearing opposite a split second before Spanner took off running.

"Crystal. What the fuck?" Spanner leapt over the low bamboo railing and sprinted towards her.

Bent double Crystal breathed hard and fast, words punctuated by a shit load of tears spilling from her mouth.

"Easy sweetheart, I got you. What the hell happened?"

"Spanner, thank God you're here. They've taken Kate."

Luke fought to calm the fears splitting his skull. His plans and prayers spun away from him. 'What? Who?' He forced the words from his throat.

"The driver. He took her." Gasping for air, Crystal clung to Spanner's arm. "Salif was with him."

One glance at Spanner told him neither was surprised.

"After we left, the idiot drove like a bloody maniac, surfing every bump and ditch. Kate was in pain and needed her pills, but we hadn't eaten. We, oh, God, I asked him to stop. Spanner, we have to help her."

"Crystal, pull yourself together." His face now an inch from hers, Luke's fingers snaked around her arm, shaking her, unable to reign in the terror seething inside him.

"Shit, Doc, back off. Take a fucking breath." Spanner shoved him against the wall.

The arm pinning his throat brought him to his senses. "Okay, okay. Take your hand off me." Spit sprayed from Luke's mouth along with the choked words. Attempting to dampen the rage roaring in his blood, he sucked in a breath. "Sorry, sorry. Crystal, where did he grab Kate?"

"It's okay. Spanner relax. Not far. A small café. The place was deserted except for the waitress and her baby. Kate needed to pee. I should have gone with her, but she wanted me to order. It happened so fast. He forced her into a car."

Luke scratched his head. It made no sense. For the life of him, he didn't understand why Seckou snatched Kate. *Revenge?* Now that scared the fucking shit out of him.

"Take Crystal, find Knight," Luke spat the words at Spanner. "My last vial of morphine says they've taken her to the farm."

"Get your hands off me." Kate clawed at the blindfold covering her eyes and lashed out with her right leg. *Stay calm. Think. Where was Salif?*

"*Ne bouge pas.*" The wrench to her injured arm sent agonising tingles from her shoulder to her fingers. Lesson learned, Kate didn't resist the next time her attacker dragged her wrists behind her back and insisted she didn't move.

In hindsight it was stupid leaving the café alone, right now, she couldn't get lost in what should have been if she hoped to escape this mess. She sucked in a shaky breath, focussed on her surroundings, searching for any clue to where they were taking her.

The smell of petrol flooded her nostrils, strong enough she could taste it. The screech of wheels and frequent bumps clues to how fast they were driving over uneven terrain. For some reason, she was positive they'd double-backed and were on their way to Dori.

Luke would figure it out. He would find her. Kate shrugged, angry with herself for giving in to the temptation, the fantasy that anyone would care enough to come for her.

Suddenly, the van stopped, throwing her forward. The tight grip on her wrists returned. "Please, where are you taking me? What do you want?"

"*Tais-toi, Putain,* or my young friend will end your life. No more questions."

"Salif. Help me."

"I tell you this happen. This is your fault." Salif's voice shook with fear and anger.

Leaving her wrists tied, the man grabbed her hair and ripped away the rag covering her eyes. Blinded by the sudden flash of light and not wanting to be dragged in the dirt, Kate struggled to keep her feet underneath her as he kicked her forward.

"*Ouvre la porte*," he growled at Salif.

The door creaked as it scraped along the ground. The squawk of wild chickens rang in Kate's ears.

"*Allez*. Get in." One last kick sent her crashing to the grimy floor.

It was pitch black. The stench of animal manure filled Kate's nostrils. Bill lodged in the back of her throat, and she gagged. Terrified the driver might come back, she sat quietly, concentrated on her breathing, and blocked out everything but the good things. Tender hands, soft touches, Luke's constant concern.

She ducked instinctively at the rustle to her right and scrambled to a sitting position. Fists balled tight she would fight anyone who tried to hit her again.

"Miss Kate, *c'est moi*, Amina."

She'd never been more thankful to hear anyone's voice in her life. "Are you okay?"

"*Oui*. Wait. I untie you."

"Yes, yes, hurry."

Amina crawled out of the darkness and released her wrists. A deep ache throbbed through both her arms, but nothing felt wet or sticky. Hopefully, her stitches were intact. "Where are we?"

"Yacouba's barn."

Slowly, Kate's eyes adjusted to the slithers of light creasing the walls of the outbuilding. She shivered, she was right, they'd returned to Dori. "Who else is here?"

"I don't know. I see only my brother and my mister. Yacouba. I think he is waiting for Seckou."

"Did he hurt you?" Caught up in her problems she had selfishly forgotten to check Amina.

"No. I'm hungry."

Kate drew the girl into her arms, shuffled backwards until her back hit the barn wall. Determined to be strong enough for them both, she stroked Amina's back. "It's okay. They are coming for us. Dr Luke will be here soon." Hell, she hoped Sentinel were as good as Knight believed.

The door flew open. Amina trembled. For a second, the light blinded her. A man wearing a blue headdress, a Tuareg, rushed towards them and clamped his hand over her mouth. Clinging to Amina, Kate sank her teeth into his hand. The man swore, his smack to the side of her head sent her blood spurting onto his boots.

Amina screamed.

"You are dead," the man reached for her again.

No way would she let this bastard see her fear. Kate stuck her chin in the air and shoved Amina behind her. The man drew his knife from his belt, laughed and twirled the blade in the shaft of light streaming through the open door.

"*Arrêtez.* Stop. Bring her to me." Out of her bruised, half-closed eye, Kate recognised the man standing in the doorway. Yacouba.

"Playtime over, *mon ami.* Seckou say the nurse come with me. Later, you can have fun with her. Do what you wish. Salif, bring your sister."

CHAPTER TWENTY-ONE

The Boss got called many things. Luke had to admit time waster wasn't one of them. Dressed in camo pants and a black t-shirt, Knight listened, no wasted breath on dumb questions, while he did his best not to take off alone and relayed their situation.

"A doddle, give or take a few tangos," Knight joked. The slap on Luke's back meant to encourage him. "If you're right, Doc, we were heading that way, just sooner rather than later. Issouf, the truck ready to roll?"

"*Oui*. I bring here."

Was Kate injured, alive? Dwelling on what they might find at the farm did fuck-all for his mental health. He checked and re-checked his Bergan, stuffing it with enough supplies to cover any eventuality. When Issouf drove up, he was more than ready.

Kate is alive. His soul would accept nothing less.

"Spanner, you're with Issouf and the others. Doc, with me in the Jeep." Orders issued, Knight revved the Jeep and silence reigned over the comms. Every man was running the game plan in their heads.

A mile from the farm, Issouf pulled over to the side of the makeshift road. Everyone gathered gear and weapons. Luke made one last check of his medical bag before slinging it over his shoulder and tucked a SIG Sauer into the holster on his belt. His high and mighty morals buried in the dirt at his feet.

An hour max left of daylight, this close to the equator. Plenty of time to jog the remaining distance and be in position before dark. Knight took point, from here on in, hand signals their sole communication.

Under cover of the sparse trees around the farm, everyone took their assigned position.

The Boss' voice crackled in Luke's ear. "Snake. SITREP. Weapons?"

"AKs mainly. Don't rule out an RPG. Over."

Great. A rocket-propelled grenade. These fuckers weren't mucking around. One by one, lights went out in the hut and surrounding outbuildings.

"Looks like they're turning in for the night, gentlemen. Okay, you all know what to do," Knight confirmed.

"Roger that. Anyone have eyes on Kate or Amina?" Luke asked, refusing to consider Kate was anywhere else.

"Negative. Now shut the fuck up, Doc. Over." The Boss had no patience for chit chat.

The hairs on Luke's forearms stood to attention. Two guards armed with rifles stepped from the main building, slapped each other on the back. All set to patrol the perimeter, one guard paused and balanced his hip against the side of a beat-up Land Cruiser, checked the sole of his boot and cursed. *Yeah, shit happens dickhead.*

The other lit a cigarette and headed towards a small barn. The dickers had no clue of the shitload of pain set to rain upon them. His spidey sense fully engaged Luke's gaze remained on the barn.

Kate's in there. He was sure of it. Moving wheels rumbled in the night taking the edge off his triumph. Vehicles were approaching.

"Snake, how many? Over," Knight asked.

"Two vehicles. Hard to tell. Possibly eight men. Over."

"Copy that."

"Ready to shoot on your signal, Boss." Snake's assurance should have taken the edge off his nerves.

He concentrated on the big guy outside the barn. The prick hadn't moved.

"Hold for my signal," Knight commanded. "Okay, watch your backs —let's finish this. Snake hold the perimeter. Spanner, Doc, stay where you are. Oumar, you, and your men move with me on my three. One. Two. Move." Knight stayed low and lunged ahead of them.

"Moving," Oumar confirmed.

Seckou's reinforcements were closing in, another thirty seconds tops. Luke adjusted the weight of his Bergan, ready to run if and when needed. Spanner coolly hooked his index finger around the trigger of his rifle.

In front of them, the gleam from the barrel of a weapon caught Luke's eye seconds before bullets sprayed the night. *Fuck.*

Alerted to their intrusion, guns blazing, men swarmed out of the hut fleeing in every direction. The first guard ran straight for him. Adrenaline set his body on fire as he reached for his weapon.

"I have him, Doc." Snake's voice, as steady as his gun hand, hissed over Luke's headset. A single shot rang into the night, and the guard's chest arched to the sky before he toppled into the dirt, drowning in his blood.

Luke released the breath caught in his throat. His hand shook, the nozzle of his gun pointing at his feet. Once again, he'd been saved from firing his weapon.

"Beers are on me," Spanner sniggered.

"Okay, don't put your feet up yet dickheads," Knight snarled.

Panic whiplashed through every cell kicking his heart rate into over-drive. Memories of 'B' patrol under fire, Mike's blood streaming through his fingers snatched his attention, froze him in time.

Spanner tugged on the strap of his Bergan. "Doc?"

Pull yourself together. Luke shoved Spanner's arm from his sleeve. All he could see was Kate, a perfect shield for Seckou, getting hit by a stray bullet.

Get her to safety. Nothing else mattered. They couldn't wait, no more pissing about, he had to do something, or he'd go insane. *Do no harm*. The oath warred with the certainty he would do anything to protect Kate. Anything.

Positive she was in the barn he jumped to his feet. "Snake, cover me, I'm going in for Kate and the girl." Breaking free of their cover, Luke took off, his eyes peeled for any stray insurgent. He'd fight any obstacle that came in his way.

"Right behind you." Spanner stumbled after him.

"Shit. Roger that," Knight groaned.

All around him, Issouf and his team were in the thick of it, taking parting shots from Seckou's men as they piled into their vehicles. Dust, stirred by the spinning wheels, made it impossible to score any more targets.

"Fuck me, dead! He's getting away," Knight bellowed. "They're heading towards Dori."

"Crys." Spanner's anguished cry vaguely registered.

"S'okay Sergeant, Issouf is with her. She's safe."

Luke held tight to his weapon and kept running. He'd been a shit to Crystal. "Spanner, I—"

"Save it doc." Spanner winked. "We going into that barn to get your girl, or what?"

Seconds later, they were either side of the wooden door. Spanner bashed the metal latch with the butt of his rifle, flipped the metal latch and kicked it open. Safety off, he led, alternating hand signals between a fist and a wave.

Luke bit his tongue and willed Spanner to get a fucking move on before he lost it. "Kate, where are you? Talk to me."

"Here," Kate's voice rose over the mayhem outside.

Luke didn't need to see her face to know she'd been through hell. She sat in the middle of the filthy floor cradling Amina.

"Kate, I'm here. Right here. Look at me." He turned her face to his and watched her eyes fix on a point over his shoulder. An enormous bruise covered the side of her face.

"Sitrep," Knight's words spat into Luke's headset.

"Targets acquired. Over." Spanner replied and knelt beside him. "Let's get them out of here, Doc."

"Kate, look at me. Spanner, take Amina." He waved his palm in front of Kate's face.

Stunned, she didn't blink, her fingers locked on the girl's shoulders. "No. Luke, check Amina … the baby."

Looking to him for his next order, Spanner eased back.

"I will as soon as we have more light. Let Spanner take Amina."

"I told Amina you'd come for us." Kate loosened her grip on Amina's arm.

"Never doubt it. Can you walk?"

"Yes. I think so."

Luke locked his arm around Kate's waist and helped her to her feet, and for the first time in hours, his breath made it past the tight fist in the middle of his chest.

Boss. Coming out, carrying Amina. Doc and Kate are walking. Over," Spanner reported.

"Copy—Head for the trees. Doc, you lead. I'll cover Spanner's six. Over."

Spanner placed Amina gently over his shoulder. Not the most comfortable, but the best way to carry her and keep his gun hand free.

"Go." Heart pounding, Luke moulded his palm to the curve in Kate's back, shielded her head with his other and bolted.

Safe under the trees, Kate clung to his hips, pulling him closer. They were both shaking. Damn holding back, doing the right thing. He was desperate to get her alone, to clamp his mouth to her delicate pink lips, suck in her sweetness and celebrate the fact she was alive.

Taking hold of her wrists, he brought them to his chest, creating a space between them. "We need to get you out of here." Once they were safe at the hotel, he would confess his part in her brother's death and pray she'd let him kiss her.

Minutes later, Snake guided their truck into the clearing. Luke settled Kate inside and handed her his canteen. "Drink."

"Amina?" she gulped the water.

"Easy. Amina's right here."

The door opposite swung open, and Spanner placed Amina into the seat next to Kate. He joined the rest of the team in the back of the truck.

"I'll drive." Knight put the key in the ignition.

Luke squeezed in beside the Kate and Amina, a tight fit, but he wasn't letting them out of his sight.

"We ready to move, Doc?"

"Yes. Let's get the hell out of here." He slammed the door.

Knight rammed his foot on the accelerator.

Luke leaned over and placed the canteen to Kate's lips. She shivered. "Amina will be fine, Kate. Take another drink. Slowly."

"Are you sure?"

Luke reached for Amina's wrist. "Her pulse is strong. We'll check her at the hospital. Together, okay?"

"Her baby, I have to make sure she's—"

"A girl, hey?"

Kate's mouth trembled. Luke dragged a smile from his boots and wiped a tear from her cheek.

"*Mon bébé*?" Amina wailed, and her hands clutched her bump.

Luke grinned. "Step on it, Knight. We're having a baby."

"*Blimey.*"

CHAPTER TWENTY-TWO

Kate wanted to curl on the floor and snore. For a day. Make it a week.

After eighteen hours coaxing Amina's baby into the world, her body ached. Pummeled to a pulp as if she'd gone ten rounds with Crystal's cousin, an Olympic hopeful in the middleweight boxing division she slumped in the chair next to Amina's bed.

Luke cradled Amina's baby to his chest, humming a nursery rhyme. His rich tenor voice rolling over them. Transfixed, head on her hand, she released a heavy sigh and remembered how her father sang to her when she couldn't sleep.

"Come here." Palm up, Luke offered his hand.

Drawn to him swifter than snow to mountain peaks, Kate stared at a future she didn't dare claim. Avoiding his hand, she nuzzled into the gentle 'c' curve of the baby's spine, her smell as sweet as a summer berry.

Luke's fingers glided over the bruise on her cheek. Despite the alarm bells ringing in her head, Luke's touch was worth the sting. If she weren't careful, she'd end up wanting to hold more than Luke's hand.

"You do this every day?"

Dream or deliver babies? "Most days. Come on, Doc, don't tell me this gorgeous girl is your first."

"Outside of med school? 'Fraid so. I never considered obstetrics. It was always trauma medicine for me, much to mum's disappoint. Before retirement, she was an obstetrician." He cleared his throat.

More to that story, she was curious to hear more, but when he didn't continue, she didn't press. Sharing meant caring. It wasn't right, the flash of sadness in his eyes, not for the man who rescued women from gun-toting dickheads and soothed newborns with *Twinkle twinkle little star.*

"I can see why your mum thought you were destined to follow in her footsteps. You're a natural."

"Waaargh." Amina's baby shot from a purr to ear-piercing wail, shattering the moment.

"Oh, oh. Kate?" The expression on Luke's face was priceless. No joke. He didn't have a clue what to do next.

Kate laughed. "Don't worry, Doc, she's hungry. Time to surrender your prize to mum."

"Er, okay, nosh time, little one." Arms outstretched, Luke presented his bundle to Amina. "Er Congratulations. Your baby is …"

Out of his depth, Luke stuttered to find words. Odd, she'd heard him speak French and Mossi. Kate jumped at the opportunity to rescue him for a change. "Baby is … *très belle.*"

"Yes, *belle*. Beautiful." Luke kissed the soft, delicate skin of the baby's forehead.

It was odd that he should have trouble with beautiful, given it was the first word that came to most people's minds when they came face to face with a newborn. Before she had a chance to mention it, a tear pooled in the corner of Luke's eye. Without thinking, she captured it on the edge of her thumb.

"Sorry, I was sure there was something in your eye." The teetering tear shone brighter than a speck of gold. *Too close.* Heat flushed her cheeks, she took a step back and stared at her toes.

"Okay, you two—stop torturing the poor child. They can hear this honey in *Wagga*." Crystal to the rescue. "It's time for you two lovelies to take a shower and nap."

Crystal twirled in front of them, the gleam in her eye working overtime.

Luke naked in the shower, her tongue tracing kisses along the line of dark hair that trailed from sternum to his navel. The flush returned to Kate's cheeks. *Steady.* Her girlie bits sang despite the thousand reasons for not sleeping with him again.

A quick shower was a great idea, get rid of the stench of Yacouba's barn clinging to her clothes and skin. Last night, Amina had earned a reprieve. A woman in full contraction proved too much for Knight. He and Spanner opted for the local bar, promising to question her this morning. Kate had every intention of being there when he did.

"Luke, what time will Knight be here?"

"Didn't say, but if you're worried, I'll check." He reached for his phone.

"Please. When we get to the motel."

"Okay, I'll make sure we're back in time."

She trusted Luke to keep his promise.

"Sleep Amina, we'll be back soon." Kate couldn't resist one last peck on the baby's cheek.

In the overcast car park, the stink of cooked fish and cabbage hanging in the air, made her stomach roll. Djembe drums echoed in the distance. She missed those lazy evenings, dancing and singing with the other nurses on a Friday night, a reward after a tiring day at the clinic.

"Up for a walk or do you want to wait while I fetch the Jeep?" Luke's voice rolled with the gathering thunder.

"A slow walk. That's a brilliant idea." She resisted linking her arm through his, but he stayed close as they strolled in silence, occasionally catching each other's gaze when they passed something the other found interesting. As sure as candles in a church, saying goodbye to Luke would be hard.

Large puddles formed a moat around the entrance to their room. Feeling like a little kid, Kate grinned and waded through them.

"Hey, watch where your splashing." Luke grabbed her by the waist and lifted her over the ditch of water.

"Luke, please, you'll drop me." God, it was good to laugh.

"Never." Put this other arm around my neck." He reached for her uninjured arm.

The tenderness of Luke's gesture washed through her warmer than a summer wave. Still laughing, he carried her the last few feet where they fell against the door.

Luke wanted her. Desire gleamed from his dark eyes filling the shadows with a heat that warmed her to the core. It would be more than easy to let him know it was okay to take a step closer.

"This hurt?" The caress of his finger from her chin to her cheek sent tingles running haywire along her spine.

"Huh?" Kate raised her mouth and closed her eyes.

"Here." The tip of his thumb pressed the bruise.

"S'okay. How's it look?" She sniffed.

"*Très belle*." Luke chuckled; his thigh brushed the inside of her leg.

"Mm, you're a quick learner."

"Better believe it."

School's open, the words were on the tip of her tongue. Luke's breath danced over her lips and tears streamed from her eyes—rotten timing for the waterworks.

It tore Luke up, seeing Kate in tears, scooting under his arm, and scraping the blood spots on the front of her shirt. "Please don't cry."

The desire to get personal with her mouth, silence her sobs with a kiss fought with every rational bone in his body, threatened to tear down the wall he was working so hard to build between them, made him want to take her right there against the fucking door.

He put his hand in his pocket and searched for an imaginary tissue.

"Luke. Look at me."

Done looking—he wanted to taste, to feed off the one beautiful thing in his madness.

"I'm filthy," she said.

"A little bruised and bashed ..." Maybe he should offer to wash her back, her legs, her ...? "Want me to wash your hair? Mum used to say getting her hair done every Saturday set her up for a better week."

"A good place to start."

His heart raced, thinking of how he would love to explore and lose himself in every inch of Kate Gibson. What did she eat for breakfast? Did she have a favourite colour? Flower?

She was everything bright in the world. Brave, gorgeous, and kind. Kind, the word didn't do her justice but damn if he could think of a better one. Not now, not when she stared at him with eyes bluer than Ceylon sapphires and sincerity that devoured his reserve and challenged his honour.

Tell her.

Washing her hair might be the sexiest move he'd ever make when it came to Kate Gibson.

Sucking in a breath, he turned the key in the lock. "In."

Kate laughed, and he joined her, anticipation playing in the air between them. Perfect breasts, tight nipples poked against the buttons of her shirt.

His balls ached, swollen and tight, he just might explode, imagining bold, brave, Kate riding him into oblivion.

The sound of a Bollywood raga destroyed the blistering possibilities. "Swear I will burn every fucking mobile on the planet."

Kate's breath hitched, and she bit her bottom lip. "After me, you're first."

"Don't answer it."

"I must. It's Crystal."

"Lost her toothbrush? Sorry," he mumbled. The jibe unnecessary.

She smiled. "The phone. It's in my bag."

Luke tossed her bag onto the bed. This close, the citrus scent that always followed her, filled his nostrils. "I'll be outside when you're done."

Time to hold a cigarette and thank Crystal for saving him from devouring Kate's perfect mouth.

CHAPTER TWENTY-THREE

Luke hunched over the butt of a cigarette, sheltering it from the rain.

Rattling windows and shaking doors bombarded the morning. Not even the birds hung around the trees.

George, his ears pricked, trotted beside Snake who furtively glanced over his shoulder as he strode towards him. Situational Awareness an essential tactical skill drilled into them in training.

Locate your enemy before he got a chance to blow your brains out —survive.

"Morning, Doc."

Talking of dogs, Luke nodded at the man who, since the day the Boss invited him to join Sentinel, morphed into Knight's favourite pit bull.

"How's your new friend?"

George shook the rain from his fur, showering it over the bottom of Snake's pants.

"Him?" Snake curled the piece of rope tied around the dog's neck once around his hand and patted the dog on the head. "He's good, aren't you boy?"

"No shit." Luke could swear there was an answering glint from Mike in the dog's eyes. He chuckled, it was no secret, everyone was glad George was a part of Sentinel. "What can I do for you?"

"Boss sent me. He's spoken to Amina."

"Shit." Luke ground the butt of his cigarette into the dirt. When he told Kate, he was in for a world of pain. "And…"

"Hotels are the fave target of the month, and Uncle Seckou plans to bomb another, one of the major ex-pat jobs in *Wagga*. The problem is Amina couldn't confirm which one." Snake scratched George behind the ears.

"Aha. Suppose we're not taking the women to *Wagga*? Where to?"

Snake straightened. "Not so fast. The plan stands."

Luke's blood turned to fire in his veins. "Has Knight lost his ever-loving mind?" Fuck revenge. The Boss could think again if he planned on using either Amina or Kate as bait and sending them into the mouth of the lion.

Snake smiled. "Nope. Hide in plain sight. Plus . . ."

But wait, there's more—Knight and his endless supply of fucking steak knives.

"The Boss has contacted the local militia and offered our help with their operation. As Sentinel has no vested political interest, it was a suggestion they couldn't refuse. When we get a bead on where Seckou's gone to ground, Oumar will head there. Our friend gets around, has contacts everywhere. He's certain he can infiltrate the group and secure intel. I'll go with him."

Luke seethed, kidnapping Kate and Amina crossed his mind, hide, and protect them until it was safe to return. But there was safety in numbers. Fine. For now, he'd go along with taking Kate and Amina to *Wagga*, but the first hint of trouble and they were ghosts. "Salif? Any sign of him?"

"Not yet. Oumar's on it. If Kate's okay to travel, Boss wants you to bring her to breakfast. We're leaving straight after we've eaten." Snake dug his hands in his pockets and whistled for George to follow. "Later."

"Yeah, tell Knight we'll be there."

Neither he nor Kate had eaten, but first he sure as hell needed a shower. A place to hide once he broke the news to Kate. She stood by the bed, a bunch of what looked like old papers and photographs in her hand.

"Everything okay? The phone call?" Luke wiped the rain from his forehead and resisted the urge to lick the pulse quivering beneath the open neck of her shirt.

"Yes. Nothing serious. Amina's having trouble feeding her baby. Crys asked when we'd make it to the hospital."

"Isn't Crystal qualified to …?" He stopped himself, no use starting a fight. His beef was with the Boss and his pawn shuffling. "Has the baby got a name yet?"

"No, mum wants to wait a few days." Kate's face turned a sexy shade of pink as she crumpled a black, lace bra in her hand and shoved it in her bag.

Luke's mouth watered. "Why? Babies deserve names."

"What's up, Doc? Why are so grumpy?" Kate cocked her head to one side and waved her hand, dismissing him before he could apologise for being an arse.

"She's superstitious. Not long before this pregnancy, she miscarried. Amina, like many women in her village, believes it's best to wait until a baby survives its first week before giving it a name."

Kate's bottom lip trembled. Careful not to make any sudden move, Luke moved to her side. This close, the red blotches marring her pale skin made him feel like a useless dick. Add sunburn to the bruises, the shit job he did of keeping her protected. "Have you got a hat?"

"A hat? This conversation is getting ridiculous. What the fuck, Luke?"

Luke could smell Kate's anger. Arousing, the way she saved her potty mouth for special occasions. Instantly hard, he shifted slightly trying to ease his growing erection.

He tapped the top of his head. "The hat—for the sun."

"Oh. Sorry."

Her lips formed a circle, the perfect shape to mould around his cock. *Sweet heaven. Randy Ralph. Get a grip.*

"S'okay. Listen, while you were talking with Crystal, I saw Snake. We're re-locating to *Wagga*." He'd have preferred a bullet to his brain to the veil of disappointment dimming the light in Kate's eyes.

Kate squeezed his shoulder and gave a mock salute. "I'm sure it's for the best. I'll hop, skip, and jump when we see Knight. I'll finish getting ready, and you can drive me to the hospital. Amina's vulnerable enough without facing Mr Tsunami's interrogation alone.

"Too late. Knight questioned her shortly after we left." Kate's shoulders sagged, deep resignation clouding her face. Defeat didn't look good on her. He had to admit he was surprised she hadn't put up a fight. He didn't enjoy mistrusting her.

"No wonder Amina is having trouble feeding her baby. I'm sure Knight's scared her half to death."

He hated the shrillness in Kate's voice, the mix of fear and fury, so he offered a piss-weak apology. "There was too much at stake, Kate. The Boss couldn't afford to wait. Amina's information tallies with intel he received from Mali."

"What intel. Will they come for her again?"

Kate's hand ran over her stomach, the way it often did when she was nervous.

"I doubt it." A grim shadow settled low in his gut. Kate was a smart woman, must have guessed he was talking out the back of his head, but she didn't push. "Too busy fixing to blow up a hotel."

"Where?"

He reached for her hand, pulling back at the last minute. He wanted to haul her to him, feel her heart meet the pounding of his own, tell her everything would be okay, but he couldn't trust himself not to go further. In any case, she should be terrified. This business with Seckou was no game.

"*Wagga*. Everyone's having breakfast. You can hear it from the Boss. But, first, we both need a shower. You first." Kate nodded and brushed past him. If he lived past this week, he'd never get enough of her sweet, tangy scent.

From the first time they'd locked eyes, Kate shone a light in the black spaces of his soul. Spaces destined to darken when she found out what he'd done? He'd die rather than see her hurt. But, she deserved better than her brother's killer.

He'd made up his mind. Once they located Seckou, he'd tell her everything then offer to take Snake's place and leave with Oumar. Knight and the team could protect her.

While Kate showered, he sorted clean clothes, opened the door and held another cigarette. At this rate, they were turning into a two-pack a day security blanket.

"All done. Your turn."

"Great, thanks, why don't you go ahead and eat. I'll be there soon."

"Okay, but you'd better hurry before Spanner eats everything plus the table."

He took one last look at Miss Gibson, the eyes designed to slay dragons, and headed for the bathroom. He was more than his damn cock. Twenty minutes later, clean-shaven and still achingly aroused, he joined the party.

Behind where Kate sat, shafts of sunlight streamed through the window, teasing the ginger highlights in her hair. Even with *hungry-not-planning-to-eat* etched into the faint lines on her face, Luke swore he'd never seen a more beautiful woman.

He slid into the seat beside her, broke off the end of a baguette and slathered it with peanut butter. "Eat."

"Thanks." Kate's smile fell, lifeless, as she took it from his hand.

"Time to move, boys and girls. Luke take it with you." The cane chair creaked under the weight of Knight's solid frame. "Spanner, pay the bill."

"Not me, Boss, I'm out."

"I have it." Kate took her purse out of her pocket.

"Put it away, Kate." Luke tossed several francs on the table, more than enough to pay for their meal, and moulded his hand to the curve of her lower back. "I'll help with Amina."

"No, all good. Stay. Eat. The pineapple is delicious. I can manage." Kate's fingers brushed his forearm. The feather touch landing with the force of an avalanche.

"Will do." Not caring who saw, he sucked in a breath and dropped a kiss on the top of her head. What he'd give to wear out the spot. *Quit kissing her*. She'd walked into his life as if she were strolling in Hyde Park and collected every one of his missing pieces as though they were conkers tossed by the autumn breeze.

"Rolling in ten," Knight yelled from beside his Jeep.

"Thank you. For everything," Kate whispered as she sidled through the space between him and the door.

The finality in her voice made him tremble. Her fucking smile, he'd spend the rest of his life missing her smile.

CHAPTER TWENTY-FOUR

What made Doc so bloody special he could stir her deepest insecurities to boiling point? The heat of Luke's touch didn't scare her. No. It was the way she leaned into it that terrified her.

Face it. A brush of Luke's fingers anywhere on her skin and Kate's lungs took orbit.

No false modesty, a lot of men found her attractive. Playing touchy-feely with six-foot-plus of a strikingly good-looking male whose sensuality left her panting? She'd have to be dead not to respond to the welcome digression from the madness wreaking havoc on her world.

Her friends fell in and out of love with the phases of the moon. Not her, she was under no illusion that sex meant anything more than mutual pleasure—relief from inescapable daily stress.

Luke wasn't interested in her beyond his promise to Mike to watch out for her, and maybe, he felt a little shitty for the way he upped and left after their explosive night of passion.

Until she met Luke, a steamy roll in the sack, no attachments, suited her fine. Love 'em and leave 'em, one of her grandmother's favourite sayings. Mike's death, coupled with the memory of dad deserting her, had left a bone-deep emptiness inside her she was having trouble shaking. Allowing Luke to fill that space only to have him walk away might finish her. *Yep. Petrified.*

"Amina okay?" Arms crossed over his chest. One leg hooked lazily over the other, Luke leaned against the Jeep, waiting, flashing a smile that flipped her heart and made her legs weak.

"Yes, she's right behind me. Thanks for getting my bag. Dump it over there. I'll ride with Crystal." A little distance might cool the flush of longing invading her body every time she laid eyes on him, but she didn't move fast enough.

"You don't want to ride with me?" Luke stood in front of her, his brown eyes dancing with laughter.

She almost caved. Almost. "Aren't you sick of babysitting me, Doc?"

"Not even close."

Damn. Kate cleared her throat. "Spanner mentioned Crys wants you to give a talk to the trainees at Yalgado Hospital. You can work out the details on the trip to *Wagga*. Let's tell her she can ride with us." Could she sound shriller, no, she pressed her fingernails into her palms.

"Sure. Sounds good."

The hint of his thigh pressed beside hers, encouraged her to fall in step with the fluid movement of his long legs. Her breath hitched. If Luke noticed, he didn't let on as they approached Spanner's bike.

"Crys, ride with us, it's more comfortable in the Jeep. You can sit up front with Luke and lock him in for those talks at Yalgado," Kate pleaded.

"Thanks for the offer, Kate, but I'm happy riding with Spanner." Crystal wobbled.

Spanner grabbed her outstretched hand, supporting her while she climbed onto his Triumph Tiger. Fresh ink, a Spiderman tattoo, circled his thick bicep. Mind-boggling what the SAS got up to when they weren't protecting queen and country.

Spanner grinned and locked Crystal's arms around his waist. "Hold tight. No falling asleep."

"If you think you're the first boy that's ever had me on his bike, you're mistaken." Crystal's cheek snuggled into the spot between Spanner's shoulder blades.

Spanner adjusted the strap on his helmet. "A challenge. I love it. Be sure, Crys. I will be the last."

Kate was happy for her friend, but her smile didn't make it to her lips. Honestly, she was a little jealous, make that sad that she'd never experience the loving banter Crystal shared with her man. Unable to watch any longer, she looked around for the Boss. "Where's Knight?"

"Long gone." Spanner disengaged the clutch, smiling when the Tiger's engine purred. "Drive safe Doc, precious cargo on board." He nodded at Amina and her baby.

"You too. See you in *Wagga*. Climb upfront Kate while I'll settle Amina."

Happy or not, she was riding with Luke, the man with the smug grin plastered on his face. She shrugged, it could be worse, her head ached less, and the Jeep was air-conditioned.

They hadn't gone two miles before Amina and baby were sleeping soundly in the back seat. Despite the crosswind accompanying them for the long haul down the N3, she was determined to join them. Closing her eyes, she slipped into a restless doze.

Hours later, eyes itchy and bleary, she peered out of the window. They'd arrived at Knight's villa. Typical of many affluent homes in *Wagga* a high wall surrounded the grounds. Painted the traditional sandy orange, it was complete with a barbed-wire crown.

In the middle of the road, a small group of kids playing tag made the most of the fading light.

Thirsty didn't come close to describing the sandpaper dryness at the back of Luke's throat. He'd hack heads for a single malt. The Boss was deep in conversation with a security guard sprawled in a folding chair outside the entrance to his villa. Knight waved him into a parking spot beside Spanner's bike.

Other than attending debriefs, he avoided Knight's villa. Too many ex-pats lived in the Zone du Bois region of Burkina's capital. He preferred a bunk near the military base, working out his frustrations shooting hoops on the basketball court across the street.

"We're here, Kate. You can open your eyes." For most of the trip, she'd played dead. Their almost kiss left a tension between them that neither found comfortable. Most of the drive he'd racked his brains trying to work out if and how he should apologise.

"Uh?" The shrug of her shoulder said it all. Ms capable didn't need his help rolling out of the Jeep. Her eyes focussed on Crystal who sat rigid on Spanner's bike.

"Luke, please, help Amina." Clearly worried for her friend Kate hurried to Cry's side.

Amina and her baby were awake and doing a ton better than Crystal whose face was a shade of murky green. "Take my arm." Amina didn't refuse.

Kate braced her injured arm against her side and helped Crystal off the bike.

He should have told her the woman was, yeah, going to vomit. Luke's high-school drama days sprung to mind, Richard III, he'd played the lead. *My kingdom for a horse.* Bugger the horse but make it a Laphroaig over a cube of ice. It might not make him a better man. It would elevate his mood.

Kate pulled a tissue from her pocket and offered it to Crys.

"Thanks."

"You okay?"

"Yes, don't worry, hun. I'm fine. No thanks to lover boy." Crystal tilted her head at Spanner.

Both women flashed Spanner a die-now-dog look—his friend well in the shit for riding to *Wagga* without a break. Served him right. Yes, Lukie boy, you need that scotch.

"Spare one of those?" Luke eyeballed the guard, feeling shabby when the Burkinabe tossed him his last cigarette and smiled.

"Don't worry Kate. I won't drop her." Spanner scooped Crystal, half whimpering, half laughing into his arms.

"Hey, you better not." She slapped the top of Spanner's head.

Luke turned to grab their bags. Pity, his favourite redhead didn't need carrying. The masochist in him loved playing cat and mouse with Ms Gibson.

"After you, Kate." Luke sighed. Following the sway of her sexy hips was poor consolation.

"Make yourselves comfortable." Knight disappeared around the back of the villa with the security guard leaving Spanner struggling to hang onto Crystal and punch numbers into a security keypad.

"Hey, need help here. My hands are full." Flashing teeth white enough to grace a Colgate ad, Spanner bounced Crystal in his arms.

"Move." Luke elbowed him and punched in the code.

Crystal shrieked loud enough to burst Luke's eardrums as Spanner galloped past him. "Coming through, Doc."

Kate made her move and their eyes met. He hated the glint of sadness, wanted to massage her neck, smooth away the tension creasing her forehead. To die drunk on her familiar scent, what a goal.

He'd give a lifetime's pay for things to be different, for a chance to see if they had a future, take her on a date. The air chilled as her warmth followed her into the villa.

"Knight, where's your kitchen? Any food in the fridge?" Kate called out to the Boss, who'd materialised at the end of the hall.

"Good idea, hun. While you cook, I'll help Doc get Amina settled. Spanner put me down. Where's her room, Knight?" Free of Spanner's arms, Crystal smoothed back her hair. Ready for business.

"Second door on the left." Knight pointed to the room next to the master bedroom. Always in charge, the Boss intended keeping his eye on Amina. "Kate, follow me. If you're after something to scramble, my fridge is at your service."

Cheap shot. Dead on her feet, Amina leaned into Crystal for support as he took the baby from her arms. Another one who had little interest in food.

"I got this, Doc. Come on, hun, the chair over here looks comfy. *Rest la.*"

He'd told Kate babies weren't his thing, but he couldn't resist a stroke of the sprog's soft head before he relinquished her to mum.

Spanner poked his head around the door just as the sight of the baby's tiny hands, curled into fists, found the lump to his throat.

The day he left for Africa his mum called to say he was an uncle. His sister had a boy. Uncle Luke. They'd never been a close family, but he should make an effort and catch up next time he was in London.

"Hey Doc, hidden talents, I never knew you were good with kids. Come and help me open these beers." Spanner yelled across the open plan living area.

"What's up with you, broke your arm?" Not up for hanging with Spanner, Luke grabbed a beer and aimed for the nearest exit. "I'll be back."

Surprise! His feet opted for the kitchen. Leaning against the door frame, he took a swig of his beer and admired Kate's passion for butchering vegetables. With her free hand, she reached for a copper pan and did her best to ignore him. The overplay of innocence masking her face was priceless.

"Hi, what's cooking?" He lifted the corner of the plate closest to his hand.

Kate waved her knife. "Step away, before I nick you with this."

Bring it on. Give me an excuse to pin you to the kitchen bench and…

Her giggle tripping across the air made him harder than he'd ever been. The danger of the past few weeks had robbed everyone of downtime, opportunities to play. He leaned over the counter—his erection pressing uncomfortably against the front of his pants.

"Easy, killer." He placed his palm over her fingers. I'm starving, something smells good, so I've come to check on dinner, sneak a taste."

Kate rolled her lips together and lifted her eyes to the carrots on the chopping board. "Have at it."

"Thanks. Luke took two and offered her one.

"All yours."

"Your mum teach you to cook?"

Kate tossed the knife onto the counter and turned to check the grill. "No, Mother can't cook for beans." They both laughed at the cliché pun.

"Who? I know it wasn't Mike."

"You can say that again."

Luke opened his mouth to comply, her every wish his command. Anything to keep the light shining in her eyes.

"Shh. No. I'm afraid I am a miserable fake. I have a repertoire of five dishes. Tonight, you will sample three of them."

"The other two?"

"Desserts. Tell a lie. I forgot Mike's biscuits. Damn."

Kate's breath caught in her throat, and he practically vaulted the counter. *Nice work* Luke could kick himself for leading her there.

"I'm okay. Give me a minute." Kate held up her hand.

One hand wiped at the corner of her eye. "Oh, hi Crys, bloody onions."

"Swap? It smells like you need to check something in the oven." Crystal grabbed the knife from Kate's hand. "Spanner, hun, you got a beer for me?"

"Amina, Asleep yet?" He didn't take his eyes off Kate's back as she checked the grill.

"How'd you guess, Doc? Off to fairyland. One less for dinner. What else can I do, Kate?"

"Nothing, almost done. Ten minutes. Find plates and cutlery, and bring everyone to the table, please."

Domestic goddess back in control. Luke smiled.

"Smells good, Kate." Knight strolled into the kitchen. "Amina settled?"

Luke guessed the Boss had been checking in with Snake. The SITREP couldn't come soon enough. Perfect opportunity to raise his hand to go with Oumar, wherever the fuck that might be. "Yeah, all good, she'll sleep until morning."

"Here, Luke, grab the ribs." Kate shoved the large plate into his hands, and the smell of cremated meat hit his nostrils.

"Awesome." Spanner speared a chunk before Luke put the plate on the table. "What's for dessert?"

"Ice cream—chocolate, vanilla, strawberry, or…" Crystal cocked her head to the side and flashed her dimples, Spanner's sweet tooth no secret.

Luke sat opposite Kate. Her fight to keep her eyes open impressive. A gold medal for her faint smile when Crystal threatened to crochet a fluffy pillow for the pillion seat of Spanner's Tiger.

"Doc, Kate, Amina good to travel tomorrow?" The Boss offered Kate the salad.

The food on her plate wouldn't feed a bird. Luke silently chuckled when Knight dismissed her refusal and heaped lettuce on her plate.

"Should be. It's a short drive." Kate ducked when anyone mentioned the inevitable trip to the refugee camp. She was doing it now, staring at the tiled floor as if it held a happy ending.

"Kate, come and see me before Amina leaves." Knight stabbed the tip of his fork in her direction.

Luke raised an eyebrow. Now, what was that about, the Boss didn't usually have much time for civilians.

"*Je pars, Monsieur Knight. Il est dix heures*." The security guard hovered in the doorway. Knight glanced at the wall clock. "*Eh bien*, Aziz. Tomorrow."

"*Oui, bonsoir*."

"Goodnight."

Knight's place was a fortress, but with security gone for the night, they'd take turns keeping watch until morning.

"Anyone for cards?"

"No, thanks, Spanner, not me" Kate pushed her half-full plate to the side. "I must call Aunty, sort a few things for Amina before they … before tomorrow. Which room's mine, Knight?"

"Follow me." Knight crooked his index finger.

"I hear my bed calling too. A long shower followed by layers and layers of shea butter."

"Need help?" Crystal avoided Spanner's attempt to pull her into his lap.

Luke joined the bloody Conga line, determined to make sure Kate was okay, see if she needed anything before, they turned in for the night.

"Guest rooms are on the right, take your pick. I'll take first watch, gentlemen." The Boss left them and strolled to the sofa, took his pistol from its holster, and placed it on the coffee table in easy reach beside him.

"This is me. Goodnight." Kate tapped her finger on the door in front of her.

No way, standing this close to her, could he not admire the rise and fall of her perfectly round breasts. Not a good idea, given he was on the edge of control. He'd always been careful. As a trauma specialist, keeping emotional distance was expected.

"'Night, you two." Crystal waved and slipped into the room next door.

"Sleep well, Kate." He shouldn't, given he was leaving within the next few hours, and she still didn't have the full story of her brother's death, but he couldn't resist kissing her cheek.

"You too, Luke. Goodnight." Kate swayed.

"Steady." *It's just a kiss.*

CHAPTER TWENTY-FIVE

Stuff Luke's cocky self-confidence. Kate swept her tongue across the front of her teeth and stood taller.

"Second thoughts it's a nice night. There's a garden, right? Want to join me for a look at the moon?" Her nose in line with Luke's chin, she tucked a lock of hair behind her ear and hooked two fingers under the belt of his pants.

She wanted to undress him, slowly, blistering attraction for each other had never been their problem.

Luke cleared his throat. "Sure. Go ahead. I'll grab a couple of waters."

"I fancy a glass of red, do you think you can find a bottle?" She let go of his belt and brushed the side of her mouth with the tip of her pinkie finger.

"I'll see what I can do."

Kate offered him a grin that didn't show her teeth. She wasn't usually such a tease. Hadn't she congratulated herself on keeping her distance? This pull between them was as strong as it was strange.

She was all over the place, there was a bloody terrorist out there, dead set on blowing up a hotel. If her insides ever stopped churning, she might be able to clear her head and get her sodding libido in check.

Eager—much? Luke must have sprinted because she'd barely reached the seat at the end of the path, and there he was, next to her, bottle, and glass in hand. "Nice night. You're not joining me?"

"Another time. Knight's taking the first watch, but we're all on duty tonight."

"I see." She pointed to the stars twinkling above them. They weren't the only things putting on a show.

Luke poured the wine, didn't spill a drop, impressive considering he never took his eyes off her. He took a step closer and offered her the glass. "You worried about Amina about her going to the camp? Sorry, we couldn't stay longer in Dori."

"Oh, Doc. I didn't take you for the sensitive type. You've already explained why that wasn't possible." *Score me.* Convinced Knight must be out of his mind, she was angry at being used as bait, but it was no use going over old ground.

Luke won't let anything happen to Amina and the baby. All the way to *Wagga*, she reminded herself never managing complete conviction.

"Sensitive." Wounded for a sec before he offered one of his smiles, the bow-shaped grin that brought crinkles to the side of his eyes. "It's one of my many hidden qualities."

Her body quivered. "I'm sure. To answer your question, I'm not worried. I'm tired. An early night will do me good."

"Uh-huh. Is your arm bothering you?"

"No. It's doing fine, thanks to you. Nice stitches by the way."

"Thanks. Look, as much as I like being out here with you, sharing a drink under the stars, discussing my neat sewing skills. You've been, er, prickly, since I told you we were leaving Dori. Want to tell me why?"

"Prickly? Now, I know you're sensitive. I shared the ride with you to *Wagga*. Or didn't you notice?"

"Oh, I noticed. Three and a half hours sitting next to you pretending to be Sleeping Beauty."

"Don't be ridiculous. I was exhausted. It's been a rough couple of days."

"Bullshit, Kate. What will it take for you to be honest with me? Another glass of red?" Luke waved the bottle.

"No need to be childish, insulting. It's not all about you." Kate swallowed hard. Honesty, trust, reasons why she didn't get involved, why she avoided getting close and having to deal with mixed messages.

"If you must know, I'm pissed off with Knight, you, the whole damn team. I blame myself, but I can't help thinking if I hadn't called you, maybe none of this would have happened." Now she'd said it she realised how much the truth had been gnawing at her gut.

"You can't be serious. Yacouba shot you for Christ's sake, or have you forgotten?"

"No. But if you and Spanner hadn't charged after us, maybe I could have talked Yacouba down, persuaded him to let Amina return to the clinic."

"Now I know you're making this up as you go along. You've been working in this part of Africa long enough to know men like Yacouba see Amina as their property. No different to his goats and sheep, he can do with her what he wants. Do-gooder nurses from London mean shit to him. I repeat. He shot you for God's sake."

"Yes. And Knight offers us up for bait."

"Christ, Kate, Knight, any of us, we'd never let anything happen to any of you. You are ours to protect."

"Don't shout. People are trying to sleep. You'll wake Amina and the baby. Amina deserves to fall in love with who she chooses. Start a family with a man who makes her the centre of his world." She poked Luke's chest with her finger, choking on words more to do with her than Amina.

Luke grabbed her wrist, making her cry out at the sudden move. She took a long, slow breath. The urge to sink against him, soak up his strength brought back the terror, the certainty any comfort he offered was as fragile as the glass trembling in her fingers.

"What? You think I'd hurt you?" Luke frowned.

"No, of course not. I'm sorry." She swayed a little on her feet, the glass trembling in her hands. He didn't understand. She'd been hurt too many times, but not by Luke. Never by him.

"Forget it, Kate. Time to chill. Things are getting a little too hot and heavy for both of us. I shouldn't have yelled I know how much you hate it, or assumed you are less than professional. All I want is for you to be safe."

"Safe? And how did that work out for Mike? You were there, all of you were there. Everyone came home except my brother."

Luke paled in front of her, his Adam's apple prominent as he swallowed. She braced, expecting his anger, knowing she deserved it for letting her mouth run away with her.

"Goodnight, Kate. 'll talk to you tomorrow." The resignation in his voice destroyed her ability to speak.

She inhaled, opened her mouth to call after him, to explain how his nearness terrified her, that she couldn't afford for them to get close.

Too late. Luke disappeared into the villa. For the best.

CHAPTER TWENTY-SIX

Kate traced her fingers over her throat, the muggy heat pressed in on her, even sweating didn't do any good, it trickled down her neck like tepid water from the outside tap.

Crystal sat next to Spanner on the floor of the living room, his Glock tucked in the waistband of his pants, surrounded by toys, bibs, and teddy bears.

"You get any sleep, hun? Spanner, fetch Kate a seat."

"S'okay, Spanner, no need." One hand on his shoulder, she tipped her chin at the pile in front of him. "You two look like Santa's elves. What's with the toys and sewing machine?"

"Just getting a few essentials together for Amina and the baby."

That was a laugh. "A few?

Crystal rocked her weight on to one hand and nudged Spanner's elbow with the tip of her foot. "He's making a meal of finding the perfect teddy for the baby. Other than those she's standing in Amina doesn't have any clothes. She needs some new ones, and I found this happy fabric at the market. You like?"

"Wow, you were up early. Bright." Admiring the yards of colourful batiks, she wished she could sew, cook, be more useful.

"Too much?" Crystal wrinkled her nose. Light streaming through the open window bounced off the skirt lying in her lap.

Kate shook her head. "No. It's perfect, Crys. Amina will love it." She went over it again, trying to understand how sending Amina, and her baby to the refugee camp was a smart idea? Luke's argument hadn't convinced her.

Aunty cared, that wasn't the issue, she'd do her best to make sure they were safe, but protection was Sentinel's job. Who better? Knight's villa was a bloody fortress, and he was more than confident it was a matter of days before they took care of Seckou.

She trusted Aunty implicitly, but couldn't vouch for the other refugees. For the right price, desperate people might turn Amina over to Seckou. Dread sank like a lead weight to the pit of her stomach. If Yacouba found Amina … Kate shuddered.

Her nightmare had returned last night, leaving her with a sense of terror. Maybe she'd kidnap Amina and the baby, get as far away as possible from *Wagg. Don't be ridiculous.*

"You have five minutes while I find Amina, then we're leaving." Kate pinched the bridge of her nose and left Crys and Spanner squabbling over teddy bears.

Amina sat outside the laundry, forehead on her knees. Hugs definitely in order.

"Dites moi, Amina. Tell me, why are you out here?"

"Please. Doctor Luke took my baby." Amina poked her nose above her knees and scraped her foot in the dirt. Vulnerable, alone, a mother before she finished school. Kate swallowed the tears looming at the back of her throat. Well over being miserable.

"Don't worry, *chérie.* Doc's making sure baby's okay. He will bring her to you soon." Kate slipped her arm around Amina's tiny waist, shuffled closer, and reminded herself to give Aunty the diet sheet and vitamins.

"When Katy isn't with me, I am scared." Amina huffed and rubbed her nose on her skirt.

Wide black eyes met hers, and her heart skipped boulders. What did Amina say? "Katy?"

"*Oui*, yes. Please, I name her for you." Amina lifted her hand, shielding her eyes from the blinding sun. "It's okay?"

"Katy. After me?" A tear leaked from the corner of her eye. Mike and dad were the only ones who called her Katy.

"Yes, please." Amina stared at her, an apology teetering on her lips.

Overwhelmed, Kate threw her arms around her and kissed away her frown. Did Amina think she'd refuse? "Oh, I'm not sure ..." Immediately, she regretted her ungrateful tone, but a name, unlike people, stayed with you forever. "There must be someone else. Your mother?"

"I have no one else."

"Oh, Amina, I am sorry. Forgive me. *Merci*. Thank you, *je suis honoré*." She cuffed her tears. "It's my grandmother's name, my dad's mum. Oh, she'd be so proud of you, sweetheart." Babbling like an African parrot, they were sniffing like a couple of leaky taps. Kate offered Amina the dry edge of her manky tissue.

"She has Aunty's name too, Faiza. I will miss you. And Crystal. She makes me laugh."

"Oh, trust me, Crystal can make the dead giggle." Kate blew her nose, and they burst out laughing. Fighting back more tears, she rubbed her hands over Amina's bony arms and prayed Yacouba died screaming. "Knight, his people, they are looking for Salif," she assured her.

Suddenly defensive, Amina squirmed and folded her arms across her chest. "I go find Katy now. She be hungry."

Far from supporting Amina, her words had the opposite effect. Was she worried what Knight might do when they found her brother? "If ... when they find Salif, they won't hurt him, they'll bring him to the camp."

Amina's eyes shifted nervously side to side. She had to ask. "Amina. Do you know where Salif is?"

"There you are, hun. Here's baby, safe and sound." Killing any chance of hearing an answer, Crystal joined them on the laundry step and settled the baby in Amina's arms.

"Dr Luke says your baby is as healthy as her mama. We could have told him that, right? If you're ready, Auntie's waiting for us.

Amina drew the thin cloth tighter around Katy.

"Cheer up, Amina. Spanner helped Crys pack a bag of treats for you." Kate nuzzled her nose against the baby's cheek. The unmistakable new-born smell of fresh sugared milk and clean cotton filled her lungs. "Were you in on it, Crystal?"

"In on what?"

"Baby's name. Katy."

"No. That's perfect. Congratulations. Oh, before I forget, the Boss is looking for you."

"Damn. You finish getting ready. I won't be long." The last of her energy drained from her body. She had no idea what Knight wanted, and after the fight with Luke last night, the last thing she needed was another row.

Knight sat behind a large, oddly shaped desk. She recognised it as a piece from her favourite Burkinabe designer. Running her fingers along the edge of the re-worked wood helped calm her nerves.

"You wanted to see me." She didn't wait for him to finish what he was doing, rude, but lack of sleep, not to mention, lack of closure with Luke put her on the defensive.

Knight lifted his gaze from his papers. Infuriating, the arched comment of his bushy eyebrow. A trademark mannerism. The look that said are you sure that's your best move?

"Knight, can we take the Jeep to the camp this morning?"

"Sure. Issouf will drive you." Knight arched the tips of his fingers together, pressed them against his lips and leaned back in his chair.

She'd give a week's pay to drive Amina to Aunty without escort, but the Boss would never allow it until they found Seckou. Robbed of independence and sick of feeling like a kid frustration and anger bubbled to the surface. Bloody Seckou. Surely, he was miles away.

"Thanks. But, Knight, no cavalry." The last thing they needed was a convoy descending on the refugee camp. "We'd better get going, what did you want?" She held her breath.

"How much do you know about Amina?" Enigmatic as always, Knight didn't elaborate.

"Not very much. Before this ..." She waved her hand in front of her face. "Er... I know, Yacouba bought her from her father, Seckou's brother when she was twelve. Life with him meant no questions if she and Salif wanted to eat." Disappointed with the betraying hitch in her voice, Kate bit her tongue. *Sod, the man.*

"Er. Can I get you something, a glass of water?" Knight fidgeted in his chair.

It was odd to see the Boss, a man as capable and in command as Knight, at a loss how to handle tears.

He cleared his throat and rested his forearms on the desk. "Starting next week, I've made arrangements for Amina to attend *L'Ecole du Sacré Coeur*, earlier if she's settled. Fees are taken care of, and I'd appreciate it if you would tell Aunty to be in touch if Amina or her baby needs anything else.

Kate froze, her brain scrambling to take in Knight's offer. "But ... why?"

"Sorry, I don't mean to be rude, but you've just met her." She bit her bottom lip hoping he'd take it as her apology.

"No mystery, Kate. Bottom line. The girl deserves an education. I have the means to make sure she gets it. He pushed a white envelope towards her. "In there is Amina's registration details. Please make sure she gets it."

"Thank you, Knight. I'll fetch her. You can give it to her yourself."

"No, no need, I'll leave that to you. There is no need to worry. I will always have two men posted at the camp. One of them will accompany her to school."

"Are you sure?" She had to admit she was having a hard time getting her head around his gesture, reconciling the cold, steel-hearted Boss who avoided their company and at the same time could be this generous.

"Now, if you'll excuse me, I have matters to attend to, I'm sure you understand. You'll find Issouf outside with Aziz." Leaving no room for further discussion, Knight swivelled in his chair and opened the safe on the back wall.

Kate left without hesitation. Knight's dismissal added to her sense of disorientation and unease.

Luke was outside waiting with everyone else. The sight of him standing there, hair damp from his morning shower, played havoc with her nerves and her libido.

Ready to leave, she shuffled sideways making sure she kept her distance.

"Take care Amina. Look after Katy." His eyes met hers when he called the baby by her name. A quick nod, and before she could speak, he strolled away from them.

At one hundred per cent humidity, the heavens opened the minute they rolled away from Knight's villa. Mother Nature loved Africa's monsoon season, revelled in its drama.

Drops of rain thundered on the roof of the Jeep. No stranger to wet roads, Amina dozed while Crystal whistled. Dad used to whistle. His bird imitations relaxed her, made her happy.

She fixed her attention on the side mirror, on the vehicle following them ever since they left Knight's villa. Her hands trembled in her lap, the memory of being kidnapped fresh in her mind. If she weren't sure she'd used her nine lives, she'd ask Issouf to run every red light and get them to the camp quicker.

"Hey, Kate, there's the new rollercoaster," Crystal squealed loud enough Amina stuck a finger in her ear.

On their left, a dinosaur of steel girders glistened in the pouring rain —the recent addition to *Wagga*'s fun park.

"Too high for me."

"Not me. I'm taking Spanner. Wanna bet who screams first?"

A ride at the fair, for a second, they were lost in the excitement, but it was possible to pretend the horror of the last week hadn't happened. A knowing look passed between her and Crys, the danger was far from over, normal a fantasy.

"Not likely, I don't bet on horses that don't run." Kate squinted, but the rain covering the side mirror made it impossible to see if they were still being followed.

"Crystal, can I come to the roller coaster?" Half-awake, Amina sat forward in her seat and rubbed her eyes.

"Hun. We can all go. We'll make a day of it and bring a picnic. Soon."

Kate squeezed her friend's hand. Crystal was right, think positive. The tears were back. What would she do without her ever-positive friend?

"Amina, I have some good news too. You'll be starting school next week."

Both Crystal and Amina looked at her as though she'd showered in glitter.

"No, Miss Kate, *c'est impossible*. What about my uncle? And Katy." On cue, the baby cooed.

"Oui. *C'est vrai*. It's true, Amina Knight, has taken care of everything. You will be safe. I'm sure Aunty will watch Katy, you don't have to go full-time and can come back to feed her. I'll bring her to school if necessary. It will be okay, you'll see. Now, cheer up, you are going to school."

Amina's smile began at the edges of her mouth and quickly spread to her eyes. Issouf tooted the horn, and their laughter bounced off the roof the Jeep.

Unfortunately, the rain hadn't eased by the time Issouf parked at the entrance to the camp. No use everyone getting wet. "Crys, wait here with Amina and Katy. Stay dry. I'll find Aunty."

Ignoring their protest, she hopped out and landed ankle-deep in mud. *Fabulous.* Water seeped into her boots. Rain ran over her lips and into her mouth, as she squelched along the narrow path to the camp's women's quarters.

Luckily, Aunty's tent was easy to spot. A colourful curtain hung over one of the guy-lines. A batik she and Kate had made together during a weekend break. Unfazed by the downpour, she was sitting cooking over charcoal—water from the tarpaulin roof gushing waterfalls around her.

"*Bonjour,* Kate. You're here, how wonderful to see you." Aunty rose from her picnic chair and threw her arms around her.

"You too. What's cooking? Smells delicious?"

"*Jollof.* Join us. There is plenty."

Aunty knew her weakness for the spicy chicken and rice dish. "I'd love to, but Crystal's waiting with Amina. I wanted to make sure you were here before I dragged them ..." Hoarse from shouting over the torrents of water pounding the walls of the tents, she gave up explaining.

"*Vite, vite.*" Aunty shushed her back out onto the path. "How's *bébé*?"

Again, her answer disappeared on a gust of wind.

Ever vigilant Issouf was already helping Amina out of the Jeep. A shudder chased over her skin. Ominous shadows danced all around her, and she half expected Seckou or one of his men to come charging along the narrow path between the tents.

Keeping her distance from Luke was one thing, wanting the warmth of his arms around her right now seemed a perfect idea.

A welcome sense of relief washed over her as the canvas flap of Aunty's tent closed behind them. She recognised the two women, leading Amina to a single mattress in the corner, as trusted helpers, women Aunty relied on to help newcomers settle at the camp.

Since they left the villa, she'd been working on reining in her sadness, but a sudden rush of fear, loneliness, threatened to shatter the fragile checks she had in place.

If she stayed any longer, she'd change her mind and take Amina back to the villa. She nudged Crystal's elbow, the signal for them to leave. Refusing Aunty's offer of food and tea as gently as possible, she reached in her pocket for Knight's envelope.

"Aunty, please keep this safe. It's a letter of registration for *L'Ecole du Sacré Coeur.* Amina will explain. You'll have to sort a few things out, but when you're ready, call me, I'll let you know the security arrangements.

Maintenant, it's getting late we should get back to the villa." Aunty gave an understanding nod as she pulled Amina into a hug.

"No tears Amina, I'll see you and Katy soon." Unable to bear it any longer, she gently unfolded Amina's arms from her waist and made her escape. Always by her side, Crystal grabbed her hand, and they ducked into the rain.

The hurried goodbye ripped her insides to shreds. Against the roaring gale, it took the last of her strength to heave open the door of the Jeep.

The sudden flash of headlights flaring through the deluge blinded her for a second. Heart pounding, she raised her hand to shield her eyes. Visible between the slits between her fingers, a streak of lightning highlighted the person standing in the rain.

She would have called out, but he was inside his vehicle and pulling ahead of them before she had a chance.

"Who the hell is that?" Crystal yelled from behind her.

"Guess?"

CHAPTER TWENTY-SEVEN

Luke always happy to follow Kate's delectable was right behind her as she threw open the door to Knight's office.

"I said, no cavalry!" Kate waved her finger in Knight's face.

Luke caught the flash of appreciation on the Boss's face. Guess Kate reminded him of Mike too, all fire and righteous indignation. *That's my girl.* Teetering on her dainty toes Kate's finger barely reached the Boss' chin.

Knight grabbed the finger an inch from his nose. "How did it go, Kate? Amina and the kid okay?

He claimed no ownership of Kate, but he wasn't happy with another man's hands on her.

"Take your hands off me." Kate shrugged free.

Hell, she was pretty.

"Anyone hungry?" Spanner said.

Crystal hovered next to him, blocking the doorway to Knight's office. Six meals a day, plus snacks—the man's stomach was one gigantic black hole. Thank Christ, Knight installed a gym in his basement, or they'd be rolling him into action.

"You'd be proud of me Crys. I made good use of my time while you were gone. *Poulet Bicyclette*. For you." Spanner pursed his lips and crooked his finger in her direction.

"For me. You cooked?" Crystal dug her index finger into her chin and gave him her best Betty Boop smile.

"Did I ever? Come with me, sweet thing."

Spanner snatched Crystal by the waist and spun her into the hallway. Kate wobbled at the sudden movement. Luke steadied her.

"Thanks, Luke. I wanted to say …"

What? That she drove him insane.

Kate hmphed. "Thank you for keeping us company."

The last thing he expected was thanks, but 'surprise' was Kate's slaying feature. Along with her curves, her long limbs, her eyes, try every fucking freckle.

She straightened her spine and ran her fingers through her burnt orange curls. *Please.* Luke willed Kate not to be mean, to give him her smile. Miss Gibson didn't disappoint.

His lust got the better of him. He'd give the earth for a kiss from her pouty lips, to sink so deep inside her he'd never find his way out of her heat. Yeah, and Mary Poppins was popping in for afternoon tea.

Knight pushed past them. "Doc, Spanner. Get changed. Join me in the gym."

"Sure Boss." Spanner replied and reclaimed his arm from around Crystal's waist.

Luke nodded, excellent idea, push a few weights and chase his pulse rate for an hour. "I'm in. Give me a sec to change."

A workout might elevate his adrenaline enough to drive his gutless soul. Before he left to join Oumar, Kate deserved the truth about Mike's death. "Kate, we need to talk. Join me for a drink when later?"

"I'm not sure that's a good idea. I have to catch up on paperwork."

"It won't take long."

"Okay. Come and find me when you're finished. I'll be in my room."

Luke prayed he didn't lose his courage between a workout and a glass of wine.

Knight's underground gym doubled as a safe-room, complete with a reinforced door and tunnel exit to the street. Luke loaded a barbell and placed it on the rack. "Spanner, spot me. Chest Press. One set, maximum reps."

"Easy mate. Start slow, ten minutes on the treadmill."

Feet flat on the floor back, Luke flattened his lower back into the bench, sucked in his breath and curled his fingers around the bar. A forceful exhale. Two hundred and twenty-five pounds, not the heaviest he'd shifted but hefty enough to get his blood pumping.

"Have you told Kate?" Spanner peered over him, his hands hovering in the centre ready to snatch and rack the weight.

"Told her … what?" Spanner chose Luke's last rep to lose interest in his fucking job.

"Just sayin'." Spanner's hands dropped to his sides.

"You ain't saying shit. Get. This. Fucker. Off. Me." The air locked in his windpipe. Where the fuck was Knight?

"Let him up Spanner He's turning blue." Knight flicked him with his towel.

"Sure Boss. Okay, big guy, relax." Spanner snatched the barbell and slammed it onto the rack.

His lungs starved of oxygen, gulping for air, Luke sprang to his feet and lurched for Spanner's throat. "Not. Funny. Dickhead."

"Agreed." Knight waved his finger at Spanner, a smug grin sweeping across his face.

"What the fuck, man?" Luke tightened his grip on Spanner's shirt.

"Crys knows."

"Knows what? Stop talking in fucking riddles 'cause, I swear, if you don't stop spitting shit I will break your perfect nose."

Spanner, the dumb git, batted his eyelashes. "You care?"

Luke placed his knee under Spanner's balls and leaned in with enough pressure to make bellend wince.

"Okay, okay. Mike. The full story. Crys knows what happened."

"What, how?"

"She asked. I told her. Why's it such a bloody secret? You were supposed to have told Kate ages ago."

"Enough. Doc, let him go." Knight grabbed his wrist, applying pressure, insisting he release Spanner. He did, not because he asked but because guilt sapped a man's strength.

"As fucking hilarious as your slapstick is, you lovebirds need to relax and listen. I didn't bring you here for the benefit of my health.

Doc, you've been a remorseful, sorry, pain in my arse ever since Mike's death. No one can talk to you without getting their heads bitten off. You put your hand up to tell Kate what happened before she had to read it in a goddam letter. Why the fuck haven't you done it? Pull your shit together before you endanger the team."

Luke bit the inside of his cheek, that Knight doubted his commitment sucked. The Boss considered him a danger. He wanted to turn and leave, the villa, the fucking country, but he couldn't move, he was too ashamed.

"You feel the same way? That I'd let bad shit happen to you or the others?" Luke raised his chin in Spanner's direction.

Spanner shrugged and shook his head. "No man, of course not, but the Boss is right, you should have told her. For the record, where Mike's concerned, if anyone is to blame, it's me.

I insisted Mike took my place with 'B' patrol when he didn't fork up what he lost at cards. He was getting off lightly building latrines. No one suspected fucking Seckou was out there. It should have been me blasted to fucking kingdom come."

Luke swallowed once, twice. "Yeah, over a fucking game of cards, man, a fucking game of cards."

Spanner wiped his towel over his face, his shoulders sagged. They'd had this conversation, over a beer, in the sober light of day, it didn't make a fucking difference. No matter how often Luke told himself no way could Spanner know what hell waited for them that day, he hadn't been able to get past it, it ate at his insides, devouring a tiny piece of him every day.

Squaring his shoulders, he let go of the tension balled in his fists and faced Knight. "You want me off the team, say the word."

"You don't get off that easy Doc, but no mistake, I will pull you if I don't see a significant shift in your shitty attitude."

"Point taken. I want Seckou as much as anyone." It would take more than a back-handed apology to convince Knight, but for now, he was off the hook. "Any word from Oumar?"

"Yeah, he called while you were playing guardian angel." Eyes sharp, jaw set, determination etched into every line on his face, Knight planted his foot onto the bench beside Luke and rested his forearm on his knee.

"Oumar's tapped his local connections and contacted Seckou's camp. Always room for one more skilled disciple." Knight chuckled at the air quotes he placed around his last words.

"Thanks to the *Harmattan,* a wall of thick sand is keeping Seckou put, camped in the Sahel, where nearby villagers are *sympathique* to his plans."

"Has he found Salif?" Luke asked more for Kate than himself.

"Affirmative, but the boy hasn't left his hut since taking a heavy beating from the dear brother-in-law."

"Crystal's convinced the lad's an unwilling villain, that the poor kid can't cop a break." Spanner filled his cup at the water cooler.

Bile rose at the back of Luke's throat. He nodded for Spanner to pour him one too and listened to the Boss continue.

"I'm not convinced. Crystal could be right. Amina's brother came with her when her father sold her to Yacouba. Possibly thought he could protect his sister."

"Aside from the shitty weather forecast, did Oumar say why Seckou's not heading straight for Mali?" Luke silently thanked Spanner for the water.

"Again, more guesswork, but Seckou took a call. They were yelling in *Tamasheq.* From what Oumar understood, it was one of dickhead's Tuareg *amis.* Upshot. They are not going anywhere until they've finished what they set out to achieve in *Wagga.*"

"Okay, so where's this leading, Boss?" Spanner beat Luke to his next question.

"You will hate this Doc."

Not hard. Luke had hated many moments since colliding with Seckou. "Spill."

"Blowing up hotels isn't enough for our friend. Seckou's put a bounty on Kate's head. One thousand US dollars for the person who brings it to him on a stick."

Luke's blood turned to ice, and his heart beat a fucking military tattoo inside his chest. "Why? Amina, I understand, but why Kate?" *Keep your shit together, stay professional.*

"The short of it. Seckou plans to make an example of her, show anyone thinking of interfering in his plans that the path leads hell, where there ain't no willing virgins."

Every instinct in him roared, run to Kate, but Luke schooled his features and waited for Knight to finish.

"She's not alone. Yacouba's in the shit too. Seckou blames him for Kate's escape. To prove his loyalty knob head offered to wear an explosive vest and run amok in Kidal. Blow up the peacekeeping HQ.

Frankly, I doubt he has the guts to blow himself to smithereens, but the gesture pacified Seckou enough to give Yacouba another chance. Find Kate and his wife."

"Shit, Boss. Yacouba must be shitting himself, what's the odds Oumar can turn him, persuade him to come over to our side?" Spanner might have something.

Luke paced in a circle.

"Doubtful, but Salif's worth a shot. I'll have Oumar suss out the possibility. I suggest we rendezvous here at 0700."

"Roger that. Is that it?" Luke strode to the stairs, eager to find Kate and bring her up to speed.

"Tell her, Luke." Spanner's voice followed him up the stairs.

"Crystal?" Luke had to ask.

"No, man. Never, she's willing to let you do the honours, but it's only a matter of time. Make sure Kate hears it from you. If the post-mortem isn't already waiting for her in London, it will be soon.

Shit. Fuck. Luke let Spanner pass and waited for him to leave the gym before he returned to where Knight was loading another plate onto the inverted squat machine.

"Looking for me?" The Boss threw his towel around his neck and sat on the bench. Smug sod was expecting him.

"Yeah. It sounds as though Seckou may lose his shit any minute and Oumar's on his own. I figure I should join him and cover his six."

Knight wiped his face and scrubbed his hand over his shaved head. "Weren't you charged with keeping your eye on Kate?"

"She's in good hands." He shifted nervously on both feet.

"Did you ever speak to someone about what happened?"

Odd question from the Boss, but it was no use pretending he didn't get what Knight meant. Blessed with the tenacity of a bull ant. He'd keep coming. "No. Talking won't do any good. I will never forget. You?"

"See someone? Yeah. Once, before we came here. Cleared the air. You should try talking to a shrink. Might help."

"Yeah, maybe." Where was Knight heading with this shit? The conversation made Luke sweat. "Get it over with, man. You got an extra tuppence worth you need to say."

"Hear me, Doc. It is the last time I will say this. Mike's death. Was. Not. Your. Fault. I trump you and Spanner at the blame game. I watched Mike reach for your gun, and did nothing."

Luke braced one hand against the wall, the ringing in his ears intense. He struggled to breathe. "You watched Mike reach for my gun and didn't stop him? Son of a bitch. Why?"

"Because if I were Mike, I'd have done the same. Half a man, literally. Ever ask yourself if that's why you feel sorry for yourself? Mike beat you to it, topped himself to save you the trouble."

"You don't know what the fuck you're talking about. I would never..." Christ, his heart was fit to pound out of his chest. Assisted euthanasia on the battlefield wasn't unheard of, but he swore he'd never consider it.

"If you say so, Doc." With no further argument, Knight returned to loading the squat bar. "You want to check on Oumar. Be my guest. Tell Snake. First, take care of business with Kate."

Afraid he'd lose what little courage he found in the gym, Luke didn't bother to shower. Pumped from his workout, ready to tell her the truth before he hit the road, his fist pounded on Kate's door.

CHAPTER TWENTY-EIGHT

"I love you, Katy. Wait. Wait here."

Kate sat on the bench, the fog creeping over the pier. Her socks were dirty. Mother wouldn't like it.

"Be a big girl. Don't cry. When dad comes back, we'll have fish and chips for tea. Your favourite."

Too many faces were swimming in the darkness.

She reached towards the sea, stared at the pools of blood swirling over her feet.

Daddy!

"Kate, wake up."

Bright light filled the room—a chair by the window, cornflower blue coloured curtains. A man was sitting on the edge of the bed, stroking her hair. "Mike?"

"No. It's Luke."

Damn. Another nightmare. Kate threaded her fingers through the knot of curls falling over her face and pulled the sheet closer to her chin.

She'd given up on him coming to her room and slipped into a thin camisole and shorts. A pathetic barrier between her and the man who threatened to demolish every one of her boundaries.

"How long have you been sitting here?"

"Not long. I came to see if you were still up for that drink." A shaky thumb checked the bruise on her cheek. "How's your arm?"

"Fine." As much as she wanted him to come closer, she pulled away. The memory of her father vivid in her mind.

"You were dreaming."

Kate took a deep breath, kept the sheet close to her chest, and leaned against the headboard. "It's nothing, an old nightmare, always visits when I'm tired."

"Try again. You were calling out for your father. What happened to him?"

The question rattled her. Except for Crystal, she never talked about him. "Why do you ask?"

"Curious, I guess. Mike never mentioned his family. I guess I thought there wasn't anyone but you."

The man "My mother's alive." She held her breath, still as a statue, scared Luke might see how alone she was. Growing up, mum had kept her distance and blamed her for her father's disappearance. Mike her only real family and he was gone too.

A sob stabbed at her solar plexus, and one of those treacherous, bloody tears leaked from her eye. "Sorry I'm fine."

"The hell you are. Here, let me." Luke lifted the hem of his t-shirt and wiped away the moisture dripping from her nose.

Very attractive. If Kate allowed herself to dream of forever with a man, Luke would top the interview list. "I'm a mess."

"Never. Want to talk? I'm all ears." He tugged on the soft lobe of his ear.

Such a delicate part of this man didn't deserve abuse. Curling her fingers around his, she gently pulled his hand from his face. "Not much to tell. I … was … five." Hiccups weren't pretty.

"Mum was in one of her moods, so dad and I went for a walk. He told me to wait for him on the pier. I did. My bum stayed glued to my seat until the police found me, freezing and hungry, the next morning. He never came back.

Luke squeezed her fingers. "I'm sorry. Was there an accident?"

The concern spilling from his earthy brown eyes softened the rough edges of her heart. Pathetic, but she wanted nothing more than to drown in their depths. She snatched her hand from his, kicking herself for thinking, maybe, here was a man who wouldn't leave once he got to know her better.

"No, nothing dramatic. No big deal."

"Fuck me, Kate. Way big deal. What kind of arsehole leaves a five-year-old alone, anytime, anywhere? Did you ever hear from him?"

"No. Mike suspected Mother might have, but I'm not convinced. It happened a long time ago."

She rolled her lips together and sniffed, not sure when she'd grabbed Luke's hand again. Goosebumps erupted over her skin. Best let go before the temptation to host a pity party won.

"It's okay. I stopped pining for my father a long time ago."

"I understand, but it must have been devastating, the news about Mike."

She blinked, not surprised he'd read her soul.

Unwilling to let him any further, she shook her head. "Losing Mike ... yes. I mean, you can't have a brother on active duty and not wonder if you'll ever get the call. But loss is the side of love they never warn you to expect.

I don't understand why it's taking so long for the post-mortem results, but as soon as they release his body, I'll go back to London and arrange his funeral."

Kate grabbed the bottom of Luke's t-shirt. "I'll wash it." She wound the edge of the fabric over her fingers, pulled it over his head and tossed it to the floor. "Say something."

"Still listening." Luke's mouth grazed the tip of her nose.

He smelled of blackcurrants, sandalwood, and sweat. "Sorry. I can't do this."

"Why? Arms up," he whispered. The silk top flew over her head and rested next to his.

"Listen, Luke if we're going to do this, you need to know, sex is one thing, but getting close. I can't." She tugged him to her. "But maybe, one last kiss?"

One last kiss. Fuck me. Kate beat him to his line.

All intention of telling her exactly what happened to Mike fled along with his pants and underwear.

His tongue traced the seam between her lips and sipped the breath from her mouth. Fragile, vulnerable, he snatched her wrist and anchored her to him. *Take her, keep her. Let. Her. Go.*

"With me?" Kate's words were shards of glass piercing his heart.

"Always." Luke meant it. He didn't need Mike's ghost fucking with his head to know, no matter how far apart, Kate would always hold his heart.

Protect her. No problem. Pity he couldn't save her from the pain he would eventually bring.

A single sigh from her sensual lips became his universe. Control and Kate were never a natural partnership, but he could promise her one last kiss, one she'd never forget. More if she wanted, asked for it.

He sucked the pulse-pounding at the side of her throat, not giving a shit if he left his mark, loving the way her pelvis rocked against him. A single moan and his pulse went ballistic. The clashing of their tongues nothing short of volcanic. Her cries, the stretch of skin over her neck as her breasts arched to the ceiling, fucking beautiful.

He nipped the corner of her mouth, slipped his fingers over her perfect breasts and stroked her ribs. "Whatever you want. Tell me what you want."

"More. First, I need to lose these."

As soon as she lost the shorts, his hand slid between her legs, proud to see her hand slapping at the sheets, the grimace of pleasure on her face. He chuckled. "Say the word, and I'll stop?"

"Aargh. For Christ's sake, stop torturing me."

"I want to hear you beg."

"You first." She curled her fingers around his balls and squeezed. "Surrender."

The scent of their arousal filled the room. A sodding miracle if he didn't self-combust. "No chance." He inserted one, two fingers into her wet heat and worked her sweet spot.

"Faster." Her muscles clamped around his fingers, sucking him deeper and whimpered.

Exquisite. Luke added another finger and spread Kate wider. "Give in."

"Luke." Kate tumbled over the edge.

Her eyes the colour of blue sky sneaking through clouds, snatched his soul and refused to play nice. Anyone looking to make a secure million should bottle Kate's smile, *yeah that one,* the one she surrendered when she came.

Sharp as a laser, her eyes settled on his. The tip of her tongue probed his lips, insisting on entry.

"Closer." Kate's breath hitched. Her tongue swept over his teeth and demanded he hold nothing back with each suck on his breath. Her moans drove him crazy as she attacked his mouth and pressed her pelvis hard against him.

Her curly hair smelled of spring flowers after the rain. Home. He angled his mouth, grateful when she surrendered her tongue.

It's just a kiss. Before Luke left, he'd bind Kate's smile, not her tears, to his heart. She was tearing him apart, making him wish for a future they could never share—one *last kiss.*

An hour before dawn, before the damp kiss of her breath on his skin changed his mind, Luke eased from Kate's bed. This time Captain Coward McLaren left a note by the bed.

CHAPTER TWENTY-NINE

Seckou's Camp – Mare de Dori, Burkina Faso

At a safe distance, Luke adjusted his night vision binos and zeroed in on Oumar who sitting smack in the middle of Seckou and his lethal gang.

He'd barely made it time de-brief and set up comms agreeing to remain at a safe distance, ready to move on Oumar's signal.

Seckou held court. His fat arse spread on a sofa, the colour faded from dirt and sun. His soulless eyes peered over his blue veil at a small group of his men busy eating and cleaning their weapons. A few tended their wounds with limited medical supplies.

Luke shifted right until his lens found Yacouba and Oumar sitting on empty Olevea cans a short distance from the main group. Luke tapped his headset, listening for any shit worth sharing with the Boss.

"Un autre Brakina?" Oumar liberated beers from the plastic container filled with ice beside his feet and offered one to Yacouba.

Luke raised his eyes to the sky, *please let alcohol loosen the dick's tongue.* He was sick of hanging out in the dust and heat.

"Merde! Yacouba swore loudly and almost toppled off his can. "Seckou should not have ordered me to the back of my truck." He beckoned Oumar closer and lowered his voice. "I should ride in the front.

Who do 'e think 'e is? *La connasse*—mother fucker. My air-conditioned truck cost *beaucoup de francs*. Seckou should show respect."

If they were lucky, Seckou might shoot the whiny git before Oumar had a chance.

"You were not there, Oumar, *mon ami*, but without Yacouba's wheels, Seckou never escape. Praise Allah. The English were too busy stealing my traitor wife and the nurse bitch to follow us. Seckou blame me for their escape, the easy target. I am a dead man." He shook his head.

Luke shifted his position. The man was crying into his beer. Way to go. Ace, fucking terrorist.

"*Oui.* Women!" Oumar agreed.

Man of few words, Oumar. Kate Gibson, the woman always on his mind. The gorgeous redhead who held his every waking moment in the palm of her hand. She deserved to hear face-to-face the part he'd played in her brother's death, so he didn't mention it in his note.

"Who need them? A goat's arse is as good to poke and cost me nothing." Yacouba cackled.

Mind on the job. Luke let out a long breath through his nose. Knight was right to question his ability to stay focussed.

He'd love to wring Yacouba's neck for the way he spoke about women. Throw in his abuse of Amina and been responsible for Kate getting shot and Luke breathed a silent promise into the desert air. *Next time we meet, fucker, you will have a hard time getting off the ground.*

"Salif, I should cut off your hand for not cleaning the truck. It stunk of cow piss."

Salif's name re-claimed Luke's attention. He shifted his binoculars to the boy sitting on the other side of Yacouba. Things were starting to get interesting.

Yacouba shuffled closer to the boy who held his head in his hands. Salif wouldn't see dickhead coming. Oumar's hand slipped to the dagger concealed beneath his robe. God help Yacouba's sorry arse if he went for Salif.

Whether he noticed Oumar slip his hand to the dagger at his waist,

Luke would never know. Shit for brains rocked to his left and threw his arm around Oumar's shoulder.

"You, you will save Yacouba. Seckou will thank me for bringing you. My cousin say you are a great warrior. *Oui, mon ami?*" A loud belch rang over Luke's headset.

Friend. Shit out of luck there.

"*Allez, vite!*" Yacouba shooed away the rooster pecking at his feet and turned to face a man striding towards them. The man spoke in *Tadghaq,* a language Luke didn't understand.

"Yacouba. Come." Seckou beckoned for knobhead to join him.

Trouble. A warning voice hissed in Luke's ear.

"Sit. *Y a la place.*"

Yacouba shuffled over and fell at Seckou's feet.

Oumar kept his eye on what was going on but didn't move. A man enjoying his beer except his hooded gaze never left Seckou.

Seckou stood, grasped Yacouba's shirt and hauled him to his feet. "Yacouba, your wife and the nurse escaped. Tell Seckou why he not cut off your head and feed you to the camels?"

Fuckwit. Camels weren't fussy, but they didn't eat meat. Seckou could give it a try, but not before they found out exactly what the fucker was planning. Seckou kicked the pathetic bastard and laughed when he crumpled to his knees.

"I am useful." Yacouba's whimpered, his voice scratching at the air as if oxygen were a reason not to die. "I say before, Seckou. Strap the explosive vest to me. *Al-Hamdu lillah!* Praise be to God."

Yacouba swayed to his feet, reached for a carton of Brakina and slung it over one shoulder. "I look like a delivery man, see? No one will guess. But, first, I make dinner. Yacouba makes goat taste sweet." He rubbed his index finger and thumb together under his nose and closed his eyes.

"*Alors, écout le. L'imbécile* can cook," Seckou raised his hand in the air and nodded to his men.

Oumar raised his head and stared in Luke's direction, his signal to stay alert, and joined the bigger group pretending to share the joke. *Gotcha.*

"Go, find your goat, donkey. Better you cook with the women than interfere with my plans." Seckou grabbed Yacouba by the neck and hurled him into the crowd of men watching.

If Yacouba was the donkey, Seckou was the arse in the saddle. He raised his gun and fired a single shot above Yacouba's head. A woman screamed. Seckou's men were too busy praying he didn't shoot them to notice Oumar take off after Salif who disappeared behind the hut.

Luke cursed. No visual, he had to rely on sound.

"Wait." Oumar kept his voice low. "Don't run."

The roar of flying dirt echoed in Luke's ear. Oumar must have caught up with the boy and tackled him to the ground.

"*Doucement.* I will not hurt you. I want to talk. Okay? Don't run. Amina sent me."

Salif stopped struggling. "You take me to my sister?"

"*Oui, non.* We haven't got much time. If you want to see Amina, *dites moi,* which hotel, where will Seckou set off his bomb."

"I don't know."

Luke groaned, not sure whether he believed the boy.

"*Dis-moi maintenant.* Talk." From the rustling, Oumar was shaking Salif hard enough to make him whimper.

"*Non.* Seckou tells me nothing, but he plans to do it soon. They say three days. No more. Please."

"*D'accord.* Listen to me. I will tell you where to find Knight. Go to him, tell him what you know, and he will take you to Amina."

"Where is nurse Kate?" The boy didn't trust his chances with the Boss.

Luke couldn't blame him. Knight had threatened to shoot him last time they met.

"Forget the nurse, if you want to see your sister, find Knight. Here, take this."

They were taking a chance trusting the kid, but they were shit out of options. The kid was street smart, but no his own, he sure as hell hoped no one followed the lad.

He scanned the area spotting Salif as he escaped into the darkness running as if Lucifer was on his tail. As far as Luke could see, no one followed.

"You understand, *mon ami*?" Oumar stepped from behind the hut and raised his head in Luke's direction.

"Yeah. Nice work. Time to get the hell out of here."

"*Oui*. You go. I will stay. In case I can find out more."

"Roger that. Be safe, *mon ami*."

CHAPTER THIRTY
YALGADO HOSPITAL, OUAGADOUGOU, BURKINA FASO

Not having to listen to Crystal fussing over her as though her cat died was the plus side of hiding in the supply room at Yalgado Hospital.

In a moment of weakness, she'd shown Crys Luke's note. His apology for ducking out before they got a chance to talk. An assurance they would speak when he got back. No need. She had marked the boundary. *One last kiss.* There was nothing to say, no need for an apology.

Lately, Kate's imagination had been working overtime. She could have sworn Knight took a perverse pleasure in telling her Luke had volunteered to join Oumar.

It shouldn't bother her, men disappearing from her life. When was she going to learn her lesson?

As for vanishing objects, she couldn't figure out why there was no word on Mike's post-mortem. Internet connection wasn't great in Burkina, even here in the capital. Her email asking the hospital to forward correspondence may have got lost in the ether.

Despite asking Knight and Spanner to give her details, for some reason, they declined and deferred to Luke, who conveniently wasn't there.

Should she stay in Burkina or go home, demand answers? The question kept her awake at night. Along with worrying about Amina and Katy squashed into the corner of Aunty's tent. She was desperate to see them and make sure they were okay.

Kate sighed and reached for a box of dressings—vital supplies for their visit to the refugee camp tomorrow. As much as she disliked the idea, she'd call Mother tonight and ask her to check her post box.

"Don't forget the sanitary pads," Crystal yelled from the small classroom next to the supply room.

Moment of solitude over, Kate looked at her watch. "Sorry, Crys, can you finish getting the supplies together? I promised I'd drop books off at *Le Pélican*."

She'd found the maths books for the after-school program on Foyles' bargain table. Twenty quid later, she'd bought the lot. Most Burkina kids attended free state schools but required textbooks were scarce and expensive. Many families didn't have a hope of affording them.

"It's supposed to pour this afternoon, and Knight will kill me if I let you go alone. If you wait, I'll come with you." Crystal raised her eyebrow at the trainee beside her, working out the procedure for attaching a breastfeeding pump. "Take another look at step three." She nodded at the blackboard in front of the nurse and mouthed, "shouldn't be much longer."

"No, you stay, Crys. The walk will do me good." A chance to get her head sorted. "I'll take the umbrella and tell Issouf to follow me in the Jeep." Knight had given instructions never to let them out of his sight.

She laughed, but it wasn't a joke. As much as she wanted to believe Seckou was in Mali since her ordeal at the farm, the chill invading her soul never left her.

"Okay, but I'll worry, hun. Find me as soon as you get back, okay? I remember seeing a CD player in the villa. How about we raid Knight's collection tonight. Who knows, misery guts may have some dance music. Take our mind off stuff." Crystal smiled, twirled her hips, and took the chalk from the nurse's hand. *Centre the nipple* she wrote on the board.

"Wonderful idea. See you soon." Kate squeezed the nurse's shoulder as she passed. "Very important."

It wasn't a long walk to the library. The middle of the day, the streets were busy with people, searching out an ATM, grabbing lunch, shopping, the usual stuff. Except Kate could swear every person, she passed looked at her strangely.

At one point, she checked her reflection in a shop window to make sure she hadn't grown another head.

She couldn't shake Luke's note from her mind. *Damn it.* She wasn't a stranger to trauma. It would take more than a few days to get over being shot and kidnapped. Was it any wonder she was a tad paranoid?

By the time she reached the entrance to *Le Pélican*, the butterfly wings fluttering in her stomach were beating a full force gale. Either she'd completely lost it, or someone was watching her.

She leaned against the entrance and tried to catch her breath. She kept her eyes fixed on the windows as she approached the older woman sitting at her desk.

"*Bonjour.* I spoke with *Madame Escalier.* She said it's okay for me to leave these books." Kate held up her bag and nodded towards the donations drop-off.

"*Bien sûr.* Thank you," the librarian said and adjusted the glasses on the bridge of her nose.

Aside from the rustle of turning pages and the tip-tap of fingers skipping across a computer keyboard, the library was quiet except for the footsteps that stopped the same time she paused by the CD section. Kate glanced over her shoulder, convinced she could feel their breath on her neck.

"You okay, Miss?" A schoolgirl, seated in the corner, peered over the top of her book.

"*Oui, j'ai chaud.* Hot. I'm fine." Embarrassed, she fled into the ladies room, bent over the sink, and frantically splashed water on her face. The woman washing her hands next to her jumped sideways as Kate heaved.

"Sorry." She ducked into a cubicle, locked the door, and flopped onto the loo. Cradling her cheeks in her palms, she begged her hands to stop shaking. Ten seconds of peace before the crash of a door shook the walls.

"Who's there?" No reply. "What do you want?" Kate wiped the back of her hand across her mouth and raised her voice.

"Amina, where is my sister?"

"Salif?" The boy's knack for scaring the life out of her was wearing thin.

"*Oui*. Take me to my sister."

He was doing his best to sound tough, but the tremor in Salif's voice was a giveaway. He was as terrified as she was. Praying she wasn't making a massive mistake she drew in a sharp breath and opened the door.

Salif took a step back and curled his hands into fists. The ever-defiant gleam in his eye, he swayed in front of her. His feet were bare, and blood caked around a cut above his left eye. She reached for his elbow, but he shrugged out of her hand.

"She's okay, Salif. Amina's safe. How did you know I was here?"

"I follow you from the hospital."

"Your sister's worried. Knight's been looking for you everywhere."

Salif cringed.

"It's okay. Knight's not here."

"Where is he? I must speak with him. Oumar sent me."

"Oumar? What about Luke? The doctor?" She should focus on Salif, but not knowing if Luke was safe was driving her insane.

"I don't know. I see only Oumar. He tell me to find Knight, but I come to the hospital first."

"Okay. Let's get you out of here."

The woman Kate spoke to earlier, several books clutched to her chest, stood outside the loo.

"What is he doing in there?" She pointed to the sign blazoned over the door. *Ladies*.

There was no time to explain. "Come on, let's go." She grabbed Salif's hand and dragged him limping behind her to the exit.

At her wit's end, desperate to get back to the hospital, she forgot about Issouf and piled into the share-taxi, dropping kids off in front of the library.

Squeezed between two women on the back seat, Kate clung to Salif. From now on, she was stuck to him like apple to pie. She inhaled the breeze coming through the open window and formed a plan. Collect Crystal. Call Knight and tell him they were on their way.

Kate shoved Salif into one of the ground floor treatment rooms. "Stay here. Don't move. I'll be right back." She closed the door. Crystal, thank God, wasn't too far away, chatting with a patient at the nurse's station. "A word?" She rolled her eyes in the direction of Salif.

"Er . . . Sure, hun." Crystal directed her patient to X-ray. "You okay?" The puzzled expression on her face told Kate she wasn't the mind-reader she'd hoped.

"I'm fine." Biggest over-statement of the century. "It's Salif." She dragged Crys to the treatment room and hit Knight's speed dial.

"Kate? What can I do for you?"

No use wasting time talking about the weather. "Hi, Knight. Salif is here." Kate stretched her phone to arm's length avoiding Knight's colourful expletives.

"Stop being such a drama queen, Knight, and listen. He wants to talk to Amina."

"I bet he fucking does."

Kate rolled her bottom lips together and pressed on. "He says Oumar sent him."

"Tell Issouf to bring you all to the villa, and Kate, don't ditch him this time." A soft click ended the call.

Crystal stood by Salif, tending to the nasty cut above Salif's eye. "Let me see hun." She tilted his chin. "What's Knight say?"

"We're to bring him to the villa."

Salif jumped off the table and swayed. Kate grabbed his arm. "No. Don't run. I won't let Knight hurt you." By the glazed look on his face, he was unconvinced. "We'll take you to Amina. And, your niece, Katy."

Salif's undamaged eye filled with the pleasure meant for both. Encouraged, she pressed on before he could change his mind.

"You want your new niece to see you at your best, let Crystal take care of you."

Salif grunted.

"Amina's going to school. You can too."

Salif shook his head.

Hell, she'd pay the fees herself, anything to convince him it was true.

"Crys, call Issouf. Have him bring the Jeep to the entrance. I'll tell Reception to cover us for the rest of the afternoon. We have an emergency."

CHAPTER THIRTY-ONE

"Boss? What's up?"

"Salif's here. Where are you?" Luke could hear the Boss tapping his foot on the other end of the line.

"Pulling out of Kaya, heading to the gendarmerie at Saaba."

"Oumar?"

"Hanging in with Seckou, hoping he'll spill where and when this fucking bomb will blow. The poxy git is keeping it inner circle. Yacouba's not among the chosen."

"Yeah, fuckin' figures. Forget Saaba. I need you back in *Wagga*."

Not happening. One look in Kate's eyes. Eyes as deep as the sea, as uncertain as a storm and he wasn't sure he'd have the courage to leave her a third time.

"I'm glad Salif found you, I wasn't sure he'd make it in one piece." The lad had made good time.

"In a way. He found Kate."

Luke gripped the steering wheel, fear coursing through his fingertips. "Where, when? She okay?"

"Relax, Doc. Kate's fine. She's at the villa. I need you here." A sharp click ended the call. Knight could handle ops in *Wagga*.

Damn it. Luke swung the Jeep into a U-turn and heading back to *Wagga.* Fate had a nasty way of forcing his hand. Telling Kate about Mike was going to be harder because he'd left it this long.

Knowing she'd hate him, crushed him. *You're in love with her.* Yeah, let's keep that you ourselves.

Kidding himself, he'd get himself together, settle before he faced her, he'd taken one step inside Knight's villa before he glimpsed Kate heading for the courtyard. The streaks of gold in her hair glowing in the afternoon light, a siren's call beckoning him to follow.

"Kate," he called out, his voice softer than he intended. Perhaps he hoped she didn't hear.

"What are you doing here?"

Drawn like the sun to a fucking beach, he longed to touch her, to smooth her wild hair back from her face, to brush his thumb over the frown he put there—kiss her until the sun came up on another day.

"You okay? Can we talk?"

"Luke. I …" Kate's voice trembled, making him feel like shit for leaving her and selfishly craving her more than his next breath.

What did he expect? She had every right to be angry. Fuck the conse-quences. Luke stepped closer.

"Luke, step back." Both hands on his chest she pushed. Not hard enough to send him anywhere.

What the fuck? The shove was enough to bring him to his senses. He'd never used his size against any woman. "Sorry. Please, let's talk." Grasping her fist, he blew gently across her knuckles, hoping to take the heat out of the moment, to have her simmer down enough to hear him out.

"There's nothing to say, Luke. Shouldn't you be with Oumar?"

The glare from her steely blue eyes drilled a hole in his gut, held his gaze for a moment before she left him standing there feeling helpless, deserted.

Kate closed the door, fixed one hand to the wall, and waited for the room to stop spinning. Luke waltzed in and out of her life faster than a ride at the Easter Fair on Hampstead Heath.

She couldn't take much more. A warm bath. A bottle of red. Magic words in any order. Fortunately, at Knight's, there was no shortage of either.

Kate sat in the bath, the warm water, thinking of getting out before she turned into a wrinkled prune when her phone rang. Mother—the name blazed loud and clear across the screen. "Hello. How are you?"

"What time is it there?"

For Christ's sake, if it mattered, why did she ring? "Not sure. Have you been to my flat?"

"Yes. There was nothing in your letterbox from the air force."

"Just a tick." The lukewarm water sloshed around her ankles as she gave up her bath and put on the robe lying at the foot of the bed. Knight had great taste. The silk flowed over her skin, waltzed over every sensitive curve of her body, as near to heaven as touch could get. *You lie girl. Luke's hands are the ...*

"Kate. Are you there?"

"Yes, I'm here. Are you sure there was nothing there?" She topped up her glass and waited for Mother to finish her tuts and sighs.

"Are you calling me a liar, Kate?"

From whoa to go in the space of two seconds. Kate was used to it. "No, I'm sorry. I'll call the Visiting Officer and try to find out what's going on."

"I can do that."

Kate took another drink. Unusual for mum to be this helpful. "No, it's okay."

"Kate. When are you coming home?"

"I'm not sure. Sorry, I have to go, someone's knocking at the door." Grateful for the interruption, Kate pressed 'end', dropped the phone onto the bed and pulled the edges of the robe closer together.

Luke said they had to talk. She sucked the insides of her cheeks damn sure she didn't want to hear him say he was sorry again. But now was as good a time as any, then she could get on with pretending she was happy without him.

Still angry for the way he left, Kate blew out a breath, flung the door open and almost crumbled at the lines of concern creasing his eyes.

"Kate? Can I come in?"

Holding tight to the door as the world spun, she managed a hoarse whisper. "Sure. Come in. A glass of wine?" Kate stared at her empty glass. She needed to eat. Blinking hard against the dizziness she made it to the sofa and the nuts that were in the bowl on the coffee table.

"Not for me, thanks. Can I make you some tea?"

Kate snorted. Subtle. "Nope. Sit down. You said you wanted to talk. Talk."

"Now is not a good time. I'll leave you to it. Maybe tomorrow."

Luke was right. She'd had more alcohol tonight than she'd drank in a month, but who the hell was he? The red wine police?

"Oh, for Christ's sake, Luke. What do you want?"

"You."

They moved towards each other at the same time.

Luke took her in his arms and held her as if he didn't want to let her go, although she suspected that was precisely what he wanted to do.

If he intended swanning in and out of her life when it suited him, he could think again. She didn't want or need him. They were a mistake, his note said so.

She gripped his ears and pulled him to her. "Closer." Luke's eyes sparkled. She nipped his lip, a punishment.

"Take off your clothes." Fair—she was naked under Knight's robe.

"Bossy, Miss Gibson." One eyebrow quirked upwards.

"You better believe it." The stubble on Luke's chin grazed her cheek sending hundreds of tiny electric shocks zipping straight to her pelvis.

A speedy stripper, Luke was out of his shirt and pants before she untied her robe. Six foot four of no-mistake-male hovered over her, a lion inspecting his prey. Underneath the smattering of hairs on his chest, she spotted her target—light brown nipples—small and sensitive.

"Close enough for you?" Luke bit his bottom lip and sucked in a gasp. Unable to resist torturing him, she ran the tip of her little finger across the head of his cock until he hissed. She chuckled when he flinched. Payback for the damned note. "Sorry."

"Don't be. Arms around my neck." Luke lifted her hips, wound her legs around his waist and stumbled to the bed. His elbows pressed against her thighs, spreading her until her hips pinched.

He sank two fingers into her heat. Fucking delicious, inept words to describe the fullness building inside her. Luke's unmistakable male scent, tart blackberries and musky hell surrounded her, and she wanted to taste. Her tongue darted over his skin, her prize, Luke's groans of pleasure and appreciation.

Her orgasm hit with the power of a tsunami robbing her of breath and brain. "Please."

"Please, what?"

Bastard. Kate pinched Luke's bicep. He didn't flinch. She didn't want to talk—she wanted to fuck. Wanted to forget how mad he'd made her because she'd always be glad he was in her arms. She wanted to enjoy him as she had a few nights ago before she'd said, *one last kiss,* and he'd raised the stakes with his stupid note.

"Condom." Luke took one out of the drawer. Boy Pad—Knight was worth his weight in gold.

"Christ Luke, you're killing me."

"Not possible. I'm the one dying here."

"Let me." Luke groaned as she ripped the wrapper with her teeth and took her time rolling the condom over his cock.

Luke pulled her on top of him. "Put me inside you."

His powerful hands gripped her hips, but Luke would never hurt her. Never physically. Her heart was a different matter. "My pleasure."

"Okay?" He pulled her to him and suckled her breast, holding her while she adjusted to his size.

"Mm, yes." More, she needed more. A slight tilt of her pelvis and his cock hit her sweet spot. Her gaze fixed on the point where they joined. Her orgasm a breath away. She raised her hips and turned her pelvis in a slow circle around him. "Oh. My. God."

The scent of their joint arousal sent a familiar throbbing straight to her core. She was on fire, riding Luke, pleading with him to come.

"Fuck." Luke's strangled cry tore through the room.

Kate circled her pelvis, loving the way Luke trembled just as he had that fantastic night at Mike's.

"Funny?" Luke pinched the sensitive nub between her thighs, and she came hard, spinning to the stars, pleading with him not to stop.

Luke pounded into her, fucking her through her release before he flipped her onto her back and began a steady thrust guaranteed to return her to the edge.

"Squeeze me, Kate. Harder."

The slap of skin to skin rang in her ears along with a torrent of filthy words as she clenched, sucked him deep inside, to prove how she missed him.

"Shit, Luke, you are beautiful." She slipped her fingers between her folds and stroked her clit, the sting so good she held her breath.

Luke didn't break eye contact as he shifted his weight, changed the angle of his hips and let himself go. The room shook with their shouts, and they surrendered, coming apart in each other's arms.

"You okay? I didn't hurt you?"

"No." Luke's eyes were incredible, whisky brown, sprinkled with sparks of gold and shadows of ebony. Lazy mornings and wicked nights sprang to her mind.

"Good. Come 'ere." He rolled on to his back, dragged her into the space beneath his armpit and kissed the top of her head.

She had broken every rule and let him in, but, as sleep claimed them both if she expected a declaration of devotion, it never came.

Kate wasn't sure what woke her - after the best sex of her life, she should sleep for a week.

"Luke, are you awake?" She turned on the bedside lamp. Dead to the world, a light snore escaped Luke's nose.

As wonderful as making love with Luke had been, the threat of Seckou was very much alive. Salif had agreed to talk with Knight, but it wouldn't be long before he was demanding to see Amina. Kate threw the sheets over her legs and tried to figure out how she was going to shift Luke's arm from her waist without waking him.

"Going somewhere?" Luke caressed her nipple with his thumb.

Her head fell back, and she moaned. Kate ran her fingers over the hard planes of Luke's abdomen. The early sun poured over his smooth skin, highlighting every contour of his muscled torso. She wanted him again, but something held her back, gnawed at her self-confidence.

"What's the matter, Kate?" Luke rolled onto his back.

Kate blushed. There was no mistaking the erection half-hidden by the sheet.

Luke looked at her with a mix of lust, pain and tenderness. Confused, she ran her thumb over his brow, trying to figure out what his expression meant.

They still didn't fully trust one another. *Get over it.* Kate was sick of living in the past, scared of being left on that pier. If Mike were there, he'd be telling her to celebrate life with every inhale.

Luke rolled on top of her and braced his hands on either side of her face. The hard length of his erection pressing between her legs sent pleasure cascading through her pelvis.

Deep down, whatever this was, it was bound to stay with her beyond the moment, and no matter how much time they had together, she intended to enjoy it. Raising her head and teased Luke's tight nipple with her tongue, revelling in the sweet agony gnawing at her clit.

Luke sucked in a breath. "Bite me, he groaned.

CHAPTER THIRTY-TWO

Hell. Kate swiped her hand over her shirt; the sting of spilt coffee made her curse. She hadn't noticed the cup tilt as she scrolled through the list of missed texts from Mother.

I'm about to board the plane.

I land at 9.15 a.m. your time.

Should I catch a taxi?

Where are you?

Damn, damn. Kate typed and erased the message telling her not to bother. Going by the time stamp on the texts, she was too late. The plane had left Heathrow. Instead, she left a message asking her to take a taxi from the airport and forwarded Knight's address.

Resigned to the impending visit she decided to keep busy. Heading for the kitchen, she pulled out pans and raided Knight's fridge. Everyone was tense, doing their best to figure out Seckou's plans. The least she could do was make the team breakfast, Crys was happy to help, her cheery encouragement when she told her Mother was on her way better than the stiff drink she seriously considered.

They piled plates with eggs, bacon, tomatoes, and toast, extra for Spanner, and two pots of strong coffee. Luke winked when she entered

Knight's war room, parading the feast above her head, and caught her wrist when she turned to leave.

"Stay." Luke stood and gestured for her to take his seat.

He laced his fingers through hers, and their palms pressed together, and a shaky breath shivered in her chest.

A thick French accent poured over the phone on Knight's desk. The gendarmes had raided the camp Seckou was gone. "No hope of immediate capture."

Kate's knees trembled. Terrorists, they must be made of smoke the way they came and went. A high-pitched sounded in her pocket. Reluctantly, she let go of Luke's hand.

Plane has landed. I am in the taxi.

Kate flashed the screen at Luke. Puzzled, his head tilted to one side. She kissed him on the cheek. "I'll fill you in later."

Forcing a smile, she stood. "She's here." Her whisper, plus the pressure she exerted on Crys's elbow worked. No questions asked she followed her out of the room.

Kate scraped messy strands of hair off her face. Before she could find something to tie it, maybe change her shirt, the doorbell rang.

"Showtime." Luke stepped out of Knight's office. She risked a glance at his face and immediately wanted to kiss him, sorry for causing the crease between his eyebrows.

What was she, six? Her hands were shaking. She pulled a breath in through her nose, resisted grabbing Luke's hand and stepped next to Crystal.

"You made it." The woman who must have spent the entire plane ride from London dressed in her winter coat. "Mother. Aren't you hot?" *Who wore gloves in Africa?*

No kiss, no hug, her attention zeroed on Luke.

"Pleased to meet you. I am Fiona Gibson. Call me, Fiona."

"Likewise, Mrs Gibson, Fiona, I've heard a lot about you."

If that felt awkward, wait. *Don't hug her.* Kate's silent plea answered as he opted to shake her hand. Her heart swelled, time to rescue the big guy.

"Let me take your bag." Kate reached for the overstuffed suitcase. Christ, how long was she planning to stay?

"Don't fuss, Kate." Mother clenched her case.

"Let me, ladies." Luke eased her fingers from the handle.

"Thank you, Luke." Mother batted her eyelids. Kate wanted to fall through the floor.

"Mrs Gibson. It's been ages since I last saw you. How are you?" Crys flung her arms around Mother's neck.

"Yes." Mother stiffened and wriggled out of Cry's hug.

"Er. How was your flight?" Luke asked.

A string of complaints followed: her seat; the lack of legroom; the plastic food; the incompetence of flight attendants. Kate let her mind drift, more interested in getting Luke alone and finding out what happened after she left Knight's office.

In the lounge area - Spanner and Knight joined the welcoming party. A warm sensation settled in her stomach. She wasn't alone.

"Good to meet you, Mrs Gibson. Kate's told us a lot about you." Spanner grabbed Crystal's hand. "Back soon, Mrs Gibson. Crys, with me, in the kitchen."

As Knight added a frosty welcome, Kate envied her friend's escape. Luke sank next to her on the sofa, their knees a safe distance apart. She counted the minutes until she could let down her guard until she could feel Luke's hands stroke her skin, his kisses ease her stress.

Luke was nervous at meeting Mother for the first time. A natural reaction, she had that effect on most people.

"Tea, Fiona?" Luke offered.

"No. Thank you. But if there's a bottle of Gordon's lurking somewhere, Luke, I'd murder a G and T. Easy on the tonic. No ice."

"Okay, I'll see what I can do."

Kate closed her eyes and sighed.

"How about you, Kate?"

"That would be great. In a minute." She wasn't ready to be left alone.

After meeting Fiona Gibson, Luke could understand why Kate never spoke much about her mother. Nothing he could put his finger on except creepy sensation running up and down his spine—an expert at pushing buttons.

Kate sat on the sofa, back ramrod straight, eyes darting around the room, looking for her nearest escape.

Fiona's litany of complaints continued. Kate sighed and raised her eyes to the ceiling. He shifted closer to her, fighting the impetus to take her in his arms.

Luke admired Kate's strength, her soft smile, the way her breath hung in the air. He met Kate, and it wasn't long before he had no choice. Wanting to share his life with her became his future.

Before he could make love to Kate again, Knight was right when he said he needed professional help to deal with what happened. First, he owed her the truth about Mike. Something he planned to rectify as soon as they settled Mother.

Kate moved further away, knees pressed together, she'd fall off if she sat any closer to the edge of the sofa.

"Why are you here?" Kate asked abruptly.

Like him, her patience was at an end. Enough of the creepy crawlies.

He was proud of her. The expression on Fiona Gibson's face would have made many warriors turn and run— he had no idea how Kate handled it.

"You called me, remember, asked me if you'd received a letter from Mike's regiment." Fiona pinched the ends of her fingers. The gloves were coming off.

"I remember. You said nothing had arrived. I told you to send anything from the RAF to me." Kate bit her bottom lip.

"Well, I checked again and decided to deliver it in person."

"Why? I said I'd return to London when they released Mike's body for the funeral."

"That's the reason I came. The funeral." Fiona's mouth twisted, the corners of her mouth shaping halfway between a grimace and a grin.

Luke kept his distance.

Kate sighed heavily. "What is so important it couldn't wait until I got home?"

"We can't bury him, Kate—not at Our Lady's."

Kate scrubbed her forehead. It must be throbbing judging by the worried look in her eyes.

"Why the fuck not?"

"Ask Luke." Fiona pointed at him.

Oh, fuck. Luke stood, his hand hovering a warning in the space between them.

"Mum, please, I can't take any more of this."

"Kate. Please, no histrionics."

"Histrionics. You have got to be joking. Who uses the word anymore?" Kate sprang to her feet, shoved him aside. "Ask him what? Why can't we bury Mike at Our Lady's? It's what he wanted."

"That may be the case, but it's not possible."

"Mum, please. Whatever game you're bloody playing. Stop."

"I'm not playing games, Kate." Fiona stood, hands on her hips, prepared to argue.

"Enough. Tell me why we can't bury Mike and leave out the rubbish."

"It's against everything the Church tells us." She pulled an envelope from her handbag and tossed the letter at Kate.

"What Church? Last check we were atheists."

Her mother glared at Luke. "Tell her. Tell her what happened."

"Luke? What the fuck is she talking about?"

"I …" Not like this. He'd never wanted to tell her like this.

"You are the medic for the team, correct? You were there when my son died? Tell us how it happened." Fiona Gibson was unrelenting.

"Mum? Maybe Luke doesn't want to talk about it." Kate's voice skittered around the periphery of the room.

Luke's heart hammered in his chest. "It's okay, Kate."

He grabbed her hand. "I've tried to tell you every day since I came to you at Mike's flat, but I haven't ..." He stopped, took a breath, his heart hammering in his chest, looked her in the eyes—he owed Kate nothing less.

"I was at The Boardwalk, grabbing a burger. My beeper went off. Man down. An anti-tank device detonated, ten miles out in a nearby village."

Kate gripped his hand, and he held on, knowing very soon she'd snatch it away and he'd have to let her go.

"I picked up my med equipment and chased Knight to the ambulance. At the site, we made our way to the casualty." Luke stopped speaking, swallowed, searching for his next breath, his courage. He'd never been more shit-scared when Kate let go of his hand and started beating her thigh. "Kate?"

"It's okay, Luke. Go on. I want to know." The brush of her thumb over the back of his hand brought a lump to his throat. He swallowed hard.

"Luke, please. Go on," Kate pleaded.

"Both Mike's legs were gone. One arm was untouched, but nothing remained of the other below the elbow." His kept his voice steady, clinical —his tone ice.

Kate gasped and shivered, and Luke watched his entire life, the life he imagined with Kate, flashing before his eyes.

He bowed his head, not strong enough to look at her, couldn't bear to see the light for him in her eyes fade to nothing, to hatred. His legs refused to take his weight when he tried to stand.

"My God." Kate entwined her fingers tightly around his.

"I grabbed a syringe of morphine from my bag, and within seconds, Kate, the pain ended as soon as the drug hit Mike's bloodstream."

Kate's expression changed, tears rolling over her cheeks. Had she guessed, he was holding back, hiding something?

"But my son didn't die from his wounds, did he?" Fiona kept coming. A fucking Sherman tank locked and loaded.

"No." Luke followed Kate's gaze to her mother. The Taliban should package Fiona Gibson and let her loose on the infidel.

He couldn't tell Kate in front of her. She needed space to yell, scream at him, without her mother breathing down her neck.

"Come with me." He snatched Kate's arm and pulled her to her room.

"Luke, let go, you're hurting me."

Shit, shit. "Please. Sit down."

"What's going on? What does my mother know that I don't?"

"Mike committed suicide with my gun." Words said he wanted to disappear.

"Impossible."

A part of him died at the one-word denial.

"God, Kate, I'm sorry." Like father, like son. Mike left her, and he had helped him do it.

"Luke. Answer me. The gun, did you give Mike the gun?"

CHAPTER THIRTY-THREE

A burning rage was destroying Kate from inside, obliterating all sense, she wanted to harm someone, mostly herself, for not being good enough. How could her brother, a man who sank more into a day than she did in a week, kill himself?

Mike committed suicide with my gun.

Knight insisted Doc was not responsible for Mike's death, that they were all there and that any of them could have stopped her brother, but she couldn't shake Luke's words from her head.

No excuses, he should have told her the truth sooner. She'd trusted him, allowed herself to wonder if they might have a future. They'd made love for Christ's sake. Was that a lie too?

She'd broken her rule and fallen in love with Luke, and there was every chance she'd never forgive him, but she did make herself a promise. When the nightmare of Seckou was over, she'd find him, tell him she didn't blame him for Mike's death.

The pain in his eyes when he'd left haunted her every breath, struck colder than autumn after the August heat. It took all her energy to sit and stare out of the window and watch clouds float in the endless sky.

"Kate. Come out, hun. You're scaring me. You haven't left that room, except to pee." Crystal had been knocking on the door for hours.

"Go away."

"Five minutes then I'm coming in, Kate," Knight's promise sailed over Crystal's protests.

"Hey Knight, get a grip and stop terrorising my friend."

"Four minutes," Knight persisted.

The man was an arse. She pitied any woman who found him attractive. Kate burrowed her nose in Luke's shirt, the smell of wild berries and musk created havoc with her willpower.

"Please, hun, don't listen to him. I will sit on my bum here until you come out and talk to me."

Kate smiled. Crystal, protecting the doorway, wasn't past flinging herself in front of Knight's boot.

"Your mum's gone. She left a note."

They both snorted.

"Amina called. She is looking forward to seeing you at her new school this afternoon."

Kate groaned. In the past week, Amina had settled in, made friends, and made Kate promise to come and meet her teachers.

"Come out and eat. Spanner baked a cake."

Kate stared at her jittering hands. Bloody, bomb threats and Spanner cooked. Her stomach rumbled. Lying on the floor didn't get her closer to breakfast.

Her knees cracked and complained until she finally straightened her legs. She reached in her pocket for something to clean up the tears caked on her face and landed on the tightly screwed up ball of paper—Mike's PM results. Fresh buggers streamed over her cheek.

It was time to get her arse on a plane to London and wrap up Mike's affairs. Get his funeral over and done with, then she could come back to Africa and continue what she loved.

Grateful Knight decided not to split her door off the hinges she wasted no more time and stuffed her dirty laundry into her suitcase.

Sniffing in a long breath, she opened the door and dived into a hug tight enough to collapse a lung.

"Where are you going?" Crys released her hold and stared at the suitcase.

Her mind rushed ahead, offering Crys explanation, promise, a normal conversation, but her heart remained stuck behind the roadblocks in her throat. "London. I need to arrange Mike's funeral."

"And Amina?" Crys was clinging to Spanners arm, her voice was shrill, her knuckles white.

Kate gently laid her hand on Crys'. "I won't let her down, don't worry. I'm sure I can get a flight out of *Wagga* later today.

Salif will need a ride to the school. I'll pick him up at the camp and say goodbye to Aunty."

"Good luck with that, Aunty says he hasn't been around for the last few days."

That was the first she'd heard of it. Fingers crossed Salif was there when she arrived. She'd hate for him to miss out.

"I'll find him and make sure Amina and Katy have everything they need."

"And what if you can't get a flight out today, there might not be any seats."

"I'll stay at a hotel close to the airport and leave tomorrow."

Crystal shook her head, ready to protest. Knight beat her to it.

"Dumb idea, Kate." The Boss, leaning against the wall, arms crossed, brow raised had spoken.

Kate shivered. Thanks to the blast from the ever-efficient air conditioning, the villa was an igloo. "I'm not asking permission."

Knight's jaw tightened. "Too bad."

"Is Luke here?" *One last goodbye? Yeah, right.*

"Haven't seen him. I'll make a few calls, try to get you on a flight out today, but if you're stuck here tonight, you stay here."

"Thanks, Knight, but ..." Her unfinished sentence telling him to shove his help, hit his back as he disappeared into his office.

"Bye, Crys. I'll give you a ring when I'm at the airport." Kate reached on tiptoe and pecked Spanner's cheek. "Bye, Spanner, take care of our girl."

"Will do."

Determined to keep it together, Kate placed one hand on the wall and pressed her lips together. "No tears, Crys. You could come with me." The offer was a selfish afterthought. The glint in Spanner's eye unexpected.

"She's talking sense, babe. Go with her. Knowing you are safe before we go after this bastard will make it much easier." Spanner said.

"No way.

Despite the danger, neither of them wanted to leave. Unfortunately, there was little practical help she or Crystal could offer. Knight certainly didn't need to divert limited resources to look after them.

Spanner and Crys were debating the odds as Issouf closed her door and made his way to the driver's side of the Jeep. She'd call her later when she got to the school.

"Where to, Miss Kate?" Issouf grinned. She was going to miss him.

"Camp. We'll grab Salif, then head to Amina's school."

Kate was itching for one last snuggle with Katy. Her wish granted when Aunty bustled out of her tent, the baby in her arms.

"Bonjour Cherie."

"Hello, beautiful girl, how are we this morning?" The baby didn't stir. Sound asleep, a satisfied smile curling around her chubby cheeks.

By the time Issouf found Salif, they were late. Kate ducked her head out of the Jeep window. Sure they were going the wrong way she frantically searched for the entrance to Amina's school.

Knight had texted a few minutes ago, Spanner won, he'd found her, and Crys, a seat on the plane to London leaving that evening. Being in Knight's debt wasn't something she would choose, but she liked less the idea of sticking around *Wagga* any longer than necessary.

She licked her lips. A long V and T in order as soon as her bum made it onto the plane.

Issouf drove slowly along the narrow street, deserted except for a few older men lining up at the lottery stand.

"Isn't the entrance to the school on the other side of this wall?" Kate wriggled in her seat. "Salif have you been here with Amina?"

"Non." Salif shifted back and forth. He'd had a scowl on his face ever since they left the camp. She thought he'd be happy to come, but like so many things lately, she must be wrong.

"Détendez-vous, we are here, Miss Kate." Issouf flashed a cheeky grin and nodded at the wrought-iron gate.

Focussed on looking for the school sign, she'd missed the entrance. "Sorry, Issouf. It must be the heat." Long gone was the cooling effect of her shower.

They parked next to the ornate fountain between a car and a shiny black Toyota Land Cruiser blocking the drive-through exit. Most likely, it belonged to a parent, or a local dignitary, who tossed angle parking in the too hard basket.

Through the open double doors leading into the hall, a mix of excited students, families, teachers and interested others were quickly filling any available seat.

Kate tucked her shirt into her skirt, smoothed the loose hairs from her face, she ought to look her best, and glanced at her watch. Five minutes before the concert began.

"Come on, Salif, let's find a seat."

"Je m'excuse." Salif hung back, shifting nervously behind her.

"Is there a problem?"

"J'ai besoin d'aller aux toilettes."

Seriously, the toilet? "Okay, hurry. *Allez, vite.* We'll wait for you over there, by the door to the hall."

Kate shifted from one foot to the other scanning inside for empty seats. Someone official, probably the Principle, peered over the podium, tapped his finger on the microphone and sent a high-pitched wail zinging through the school.

"What's taking Salif so long?"

"Shall I fetch him, Miss Kate?"

"No Issouf, he's a big boy. He can find us when he's done."

She'd never been good at drawing attention to herself and sliding knee to knee with people while they made their way to a seat was the last thing she wanted to do especially if the concert had started.

CHAPTER THIRTY-FOUR

No one could blame Luke more than he blamed himself. Unable to face Kate he'd bailed, left her hurt and angry. While Mike's ghost hovered between them, they didn't stand a chance.

Since the day he'd met her he'd lived in denial, unable to bear her rejection yet doing the one thing guaranteed to lose her forever. Dishonest with her since they met, his desertion guaranteed to wreck any hope of gaining her trust. He was no better than her father.

When Kate wasn't around, there was no hot to his cold, no light to his dark. The determined redhead, dedicated to her work, passionate in his bed, lit every one of the dark crevices inside him. He'd give everything to claim her, spread her naked beneath him, kiss her senseless, and love her.

When he should have been explaining how her brother died, he'd selfishly given in to his lust, his desire. Side-tracked time and time again. A man without courage.

The pain in Kate's eyes when her mother outed him ripped his heart from his chest and hung it like a flag over his shame.

First, do no harm. His oath broken.

When this was over, and Kate was safe, he wouldn't stop until he'd made up for the shit way he behaved.

First, he had to get his head straight. If taking Knight's advice and seeing a shrink was the only way he'd give it his best shot because life without Kate wasn't worth shit.

"You with me, Doc," Knight said.

Luke sprang to attention.

Spread across the Boss' desks were the floor plans for *Wagga*'s premier international hotel. They were ninety-nine per cent sure of Seckou's target. Spanner and Snake checked and re-checked, from the basement to the air conditioning vents. A single detail forgotten or overlooked, and people got killed.

"Where's Kate?" Luke asked and pulled up a chair.

"At ease, Doc. Issouf drove her to the school."

"When did they leave?"

Knight checked his watch. "An hour ago."

"Who's with them?"

Knight shook his head. "Relax, they're not alone. Two of the local militia are riding convoy. She'll be fine. Right now, you have to focus on the job. Copy?"

Luke held Knight's gaze. Kate should be on a plane out of *Wagga*, not paying visits to schools. But, as much as he wanted to charge after her, his skills were needed here. "Copy."

"Moving on. The militia is on alert with covert operatives here and here. Sentinel will take point at the front and back entrances. Everyone coming in or out of the hotel gets searched, I don't give a damn who they are. Are we clear gentlemen?"

"Yes, Boss," Snake spoke for the team.

"You with us Doc?" Without waiting for his answer, Knight carried on with the briefing.

"Crystal and Kate will be on a plane for London as soon as Amina's concert finishes. Issouf will drive them to the airport. Snake you will drop Crystal, collect Amina from school then take her to the refugee camp. Once she's there, you will rendezvous with us at the hotel."

Ears pricked to attention George sat at Snake's feet.

Luke swallowed. The back of his throat dry, his hand shook with the need to hold a cigarette. "Any word from Oumar when Seckou will strike?"

The question hung in the air as the ground shook beneath Luke's feet. Windows rattled, all hell rumbled around them. Close. Too fucking close.

A symphony of mobile phone tones blasted the room.

Fingers pressed to his earpiece the Boss was at the door. "Fuck me. It's the fucking school. The bastard's taken out the school."

The Land Cruiser, the one Kate had cursed in the parking area, careered through the double doors. Wood split and glass smashed. Hissing and spitting the vehicle wedged at an awkward angle before exploding in a ball of yellow flame. A tremendous roar erupted, drowning out any other sound.

The impact from the blast sucked all the air from her lungs and threw her against the wall. Dazed and legs shaking, how she managed to stay on her feet was a miracle. The smell of thick smoke billowing along the corridor made her gag.

Her gaze jerked to the men, faces covered with masks, waving rifles, firing into the crowd. Dashing for cover, people, mainly children, collided with each other. Kate swallowed, but the bitter mix of bile and dust rose from her stomach.

"*Merde!*" Issouf swore.

Kate grunted at the sudden wrench to her injured arm. Just in time to avoid a piece of falling ceiling, Issouf grabbed her elbow and hurled her to the ground.

Cups, coloured ribbons, photographs of champions flew from the shelves of one of the many display cases. Screams rang along the corridor.

Desperate to get Issouf off her before she suffocated, she shoved against his chest not expecting the wet, warm blood that gushed in the space between them.

"Issouf!" Not knowing which of them was injured, Kate wrenched her hands free from under his torso.

"*Le lycée*, the school. Explosion. *M'aidez*," Issouf rolled to his side and gasped into the mic clipped to his collar.

"Knight will come," his weak voice stuttered over the roar of the fire eating the walls of the school. "Take this." Issouf struggled to unclip his mic.

"No. I don't know what to do." Kate refused the headset, but the man was in agony insisting she take it thrusting it into her hands. "Okay, don't move."

Where were Amina and her brother? *Please, please.* She prayed they made it to safety.

It was too dark to see very much—they must have lost electricity.

Screams and shouts echoed from inside the hall, now a pile of smoking rubble. More gunshots. Everywhere people fled.

A few stopped to help others then headed towards any slit of light while others groped in the darkness and tripped over the bodies.

Christ. Kate blinked the smoke from her eyes, clutched at her stomach trying to stop the terror marching through her insides. She searched for the pulse at the side of Issouf's neck. Faint, but alive.

"Issouf. Stay awake. I need you." She palmed the sides of his cheeks, watching helplessly as his eyes fell back in his head, and a trickle of blood slid from his mouth.

Where were Knight and his bloody calvary when you needed them?

Like a beacon, a fragment of yellow batik flashed in front of her. *Amina?* Emerging out of the clearing dust, one hand covering her ear, the girl limped towards her.

"Amina, stay there. *Rest là.*" Hoarse from the smoke, her voice didn't carry far.

"Kate?" Arms outstretched Amina kept coming.

Afraid she'd get trampled by the panicked crowd teeming from the hall, Kate spat out the fine dust encasing her teeth and tried again. "Don't move".

Kate was almost on her feet when a tremendous roar blasted along the corridor and detonated Issouf into a cloud of smoke. *No.*

Yellow pinpricks of light danced across her vision the second her head slammed against the wall. Large pieces of the ceiling crashed onto people too injured to move. Slumped in the doorway, the stench of blood and death surrounded her.

She was going to die. *Luke.* Tears mingled with the dirt and grime etched into her face. What if she never saw him again? How could she tell him she didn't blame him for Mike's death? When could she tell him she loved him? A bloody awful time for questions that should have been asked and answered.

Tired and hurting, she wanted to hug that tragedy to her chest and curl into a ball. Her eyes scanned the carpet of torn bodies a fierce determination creeping over her.

Get up. No way would it end like this. Kate rolled onto her hands and knees and crawled to the spot where she last saw Amina, unsure what was worse the nip of her teeth as she bit her tongue against the pain or the stab of shrapnel stabbing her knees.

"Amina. *Où es tu?* Where are you?"

"*Je suis là.* Here."

Her stomach leapt to her throat as she struggled to pinpoint Amina's voice.

The bastards were shooting again.

A few feet from her, Amina lay on her back, one leg twisted awkwardly underneath her. "Okay, okay, I'm here." Slender fingers twitched in Kate's hand.

"Shh, sweetheart." Terrified they might hear Amina's sobs Kate lay next to her and covered her mouth with one hand. "*Doucement,* quietly. Play dead."

Sirens blared in the distance.

Where was Luke? They must know what had happened. Her head began to swim, when had she last taken a full breath? *Stay calm.* If she passed out, she was no good to anyone. The gunfire faded. They were safe, but for how long?

"It's okay. I will get us out of here." Kate stroked Amina's forehead. No way could she carry Amina far by herself.

Wiping the grime from her eyes, she made them both a promise. *We will not die here*. Issouf offered her a resigned smile. Maybe it was the sudden draught blowing around her ankles or the cloud masking the sun, but something wasn't right.

Unease churned in her gut, she glanced over her shoulder, but there was still no sign of Salif only people yelling, waving their arms in the air.

CHAPTER THIRTY-FIVE

On the street, chaos reigned. Already en route to the school, emergency vehicles, militia, gendarmes, you name it, stormed in every direction. The pounding of their feet matched the beating of Luke's heart.

Think. The word ran in a loop chasing his fears around his head. Stay focussed. Kate, she had to be alive, denial crept in keeping him sane. They broke down on their way to the school, Amina decided not to go, it was the wrong fucking day.

"Hold up, Doc. We go together." Knight's voice sang out behind him.

Luke checked his stride.

"Sit." Nose sniffing at air George waited while Snake secured his harness and lead.

"You sure the dog's up to it," Knight asked.

"I'm betting my life on it, Boss. If there are more explosives, George will sniff them out."

Big, intelligent eyes me his, the dog's tongue hung to the side panting in anticipation. Luke sensed him, Mike by their side.

"Fine. Tell me, Issouf has comms?" Luke envied the efficiency with which Knight took control. The brother you could depend on when hell broke loose.

"Copy that," Snake replied. "You'll need this." Heart in his throat, Luke caught the headset Snake tossed his way. How fast could he get to Kate?

"Doc, Snake, take the Jeep. Spanner, with me in the truck."

The Boss tore off ahead of them. Snake shifted gears and accelerated. Jaw clenched, Luke looped one wrist through the leather strap above the door and wiped the sweat from his brow.

Kate was alive. He'd accept nothing less. "Damn it man, drive faster."

Snake rounded the corner on two wheels, George whined, skidding across the back seat, as Snake slammed to a halt beside the school gate.

Now a mangled pile of iron it hung off its hinges. The walls of the main building remained, but the explosion had decimated most of the roof and the east wall. Heart pounding, Luke jumped from the Jeep and dodged the dead gendarme pinned beneath the gate.

Storming the front entrance were a dozen shooters, maybe more, spraying ammo, causing maximum havoc. Confused civilians running in every direction, fell like fairground ducks.

He couldn't get his head around it. It couldn't be random, a fucking school, for Christ's sake. Some fucker told Seckou where to find Kate and Amina. Dread sank from his head to his combat boots. If the fucker also planned to hit the hotel, no way could their resources cope.

A grim determination seeded inside him. When he found who betrayed Kate and Amina, he wouldn't rest until he did, no matter what it took, they would pay.

"Gear up, Doc."

They made their way to the rear of the Jeep. Eyes scanning the surrounds, Snake backed towards him, his sharpshooter rifle raised, covering their six.

Luke grabbed a Sig Sauer P226 and strapped a Ka-Bar and holster to his ankle. His team had always protected him, made sure he never had to draw his weapon. No lie, he would never be comfortable firing a gun. Truth, he would do whatever it took to protect Kate and make sure she and Amina stayed alive.

"Take this." Snake tossed him a rope.

More bloody bodies lay beneath the wheels of what remained of a four-wheel-drive lodged inside the entrance. Every bone in Luke's body screamed, *honour your fucking promise. Find Kate.*

Snake took off around the side of the building, nose to the ground, tail wagging, George led the way. Firearm at the ready, Luke followed, tearing a path through the tattered branches of bougainvillaea clinging to the rubble.

"Issouf, Doc here, come in. Over." As fast as he swiped it away, sweat returned to his forehead. He pressed the mic closer to his mouth. "Damn, Boss. This place is coming down. Over."

No response—nothing from Knight since they'd left the villa.

"Luke?" Kate's voice crackled through the static. His heart leapt to his throat. Kate was alive.

Surrounded by dickers firing indiscriminately into the hoard fleeing the burning building, his relief was short-lived. "Kate, hang on, we're coming for you. Issouf, you there?"

"Issouf's gone, Luke. Oh God, he has a wife, a child."

Luke blocked his mic, swore, and spat into the dirt. Kate, the most together woman he'd ever met, was close to losing it. "I need you to stay calm, Kate. Where are you?"

"We are in what's left of the corridor outside the main hall on the first floor. There's no way out."

Luke clenched and unclenched his fist. "Okay, take a breath. You've got this. Look around you."

"Er. Most of the roof is gone, oh God, there are so many people injured. Luke, you have to help them."

"Together, we will. Tell me what you see."

"The stairs are gone. Wait, there's a window." Kate's voice lifted, not much, but enough to give him hope. She was going to make it he'd accept nothing less.

"Easy. Approaching now. I'm coming. Over." Luke signalled a few feet ahead.

There weren't too many windows left in the carnage. Entering through one of them was their best bet of reaching Kate. "I'm going in."

"Roger, Doc. George and I will circle the perimeter, secure easier access for immediate evac. You are on your own. Okay, man?" Snake lifted his chin, his eyes landing on Luke's gun.

"Don't worry. Any dicker breathes close to Kate or Amina they're dead." A part of him relished putting an end to the fuckers who had done this.

"Steady Doc keep your wits about you." George stood, head up, ready for Snake's command. "Come."

Luke returned Snake's thumbs up and waited until they disappeared behind a pile of rubble. Above him, the walls groaned struggling to keep from caving.

Shots shattered the air. People kept coming, clambering from the debris, crying for help. The gunmen were concentrating their fire at the northeast corner of the building, which didn't give him much time to reach Kate. He prayed he was close to their part of the corridor.

A large, unbroken pot lay in the dirt. Dumping the contents, Luke climbed on top of it, tossed the rope over his head and aimed for the window. Twice the line fell at his feet. The lucky third found its way into the small cavity.

"Kate? You there?"

"Luke? Where are you?" Kate answered before he finished.

"Below a window. Do you see the rope?"

"Yes."

Thank God. "Can you reach it?"

"Yes."

"Good. Let me know when you've secured it. Over."

An eternity passed before Kate confirmed. Trusting the rope to hold, Luke pushed hard with his feet and grit his teeth against the burn of the line sliding through his fingers.

He hooked one leg over the broken ledge, thankful it held long enough to scramble inside the building. Arms flailing, he slid over a hill of rocks and metal and landed close to where Kate knelt beside Amina.

"Bloody hell, Luke, your hands."

The sting from the beating they took on entry paled at the sight of Kate.

Hair covered in grime and dust framed her perfect face. He wiped his hands on the front of his pants, took a long look at the woman who owned his heart. Blood seeped through the knees of her pants.

"You're hurt."

"A few scratches. No need to wrap me in cotton wool, Doc." The warmth from her fingers curled around his hands.

She flashed him the smile. Yeah, the one guaranteed to make him melt.

"We'll get out of here. The others are right behind me." Luke mentally crossed his fingers.

Kate instantly dropped her gaze. His blood turned to ice. She had to believe him. "Promise."

He cupped the back of her neck and drew her close, even the threat of a building collapsing around their ears didn't stop him wanting to kiss her.

"Doc, you inside?" Knight's voice rasped in his earpiece.

"Yes. 'bout fucking time. Where are you? Copy." Luke spoke as loudly as he dared. Shooters could be anywhere.

He moved in front of Kate and Amina determined any stray bullet would find him first. "Let's take a look at our girl."

"Heading to you. Shit. Spanner, dicker at your three." Several gunshots fired before Knight returned. "Doc. Be ready to move. Over."

"Roger that." He turned his attention to Amina's legs. Mike's torn and bloody body flashed in front of him. *Pull it together.* Amina's pulse was steady, both legs intact, but he couldn't know the full extent of her injuries until they were out of there.

A burst of automatic fire echoed along the corridor. Amina whimpered. Kate stroked her forehead. *Tranquillement cherie.* I won't let anything happen to you."

A hail of bullets hit the wall to their right. Luke pressed his finger to his lips. Rage rushed through his veins. "Boss, we are taking heavy fire. Over." Luke aimed his weapon and fired. Two, three fuckers hit the ground.

"Nice shot." Kate grinned, fingers in her ears, tears streaming in lakes over her face.

Christ, he needed that kiss. If only time would stand still. "Help me get Amina ready to transport. Okay, sweetheart? Can you do that?"

Kate opened her mouth, and he held his breath waiting for her to tell him off for the endearment as she'd done in the past. Instead, she smiled. The courage on her blackened face slew him.

Luke pulled the auto-injector from his Bergan and gave Amina a shot of morphine. A hole the size of a crater grew inside his chest, flashes of Mike's missing limbs knifed at his guts.

"Luke?" Kate laid her hand on his forearm. "What can I do?"

Plenty of cuts and contusions on Amina's legs, but they were there, and no bones showed through the skin. "All good, sit, let me take a look at your knees."

"Come in Boss. We're ready to roll. ETA? Over."

"Working on it, Doc. Currently pinned in what's left of the west corridor. Over." Knight's reply was not what he wanted to hear.

"Snake, with you? Over."

"Yep, they found us. Any exit possible your end? Over."

Luke glanced at the window. Kate, the fucking magnificent, was on her feet before he could reply. "We have a window. Over."

Thanks to the wind blowing outside, the smoke was dispersing quickly. They would get out of there. Hubris was a mean son of a bitch. The world shuddered below their feet, and a gush of heat hit him with the force of a tornado.

Fuck me.

CHAPTER THIRTY-SIX

Kate's eyes went first to Amina and then to her torn knees. How the hell? She reached for Luke's hand and stared at their only way to escape. Together it was possible. The realisation hit her as a third explosion blasted them apart.

A large chunk of cement flew past her ear and landed inches from Amina. She crouched over the injured girl covering her from any shrapnel. Tears streaming down her face, Kate raised her head and cursed Seckou.

Enough. Very much afraid it wasn't, she gulped greedily, searching for air trying to bring down her heart rate.

"Breathe through your nose, Kate, that's it." Luke's voice soared over the roaring in her head.

Siphoning air through her nose she did her best to calm her rising panic. Gradually, her breath deepened, the trembling stopped.

"Luke, where are you?"

"Here, behind you."

Her breath hitched, relief rushing through her - he was close. She inched towards him. Broken bits of debris dug into the torn skin on her bleeding knees.

Gun beside him, Luke lay slumped against the wall, one hand clutching the front of his shirt.

"Hey, no tears." Luke's hand reached for her cheek but missed.

Dull with pain, his honey-brown eyes no longer sparkled.

"Your knees, I'm sorry."

"No need, not your fault. I told you only scratches. Let me look." The blood seeping through her trembling fingers made it difficult to lift his shirt. Grabbing the edges, she ripped the damn thing open, her cry echoing Luke's shout of pain.

Luke's head swayed, and his body sagged against her hands, she tried to hold on while she swiped away the carpet of glass beside him, but he was too heavy.

She bore as much of his weight as possible in the crook of her arm, but he was a big man, impossible to lower gently to the ground.

Luke cried out. "A bit rough, sorry. Hold still while I look."

"Sure, Doc," he hissed.

A jagged piece of glass lay embedded left of his breastbone. Fear dug its claws into the back of her neck and held on knowing an inch further over, and he'd be dead. *You trained for this. Your shirt. Use your shirt.*

She steadied her hands, took a deep breath, undid her shirt, and formed a doughnut shape. Packing it firmly around the glass she secured it in place.

"Love the bra. Green suits you," Luke stuttered, eyelids fluttered.

Love for the man who tried to keep her spirits high made a meal of her gut.

"Don't talk." The words part command, part beg. "Save the fashion critique of my underwear 'til we're out of here. I'll model as many as you want."

Luke struggled to turn onto one elbow, distracting her from wondering how the hell she planned to get Amina and Luke to safety.

"Stop moving." How could he not notice the lump of glass sticking out of your chest?" Tears streamed over her cheeks she still needed to check on Amina. "I'm coming *cherie.*"

"I okay."

Trust Amina to shine, displaying courage that put her trembling to shame.

Luke's head lolled to one side, a long breath sighing from his body. *No.* "Luke. Luke."

"I'm here. Just resting my eyes." The damn idiot tried to laugh.

She had watched enough action movies to know she needed to keep him conscious, up the banter and nix the blubbing. "Sing. Can you sing? Let's make noise so Knight can find us."

"What...the...fu..." Luke slurred. "Shh, Kate. Knight's not alone out there."

Stupid, stupid, stupid. Kate thumped the side of her head. Bring the entire Islamic State running. Why not? Leave it to her to make sure they died in this sodding tomb. "Sorry. I ..."

Luke curled his fingers around her wrist and pressed his lips to her rapid pulse. "It's okay, Kate, you've got this."

Behind her, the zing of bullets ricocheted off the wall. Nowhere to hide, Kate ducked over Amina, reached for Luke, and searched for the shooters.

Heavy boots pounded closer. Kate's whipped her head around, her gaze landing on a madman tearing from the haze his rifle aimed straight at them.

Her stomach flipped, dumb move or not, she scrambled for Luke's gun and fired. Finger frozen on the trigger, she kept firing. Their attacker dropped lifeless at her feet. For a few seconds, all she heard was the click of the empty chamber.

A sob wrenched from her mouth, and the gun fell from her hands. She'd killed a man. Arms wrapped around her torso she started to rock. Were these her last moments, a killer surrounded by fire, people screaming?

No. Luke and Amina needed her. First, she checked on Amina then crawled to Luke.

"Hey… it's okay. The fuckers are gone. Don't give up on me now." Luke's gruff calm dragged her from the carnage and she sank by his side.

"Luke, I'm not sure what to do." His finger traced her lips, she closed her eyes to savour the warmth of his touch, his strength flowing through her.

"Kate."

Blood seeped through the shirt she had pressed to Luke's chest. She barely had enough breath to speak. "No. Don't talk."

"Listen to me. You must find Knight. Bring help."

Her spine stiffened. "No." How could he ask her to leave them? No way could they protect themselves.

"Kate, I know you're scared, but you can do this. Besides, you're the one who can stand." His chuckle turned to a cough.

A thousand excuses ran amok in her head. "It's too dark. I can't see."

Luke's palm brushed her cheek. "Fix your headset."

The damn thing hung from her shoulder. It must have fallen from her head during the blast.

Luke coughed again. He was losing too much blood. "No, please, don't talk." Static crackled in her ear. *Keep it together.* "Hello, anyone? Come in."

Her voice hitched. She tried to swallow the tears streaming from her sore eyes, but she was tired, so bloody tired. Struggling to keep Luke's face in focus she touched her lips to his. "Don't you dare leave me."

"I'm here. Go, Kate, find Knight."

"No, I'm not leaving. Lie back, save your strength."

"Kate, listen. You're our only chance."

She swiped away her tears. All Luke's talk about her underwear, guess it was time to pull up her knickers and get moving before it was too late.

"Go." Luke pushed weakly on her chest.

His eyes overflowed with pain and something else. What?

"Okay, okay. I'll be back for you. Stay alive. Look after Amina. I love you."

"Leave. Now," Luke moaned.

His gaze caught hers, and he smiled. The tightness in her chest released. She checked the gun made sure it was ready to fire. Her heart pounded.

Through the stream of blood flowing beneath her stinging feet. Small fires everywhere offered enough light to gingerly, stagger along the gloomy corridor. Dismembered limbs lay on the floor like broken toys in a messy kid's room.

Determined to find her way back to Luke and Amina, she traced her fingers along the wall, counted her steps and willed Knight to appear. Her throat was sore from the smoke, but she swallowed hard when no men in shiny armour materialised through the haze.

"*Aide-moi.*" A woman cried out a few feet in front of her.

"I'm here, let me help you." Kate slid to the ground beside the woman and gasped.

Blood poured over her hands as she sank them into the gaping hole in the woman's abdomen. One last inhale before her grief-stricken eyes fixed on Kate's face and life ebbed from her gaze.

A growing numbness replaced her tears. She pressed her fingertips to the dead woman's eyelids and closed the madness for the final time.

Move. One shaky leg at a time until she stood. *People need you.* A figure materialised from the darkness, but any hope vanished. Yacouba's ugly mug leered out of the smoke.

"*Alors, putain.* My lucky day. We meet again."

"Not something I looked forward to, that's for sure."

The handle of his gun glanced off the side of her face. She fell hard on one knee. The pain searing her eyeballs robbed her of her next breath and the next.

Yacouba's lips were moving, but she couldn't hear him above the ringing in her ears.

"Who else is here? The English? My wife?" Yacouba screamed.

"Too late. You missed them." Gasping for her next breath, she curled her hands into weak fists determined to fight rather than die by Yacouba's hand.

"*Quel dommage*. Salif tell me different."

His punch to her stomach made her vomit. Bile spewed over his sandalled feet. *Salif*. It didn't make sense. Her ears must be playing tricks with her brain. She shoved her hands into the dirt and shuffled her lower back into the rough surface of the crumbled wall.

Yacouba was lying, the truth too much to bear. She'd brought Salif to Amina, protected him. For what? No, it was a trick, another one of Yacouba's evil games. Salif had nothing to do with the death of all these people.

"Seckou will be happy I bring him your head." Yacouba waved his rifle.

Kate raised her chin. "What, he's not here?" No different from any general, manoeuvring foot soldiers from a distance, shedding no blood with his hands.

Yacouba growled, stepped forward and pressed the gun to her temple. So keen to kill her he missed the bloody cavalry. Men dressed head to toe in black, swarmed into the corridor. A dog barked. *George*. Kate bit her bottom lip and surrendered to the hysterical laughter bubbling in the back of her throat.

"Drop your fucking weapon, knob'ed." Knight stood behind Yacouba. Not one, but two guns pointed straight at him. "I said, drop it. Twitch and I'll put a bullet in your brain. The other is for your balls."

Yacouba hesitated, then swung his gun in Knight's direction, firing once before Knight kept his promise. Two pops one after the other and Yacouba was dead.

A shallow sense of relief swam over her aching body.

Beads of sweat glistened on Knight's forehead. "Bollocks," he grunted and clutched his shoulder.

"You're hit, Boss." Spanner grabbed Knight's elbow.

"Flesh wound. How are you going Ms Gibson?" Knight's voice was flat, unemotional as he shrugged out of Spanner's hold and scanned her knees.

"Never thought I'd say it, but better for seeing you."

"Thatta girl. Lead us to Doc and Amina."

Kate swallowed, took the offer of Snake's hand, and scrambled to her feet.

George barked and nudged her thigh. "Come on boy, this way."

Praying they weren't too late, she retraced her steps and told herself Luke had to be alive. There was so much she wanted to say to him.

"*Ici*. Here." Amina's voice, thin and weak drifted towards them.

The sound escaping Kate's cracked lips wasn't much more than a pathetic whimper. She fixed her eyes on Luke, stumbled towards him and grabbed his hand. The relief overwhelming when he squeezed her fingers.

It hurt to let go, but she had to pull herself together, keep pressure around the shard of glass, play her part in getting everyone to safety.

"Snake, you'll carry Amina. Spanner with me. Okay, Doc, we got you." Knight bent to grab Luke's legs and immediately let go. "Fuck."

"Kate, swap places with the Boss." The air of command in Spanner's voice was unexpected, equally surprising was seeing Knight hesitate.

"Please." Kate shifted forward and laid her hand lightly on Knight's forearm.

"Your shoulder. There's no other way, Boss," Spanner said.

Kate sucked in a breath, her turn to give orders. "Here, he needs you." She guided Knight's hand to Luke's wound. "Press hard."

Winding her hands tightly around the stretcher handles, she hoped she had enough strength to lift her end. She would. She had to. There was no other way.

"Ready?" Spanner winked.

"Uh-huh." She sucked in a breath and took the weight.

The building creaked and groaned as they made their way to an exit. Any minute, the rest of the roof might collapse. Part of her jumped for bloody joy at the sliver of light shining ahead. Even Knight blessed the rain as fresh air filled their lungs.

Clear of the building, they rested briefly by the destroyed fountain before lifting Luke into the back of the truck. Kate turned to help Amina and Knight.

"I'll sit with her. You stay with Luke." Knight winced and climbed in beside Amina.

Luke's face was ash grey. Tight lines pulled at the corner of his mouth. He hadn't opened his eyes since they'd begun to move him. Blood continued to ooze from the wound in his chest.

"Don't you dare leave me. I deserve one last…" Tears welled in the back of her throat. *No. No more endings.*

Knight clutched his shoulder. "Chin up, Kate. Doc's tougher than he looks."

Kate cradled Luke's head in her lap and closed her eyes. Luke's smile, the dimple, his eyes. His body started to shake. *No.*

Knight was shouting.

"Shit. Step on it Snake. Doc's coding."

CHAPTER THIRTY-SEVEN

Two Days Later – St Anne's Hospital, London, UK

Luke forced his eyes open, surrounded by beeping monitors, any movement of his head and the fluorescent lasers above his head seared his eyeballs. Maybe if he kept his eyes fixed on the wall, he wouldn't choke on the foul taste in the back of his throat. An illogical conclusion, but no one could accuse him of thinking straight in months.

A face outlined with wavy edges ebbed in and out of focus. Luke chuckled, blessing the cocktail of drugs coursing through his veins. He'd like nothing better than to sink into oblivion and dream of Kate.

"Luke, it's me."

Oh yeah, stonking good drugs.

Full of concern, Kate's voice broke through the cough racking his body, sending daggers into every aching muscle. Etched in his memory forever was the look on her face when he insisted she leave him and find help.

"Welcome back." Kate stroked his cheek.

Alive, they were alive. His hand refused to rise from the sheet, so he settled for drinking her in with his eyes. These past few weeks, she'd witnessed enough death and violence to rival his three tours in Afghanistan and acted with more courage than the toughest.

Judging from the shadows under her eyes, her uncombed curls, Kate hadn't slept or changed her clothes in a while. How could she ever forgive him?

He'd let Kate down, and there was no bunch of flowers big enough, no diamond bright enough to say how sorry he was or make up for how much he had hurt her. He wasn't sure how he could give her up only certain he must. Kate deserved better.

"Where am I?"

"St Anne's. You've been out of it for a couple of days."

London, an eternity from Burkina. "We need to talk." The words clung to the roof of his mouth, playing with his head, begging not to reach the air.

"We do. Later." Kate picked up the glass beside the bed and offered him the straw.

She didn't understand. He opened his mouth to protest and sank behind clouds of nausea.

Second time lucky, and he was determined to stay conscious. The room swayed. Kate sat by the bed. Same clothes, same… *Wow*. Beside him sat happiness, Kate holding his hand, the hint of her smile, the twinkle in her eye, could he throw it away?

"Welcome back."

"Help me sit." He squeezed her hand.

"Oh, no. The chart at the end of your bed clearly says rest."

"Come on, nurse. Give a guy a break." He snaked his hand across the sheet, palm up, pleading for her touch.

"Thanks." Luke looked towards the door. "I'm sorry, Kate …"

"For what? Sending me off to fight the bad guys then dying on me?"

"Dying?"

"Yes, damn it. We lost you. Twice."

"Then I'm doubly sorry. I can't fix the first, but I can apologise for the second. I was wrong deserting you at Knight's without answering your question. Telling myself, you couldn't handle what happened to Mike, that I had to wait for the right moment was a poor excuse."

"Not now. We can discuss it later." Kate tried again to make him drink.

"Now, sweetheart, it has to be now." Now or never. "I was a coward, unworthy of anything good in my life." Luke scrubbed his hand through his hair. "Still am."

Kate stroked her thumb across the back of his hand. "I won't pretend to understand why you kept what happened to Mike from me, but now I—"

He waited for the tears, but there were none. Tell her. She was entitled to answers. "You wanted to know if I gave Mike the gun?"

Kate shook her head, let go of his hand. "It doesn't matter. Knight told me you weren't responsible."

The air rushed from the room.

"No, don't do that. Please don't push your feelings aside because you think, oh hell, I can't pretend I know what you're thinking. I do know we'll never be able to move on unless you hear it from me. Listen, Kate. Please."

Unable to accept her drifting away from him he laid his fingers on her forearm. "Mike begged for the pain to stop. I told him to hang on—he'd be okay. The Chinook was circling overhead, but even if we made it to Base, his chances of survival were slim."

Under his palm, Kate's fingers twitched.

"He begged me to end it. Made me swear to take care of you. I lied and told him he'd be okay. You must believe me, Kate, all I wanted was to end his pain. Shit, sweetheart, Mike's screams haunt me, they will until the day I die. I couldn't think straight, I emptied a syringe of Ketamine into him and went for another."

"I understand, but you wouldn't. I know you couldn't." Kate's inhuman whimper ripped his heart to shreds.

One more dose and his suffering would have ended. "Hell, Kate. My head is so fucked up I'm not sure myself. I turned my back for a second and Mike took it out of my hands. He snatched the pistol from my belt. Kate. I killed your brother as sure as if I'd pulled the trigger. I'm a doctor —I took an oath. I should never carry a gun."

His flesh was on fire. Tortured by the tears, Kate finally let flow.

"Luke, I don't blame you."

"You don't have to blame me. I blame myself."

"You would never hurt my brother. It's not in you to hurt anyone. The proof stares me in the face. Look at what you did for Amina, me.

"No, stop. You don't understand."

"Then help me. Make me understand."

"For fuck's sake, Kate. I promised Mike I'd take care of you and I failed." He tapped the hole in his chest.

"It has to be this way Kate, no fucking note. To your face. We can't be together, not right now. Not because I don't want it more than my next breath, but I have to take care of shit first."

Luke prayed she would listen and wait for him – she said she loved him. But he wouldn't ask it of her, to love him, guilt, failure, and all.

"No, Luke, please, it's not what I want."

"It's what I want. I'm sorry." Luke kissed her cheek, fearing it might be for the last time. Luke raised his hand, and she leaned in for a caress that never happened. "You deserve more." And he was determined to be that more. "Please, go."

Needing her to hate him, a little, so he didn't take back the words tearing his heart from his fucking chest, he didn't move as the tear slid over her cheek, and she left his room.

It wasn't until he heard the soft click of the door closing behind her that he let go of his breath and let the tears fall. A grown man crying at losing a woman. His woman, the woman who would forever hold his heart.

Weeks of rehab tested his patience, several times he wanted to chuck it in, but Spanner stayed by his side, offering the kind of encouragement only a brother would understand.

Idiot that he was, it took the Boss breaking it down for him. He'd hurt Kate, again, which was never his fucking intention, but what choice did he have? Causing her more unhappiness was more than he could bear.

Why didn't she understand? They couldn't be together, not right now, maybe never. He swore under his breath. The nurses had warned him, curse out loud again, and there'd be no chocolate biscuit with afternoon tea. His sweet tooth took notice.

Wednesday morning, before breakfast, the nurse brought the discharge papers, and he signed them.

"Ready to go. Crystal's made up the spare room." Spanner patted the seat of the wheelchair.

And how did she feel about that? They'd been shacked up together for a week. They didn't need to play nurse to his sorry arse. "Thanks, Spanner, I appreciate the offer. Be sure to tell Crystal."

Spanner shook his head. "Really? You're scared of Crys. She's fine, Doc."

"If you say so. Hey, man, I need some time by myself, but I'd appreciate a lift back to mine if you're offering."

"You sure, Doc?"

"Yeah, positive." The long overdue chat between him and hell was long overdue.

CHAPTER THIRTY-EIGHT

Kate Gibson, midwife, mentor, empty shroud. Her skin crawled. For someone who dedicated her life to healing, she was doing a crap job of mending herself. They were finally burying her brother, laying him to rest.

His team were there, everyone except Luke. George by her side, she cuffed the moisture from her eyelashes and refused to think of Luke.

Grains of earth slipped through her fingers and showered over Mike's coffin. She was enough and didn't need anyone else to prove it.

One Month Later

At the end of another harrowing nightshift, Kate stumbled out of the locker room at The Metropolitan Women's Hospital, the smell of antiseptic clinging to her skin and clothes. Usually, she showered and changed preferring to leave work in a locker or laundry bag, but today was her last day.

People gathered outside the entrance moaning at London's relentless drizzle. The rain matched her tears, the hurt that threatened to shatter her confidence, turn her into a blancmange of self-doubt.

Hell. She was a professional, capable in most situations. Happy. Dad abandoning her on the pier had shaped her entire life. Perhaps if she'd given the men she dated half a chance she would be married with kids—a mother.

Lonely didn't come close to the feeling eating away at her since Mike died, but it wasn't right to blame her brother for her mistakes. Yes, he'd left her, took his own life, and it had nothing to do with her.

He loved her, hell, used his last breath to drag a promise from his best mate to look after her.

When Luke insisted on being alone, it hurt—bone-crushing, heart-stopping. Every cell in her body missed him. How many times had she called him, hung up before he could answer? She wanted to hear his voice, go to him, every moment of every day. Luke never said he loved her. No promises made.

Keeping busy was the solution, not allowing herself to count days. Kate, a flesh, and blood reminder of Luke's trauma—she wouldn't blame him if he never wanted to see her again.

They had no future, her doing what she loved in Africa and him working in London. She was leaving for Burkina and Crystal was coming around this morning, moral support for her last breakfast with Mother. Her thoughts drifted to Amina and Katy as she opened her umbrella and shut out the grey sky. It has been way too long since she had seen them.

Kate rounded the corner off Parkway and stopped dead. Mother had beaten her home. She stood beside the railing, tapping her foot, thankfully looking in the opposite direction. Kate took a sec to steady her nerves, picked up her pace and was at Mother's side before she saw her coming.

"Sorry. Have you been waiting long? I told you I didn't get off work until seven." Her back-handed apology froze in the damp morning air.

"Yes."

Kate inhaled long and deep, prayed the single word served as penalty. Fat chance. Mother gripped her handbag with both hands and reared to attention. "It's eight-thirty. I've been waiting for over half an hour."

Don't bite. Kate closed her eyes for a second and traced her fingers over the sleeve of Mother's coat. "I said, I'm sorry. Let's go in and get the heater started. You must be freezing."

Kate loped down the stairs two at a time, slid one hand into her coat pocket and searched for her keys. Mother's breath, smoky and sour, landed on the back of her neck. They say gin has no smell. To a woman, trained from a girl, to be wary of hangovers, it was a myth.

"Come in, come in. Crys should be here soon. She's bringing croissants from the bakery you love at Camden Market."

Her smile faded as Mother bolted for her kitchen, filled the kettle, and made herself at home.

"Kate. You should tidy up. You haven't unpacked." The roll of her eyes and accusation landed on the two suitcases in the middle of the living room.

Mother was a compulsive cleaner, ironed socks for Christ's sake.

"Kate, Kate, you're not listening to a word I say." Her mother's voice grated inside of her ears, demanding she listen.

"Sorry, mum. Why don't you let me make the tea, take your coat off, and get comfortable? Crys will be here soon."

Mother flipped the switch on the kettle.

Crystal tapped on the window, her face squashed against the glass, fingers clawing at the pane. *Very funny.*

"Let me in," Crystal mouthed.

"Okay, okay, coming. Breakfast's arrived, mum."

Crystal burst through the open door. Her purple coat buttoned to her throat; a bright orange scarf wrapped tightly around her neck matched the emerald green gloves she flapped at Mother. Kate chuckled and followed her into the flat.

"Morning, Mrs Gibson. Bloody chilly out there."

"I didn't notice Crystal."

Kate raised her eyebrows.

"You're lucky. I guess I'm used to African weather. London is as cold as a witch's tit. Oops."

Kate couldn't stop the laugh that bubbled from her lips.

Crystal shook several paper bags clasped in her hands. "Er ... I brought your favourites Mrs G. Yours too, Kate. Blueberry croissant and *pain au chocolate*. Point me to the plates, hun."

"Here they are." Cups rattled ominously in their saucers. Mother dumped the tray of plates and cutlery on the coffee table. "Thank you, Crystal. Bring the teapot, Kate."

The flat was small, not much room for much furniture—one sofa. Kate squeezed in between Crystal and Mother, sympathising with the meat in the proverbial sandwich. A nervous laugh bubbled inside.

"Is something funny, Kate?"

"No. I think I may be coming down with a cold." She sniffed a couple of times to make her point.

"Ugh. Don't give it to me. Sorry. That's not good, hun, maybe you should stay at home for a few days. Put yourself into isolation." Crystal took another bite, smiles rippling behind her croissant.

Kate gave her the stare. *Shut up*. She'd invited her for support, not to stir the bloody pot. Was it too early for Scarfes? Her long sigh only irritated Mother more.

"Crystal is correct. You can't be sick if you insist on returning to Africa."

"I don't have a cold." Best to fess up before Mother flew off on a tangent that could only end in tantrums and tears.

"Plans are the same. Last night was my last shift at The Metropolitan Women's Hospital. You know the contract was temporary."

Mother capitulated as Crystal filled any awkwardness with details of setting up home with Spanner.

Kate brushed the crumbs from her knees. "That was delicious, Crys. I will miss fresh pastry."

Mother sprang to her feet, cup, and saucer rattling in her hand.

"Can I get you something?" Kate asked.

"No. I have to go. I have a hair appointment at ten. Ill clear these and be off."

"Leave it, mum. I can do that."

"Very well." Mother placed her cup back on the table with studied precision. "Goodbye, Kate, I don't suppose I'll see you again before you leave."

"I'll try. Maybe not. Thanks for coming this morning. I appreciate it."

"You've never believed me, Kate, but I do worry. I almost lost you, I've only ever wanted the best for you."

"I know, mum." Kate strained to get the words out of her mouth. Affection wasn't something they practised with each other. Kate felt the cold touch of her Mother's lips on her cheek and shivered.

"Call me when you arrive. I'm sorry." Mother was out the door and up the stairs before she could take everything in, never mind react.

"Phew. You okay?" Crystal asked.

"Yes." More than fine. Great." No tears left to cry. Kate turned on the taps and dangled her hand under the running water until it steamed and pinched her skin.

"I'm so proud of you hun." Crys settled her chin on top of her shoulder.

Kate patted the back of the hand circling her waist. "Come on, spill, how are you and Spanner really coping with living together? You haven't strangled each other yet?"

"No. He's perfect. We're perfect."

"And why doesn't that surprise me. Did you consider staying here, in London? I can manage in Burkina."

"Are you mad? Spanner will cope. It will do him good to miss me. You heard from, Luke?"

Kate rinsed the last plate and faced her friend. "No. I'm sure he's busy. Knight says he has a new job."

"Not yet, but when he's cleared from rehab, the Essex offered him a place in trauma and Knight's persuaded him to stay on-call for Sentinel.

Not sure how he'll manage both, guess he'll have to decide eventually. I thought he would have called you."

Bloody tears. Kate gave them a quick swipe and dodged behind Crys for a tea cloth.

"We agreed. After everything that happened, we need time apart."

"That's crap, hun."

"Maybe, but it's the way it is. I doubt that I'll see Luke before we leave for Burkina." Kate choked on the words and shrugged out of Crys' hug.

"Kate, sit hun. You're prowling like a tiger who's lost her cubs."

Christ. Was there no sodding end to it? Every waking moment, every conversation led straight to Luke. The sooner she was in Africa and back at work, the bloody better.

"I can't wait to see Amina and the baby. Aunty says she's going back to school next week." Move on, change the subject. After the explosion, the university had offered the school temporary classrooms while they re-built.

"Have they found Salif?" Crystal asked.

"No. No sign." The sound of his name made her sick to her stomach. Amina refused to believe her brother was a terrorist, and if she were honest, she wasn't entirely convinced. "Knight won't let it go. Sentinel already has men on the ground searching for him and Seckou."

They couldn't prove Salif told Seckou where to find them until they found him and there was no guarantee he was alive.

"Crys, you know how much I love you. You're my best friend. Thanks for your support with mum, not just this morning. I couldn't have got through these last couple of weeks without you."

"Oh, hun." Crystal stretched her arms wide, tilted her head and rolled her bottom lip. "Come here."

"No. I'm fine, but I need to get on with stuff. These bags, for instance. I've been kidding myself. It's time for a trip to the laundrette if I don't want to arrive in Burkina with dirty clothes. I've organised to meet someone to look after Mike's while I'm away."

She couldn't bring herself to say tidy his grave, make sure there were fresh flowers. "I'm meeting her at three."

"Okay, I'm going, but if you need to talk after, call me."

"Thanks, but you've got your hands full with that man of yours. Go on, best get home in case he's trashed your kitchen."

CHAPTER THIRTY-NINE

Kate Gibson owned him body and soul. There wasn't a moment when Kate wasn't in Luke's thoughts. Not at the hospital, not at home, and definitely not alone in his bed.

Knowing he'd hurt her tore at his resolve each minute of every interminable day, but he couldn't risk seeing her until he was sure he could give her his best. Kate deserved nothing less.

He loved her, and if he never saw her again, it would kill him. He wanted to spend the rest of his life, making things up to her if she'd give him a chance.

For the past month, life had cruised on auto, a loop of eat, sleep, and see the shrink. He hadn't held a cigarette in weeks, that had to be a good sign.

Losing his taste for Laphroaig might be a while off, but no half-opened bottles lurked, easy to hand when the black dog came calling.

The shrink suggested he should attend Mike's funeral. Listening to the knob'ed talking of closure, he almost hyperventilated reigning in the instinct to strangle the judgemental arse.

He couldn't front the funeral and not want to pull her into his arms.

Standing a few feet away, he hid behind an oak tree grateful for its non-judgmental support and balled his eyes out.

Later, walking back over the Heath with an aching erection, he remembered the low, sexy moans of Kate reaching her climax.

Over last night's care package of shepherd's pie, apple cobbler for dessert, with a nod and a wink to Spanner, Crystal let it slip Kate was going back to Africa.

Did it terrify him that she was thinking of setting one toe in Africa, and then some, but she was her own woman, capable of saving his sorry arse, she could take care of herself *and come safely home to me.*

After he paid a visit to Mike's grave, it was time to grow a pair, front up and wish her all the best for the trip.

He lifted the edge of the curtain. Fucking pouring with rain. Perfect. By the time he'd kicked his arse out of bed, showered, and dressed, it was early afternoon.

The rain had stopped by the time he drove through the Lodge gate at East Finchley Cemetery and parked. The sun poked from behind the clouds, but he left the umbrella, according to the physiotherapist, the walk would do him good.

Cap pulled over his eyes. Luke braced against the brisk wind whistling in and out of the headstones lining *Monument Drive.* Cemeteries did themselves proud after the rain, trees sporting misty green buds and the smell of freshly turned earth mingled with the musty air. If it rained, he could dry off at the pub down the road, grab a pork pie, and a club soda before he faced Kate.

Written on the crumpled piece of paper in his hand was the grave location. One, two, three, he counted them as he passed.

What the ever-living fuck.

Five feet ahead, the sight of Kate sitting on a beaten-up camping stool robbed him of his next breath. *Stay, turn, and run?* No, done running besides she must be bloody freezing dressed in a bomber jacket and jeans. His arms twitched to crush her to her chest, keep her warm.

Kate was shaking her head, but he kept moving until his feet paused in front of her. Despite the spark of anger behind the large pair of sunglasses masking her face, he had to touch her, reassure himself she was there, that it wasn't his heart playing tricks on him.

Kate spotted Luke long before he noticed her. Her first instinct was to abandon her chair, leave, and not watch and enjoy every powerful stride of his long legs as they ate the space between them.

She tried but couldn't unwind the mix of longing and anger, tying her stomach in knots. Fitting, because in so many ways, Luke had been with her this entire time. A phantom holding her hand, he joined her in her daily habit and refuge by Mike's grave. The ghost beside her, tempting her to eat when food became a boulder blocking her throat.

Why did he have to materialise today? Her last day in London? He wanted space, no problem. She sighed as the thought of what they might have had together reached inside her chest and cracked open her heart.

She lifted her chin to the sky, inhaling the raindrops bouncing off her glasses, *go on pour*, drown her need for the man who was almost at her feet.

Hands tucked in her lap, Kate drew strength from the chilly wind biting the end of her nose, fixed a smile on her face, and braced for the second their eyes inevitably met.

The rain glistened on his eyelashes. Kate swallowed, remembering the taut muscles that rippled over his belly and chest, how they twitched with pleasure under her touch.

Here in the flesh, sharing the same air, Luke didn't say a word, the look on his face one of shock more than welcome. Crys had no hand in it then, he hadn't come to see her.

"Hello, Luke. You look a lot better than the last time I saw you." Unspoken was how long that time had been, how it had dragged with every second.

"Yeah. Sorry, Kate, I didn't expect to see you here."

She flinched and hoped he wouldn't step any closer. "If you had come tomorrow, you'd have had the place to yourself." It was hard, too hard, to turn away from his gaze.

"How come?"

"I'm going back to Burkina. Yalgado has more nurses that need a refresher." Kate swallowed the lump at the back of her throat.

"Yeah, actually, Crys mentioned it." He paused, looking more than a little sheepish. "When do you leave?

A smile lingered behind her eyes. She'd already said. Could Luke be a teeny-weeny bit glad to see her? "Tomorrow."

The blank expression on his face that allowed her to paint with miserable pictures wasn't how she hoped he would respond.

For Christ's sake, what did she want him to say? Goodbye? Stay? *Yes. Please ask me to stay.*

Bloody pathetic, but now he was here, and she couldn't tear her gaze from his mouth. She ached for him, craved that mouth on her lips which was why she didn't register Luke shift from one foot to the other. Ready to run.

Not this time. If anyone was leaving, it was her. She had to kill this obsession with Doc once and for all.

"Goodbye, Luke." She turned, her stomach twisting in knots as he grabbed her hand.

"What are you doing?" Her fingers flew from his grasp and landed over her heart. No bloody protection at all.

"Don't go." He cleared his throat. "Please stay."

"Why?" She could kick herself for the hint of desperation hanging on her voice, the way her words fell short of quiet acceptance.

Her breath hitched, a bitch when your body betrayed you. "You told me to go, remember, said I didn't deserve you."

"That's not what I said."

She squared her shoulders, prepared to quote him word for word.

Luke held up his hand. "I said that the way things were, we had no chance. I needed to work on being the man you deserved."

Her stomach twisted, flipped, and rolled, every part of her aching to trust him.

"I can't promise that I'm there yet, but I am seeing someone, getting help."

Luke's fingers brushed her cheek and caressed her jaw. She sucked air into her constricted lungs.

"I love you. Kate, forgive me. Please give me another chance."

Her heart swelled at his words, words she never thought to hear. She didn't know what to say but felt the smile creep over her lips. She rose on to her toes, buried her hands in Luke's hair and kissed him. No matter what happened next, she'd have those three words. If only she could keep Luke too.

She slid her fingers inside the warm wool of his coat, stepped into the gap between his thighs and pressed against him. His warmth stilled the shivers shaking her body. "You can never walk away from me again. No matter the reason. No matter how much you think, I deserve better. I love you too. There's no one better than you. Than us. Promise me."

Luke took her hands and circled them around his neck. "I promise. Spend the night with me. Please. Or if that's too much, let me get you warm, buy you a drink at the pub."

He took her mouth and kissed her hard. His demand, his fear, in every swirl of his tongue, as he pushed deep into her mouth. Kate pressed her forehead to his. "Yes, no drink. Take me home."

They had a long way to go, but hope was a powerful aphrodisiac.

EPILOGUE

Three Months Later

Standing by the gate, Kate's eyes settled on Knight, collar pulled around his ears prowling along River Walk, Father Thames a minor puddle at his side. If that wasn't a growl she heard, she was the lemon in the V & T.

His shoulder was healing well, which was more than could be said for his temper. He blamed himself for the lives lost at the school. According to him, he should have guessed what Seckou planned.

Kate sighed. Guilt, Sentinel's badge of honour.

"Hiya! I thought you'd forgotten me, decided not to come." Kate opened the gate and stepped to the side.

"Come 'ere. Forget you? Never." Knight hooked her waist and drew them together under her beaten-up umbrella. "What are you doing out here in the rain?"

"Waiting for you, who else?" She ducked to avoid the rain dripping onto her forehead. "Seriously, you are not the last one to arrive. I'm waiting for Lily."

"Yeah. Whose Lil"?

Did he wake every morning thinking of six things to aggravate a person? "Hey, don't let Lily hear you call her that, she'll carve a piece out of you."

Knight sniggered. "I'd love to see her try."

"Behave—Lily's our new *Afrique Santé* Liaison, used to practise as a paediatrician.

"Used to?"

"Don't ask. I haven't. I have a feeling it's a long story. Lily's never been to Africa. Her trip with us next month will be her first."

Knight raised his hands. "Hey, ask no question, get told no lies, right? How's Doc taking it, you going back to Burkina?"

Kate laughed. "You know him. I was hoping if you didn't need him, and the Essex granted him leave, he could come with me. I know he's dying to see Amina and Katy as much as I am. I was for the right moment to suggest it."

"I bet. It's okay with me, short of tying Doc to a chair, I doubt I could keep him away."

"I haven't dared ask Crys how Spanner feels, but she won't be away more than a week, long enough for us to introduce Lily to everyone at Yalgado Hospital, make sure she feels the love before she heads out to the rural clinics." Kate glanced up and down the street. "She should be here any minute."

"Here. Happy Birthday." Knight thrust a small box into her hands.

The pink paper covered in balloons made her laugh. "Thanks. Urgh, it's wet." Knight frowned. *Damn.* If she didn't know better, she'd think he was hurt, sorry would have been a stretch. Neither emotion sat well with the Boss.

Crys said he'd been married once. She couldn't imagine.

"How's your shoulder?" Kate asked, eager to dispel the tension lingering between them.

"It'll do."

"I'm sorry, Knight, I…" He turned from her hand before her fingers reached his cheek.

"Wasn't your fault."

"True, but you stepped in front of the bullet meant for me."

The hand around her waist gave her a gentle squeeze.

"The way it should be, trust me, killing is best left to the professionals."

There wasn't any point arguing with him. Knight, any member of Sentinel, would push her out of the line of fire until infinity took a holiday.

"What's the word on Seckou, Salif?" She couldn't hide the hitch in her voice. Coming to terms with Amina's brother being responsible for the bombing was difficult, occupied too much of her day.

"As I said, Kate. Leave it to those best suited to dealing with the bad guys. We rely on you to take care of the other half of the population." Knight raised his eyes to the darkening sky. "Fucking rain. Come on, inside. Where's Doc?"

"In the back garden with Spanner. Crystal's weaving her magic on the missing sun while he starts the barbeque." Kate winked.

"Sounds about right."

Spanner loved his food, couldn't cook, but, banged up in Burkina, his culinary attempts saved them from going nuts. Self-appointed Chef de Cuisine to Sentinel Security and Knights second-in-command.

Knight rubbed his hands together. "Take me to your leader."

"You go, I'll wait for Lily. She's supposed to be bringing a cake."

"Can't do that Princess, you might get eaten by a duck."

"Funny. Okay. Race you to the garden."

Spanner, Crystal attached to his hip, held court behind an oversized table groaning under the weight of red meat and onions. Looking uncomfortable, Luke stood off to the side.

"There's my man." Luke immediately relaxed in her arms. "Knight bought me a present."

"I should hope so," Doc shook Knight's hand, who responded with a nod.

"Snake here yet?"

"Inside. Trying to pick up the good-looking woman chatting up George."

"Boss, you look as though you could use a drink." Spanner's voice rose above the buzz coming from inside the French doors behind them.

"You read minds as well as fucking cards Spanner?"

"Ah Boss, as I remember it, last time we played, you took me for everything, including my camo pants.

Knight held his palms up in front of him. "What you got?"

"Heineken, or do you prefer something else? Doc bought out the local pub to make sure he catered for everyone."

"Heineken will do."

"Sorry, I lied. Out of *real* beer." Spanner handed him a Stella Artois. "It's a step-up from the Malts."

"Cheers." Knight raised his glass. "To the birthday girl."

Kate raised her free arm and dipped the neck of her bottle. Beer wasn't her favourite. Doc didn't look up, his head content to stay buried behind her ear.

"Hey, Doc." Crystal stuck two fingers in her mouth and whistled.

Spanner punched his fist in the air. "Yeah. You're making us jealous, get a room."

Kate's hand interlaced with his, and Luke was sure she saw all the way to his soul. "You need a drink? The good stuff."

Kate nodded and let go of his hand. The warmth from her eyes chasing after him as he disappeared into the kitchen. For Fuck's sake, why was Spanner following him?

Luke ignored him, focussed on finding the bottle of Pino Grigio he'd planned to save for later. The Off License insisted Sauvignon was all the rage, but Kate preferred the Italian drop. When he turned to grab the glasses, Spanner's ugly mug was six inches from his face. His head cocked to one side.

"What?"

"Scared Kate's going to leave you?"

"No." Where the fuck did that come from, for fuck's sake.

"Sure?"

"I bought a ring." Maybe it was daft, believing his denial was true.

"About time. So? What are you waiting for?" Spanner slapped him on the back.

"Easy. I lied. I'm not sure Kate will say yes, I guess."

"Fuck me. Are you nuts? She's crazy for you."

"How would you know, Crystal?"

"I need Crys for a lot of things, man, more each day if I'm honest, but she doesn't need to point out what's square in my face."

Luke's stomach rolled. The conversation too close for him to handle. "Let's get back to the party before the meat turns to charcoal."

Pretty, the word didn't come close to describing the amazing, strong, intelligent woman wrapped in his arms in front of the fire. Sharing a blanket tucked around their knees, Kate took his breath away.

Amazed Kate stayed, he pinched himself every morning. He didn't deserve her trust, not after the way he'd behaved. "Time for bed?" He buried his nose between her breasts and inhaled her perfect scent.

"Mmm. Yes." Her hand stroked the side of his cheek. "Thanks for a perfect birthday.

The tone of her voice said she was relaxed, and the nervous tension wedged between his shoulder blades vanished replaced by the familiar tightness in the front of his jeans.

Kate opened his shirt and peppered gentle kisses over the scar on his chest. He'd never forget her bravery, never be able to make up for her pain.

Luke rummaged in his pocket for the small velvet box. The ring was his grandmother's. Much loved since he was a boy and his granddad told him the story of the night he proposed.

His fingers toyed with the ragged edges. It was old fashioned. According to Spanner, women liked to choose their rings. He wouldn't mind if Kate did. Much.

He kissed the tips of her fingers and placed it in her palm.

"What's this? Another birthday present? Haven't you spoiled me enough?" She chuckled.

Never. The word stuck in the back of Luke's throat as Kate slowly opened the lid. He was glad he wasn't the only one lost for words.

The blue from the sapphire sparkled in the glow of the fire. All he could think, dream, was having her in his arms forever snuggled to the place on his body explicitly moulded for her. Shiver her bones, make love to her every night until the sun came up and he woke to bask in the light from her eyes.

This was it. He sucked in a breath. "Will you marry me?"

Kate's eyes remained fixed on the ring.

"Shit, you're trembling, I understand if it's too soon. If you need more time."

"Shh, Luke. I'm scared. Not again, I couldn't take you walking away from me."

His arms circled her waist. "Please, Kate, don't be afraid. Not of me." He pressed his lips to her forehead, and she wound her arms around his neck as he laid gentle kisses at the pulse in her throat. "I swear, I'm not going anywhere. Where would I go without you?"

Kate slid the ring on the finger of her left hand.

"Say something."

Kate tipped her face to meet his, and his heart almost burst at the smile shining through her tears. "Yes. I love you, Luke."

His heart swelled at the words he never hoped to hear. Words he couldn't live without.

"I love you Kate. That day at the picnic, I knew. After Mike died, I didn't believe we could ever happen, but there was never any doubt I was always yours." He kissed her, pushing his tongue deep, pouring into her everything he was.

"Mm. You love me. Finally, I thought I'd never hear you say it. Kiss me again and later—"

"Later." He rubbed his cheek across the top of her hair, then tilted her chin so she could see his eyes. "They'll always be a later, sweetheart. I'm never letting you out of my life."

His heart rolled over. Kate was his to protect, his to love. Forever faithful.

ABOUT THE AUTHOR

I grew up with two careers in mind: Dancer or a Professor of English Literature. Dancing won, for a short time, before I followed my grown-up path, but I never lost my love of the written word. Stories stood by me when times were tough and lovers fleeting.

Love takes courage. Retired now, surrounded by my garden, I can write about the heroes and heroines who fight for the love and pleasure they deserve. I am grateful.

AUTHOR'S NOTE

Thank you for reading Faithful. I hope you enjoyed the start of The Sentinel Security series. Book Two – *Saviour* will be out early in 2021. If you would like to stay in touch and be among the first to learn when future books in the series are released you can:

Sign up for my newsletter at www.elizarenton.com

Find me on facebook.com/elizarenton

How can you help authors if you liked their books? Tell your friends and family.

Consider leaving a review at your favourite online book retailer.

Happy reading,
Eliza

www.ingramcontent.com/pod-product-compliance
Lightning Source LLC
Chambersburg PA
CBHW020358120726
47904CB00002B/616